DEATH

WAS NOT ON THE

GUEST

LIST

OTHER TITLES BY JENNI L. WALSH

Adult

Sonora

Ace, Marvel, Spy

Unsinkable

The Call of the Wrens

A Betting Woman

Side by Side

Becoming Bonnie

Middle Grade

The Bug Bandits

Operation: Happy

Over and Out

By the Light of Fireflies

I Am Defiance

Hettie and the London Blitz

She Dared: Malala Yousafzai

She Dared: Bethany Hamilton

DEATH

WAS NOT ON THE

GUEST LIST

JENNI L. WALSH

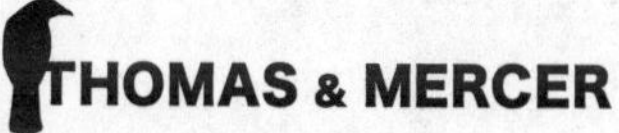

THOMAS & MERCER

Text copyright © 2026 by Jenni L. Walsh
All rights reserved.

Published by Thomas & Mercer, Seattle

www.apub.com

Amazon, the Amazon logo, and Thomas & Mercer are trademarks of Amazon.com, Inc., or its affiliates.

EU product safety contact:
Amazon Media EU S. à r.l.
38, avenue John F. Kennedy, L-1855 Luxembourg
amazonpublishing-gpsr@amazon.com

ISBN-13: 9781662536274 (paperback)
ISBN-13: 9781662536281 (digital)

Cover design by Ploy Siripant
Cover image: © Sudha Peravali / ArcAngel Images; © TWINS DESIGN STUDIO / Shutterstock; © Elisabeth Schmidbauer / Getty; © Katie Harp / Unsplash

Printed in the United States of America

For my daughter, Kaylee, my lover of mysteries. In a few short years, you'll have full rein to read my adult books.

ABBREVIATED GUEST LIST

Ginevra

Ginevra King Mitchell is the reigning queen of the Big Four. You may've heard of them: Ginevra, Edith, Courtney, and Margaret, the four most attractive and socially desirable young women in Chicago in these here 1920s. Really, since they debuted in 1914. Ginevra is charming, beautiful—her name derived from the *Ginevra de' Benci*, which Leonardo da Vinci painted—and almost always polite. Unless she's in the throes of a competition. With a drive to win like no other, Ginevra abhors losing. She also abhors gossip—about herself. Yes, she's read *The Great Gatsby*. And no, she sees absolutely no similarities between herself and Daisy Buchanan. Ginevra expects no mention of Scott or his little book at the evening's whist drive for charity. That simply won't do.

Edith

Ginevra may abhor losing, but Edith Cummings adamantly won't allow it. In golf, she's won the US Women's Amateur. And the Women's Western Amateur. That was indeed Edith on the cover of *TIME* magazine, the very first woman athlete to appear in the coveted spot. There's a reason she's earned the nickname of the Unflappable Fairway Flapper. Edith is rich and admittedly spoiled, and she has absolutely no time for any more scandal. If that sounds like the golf pro Jordan Baker in *The Great Gatsby*, then you are sorely mistaken. That woman is "incurably dishonest," and Edith refuses to tell a lie, honest.

COURTNEY

Courtney Letts has had a whirlwind of a year, divorcing one man, marrying another. She's in from Washington, DC, looking forward to a respite from her new husband and to catching up on gossip with her Big Four. Pretty as a peacock, she hasn't yet had the opportunity to tell her friends how she's been named one of the twelve most beautiful women in America. It's a real shame that Alice de Janzé is higher on the list, but it's not as if Alice has any skills beyond a well-timed tantrum. Not like Courtney, who is on the cusp of her big break as a writer. Maybe, just maybe, the muse will strike her while she's visiting Chicago, and she'll write the next Great American Novel.

PEG

Margaret Carry Cudahy—but do call her Peg—has mixed feelings about the evening ahead. She's delighted for a night with her Big Four ladies; it's been quite some time since they've all been together, and she has exciting news to tell them. However, tonight's soiree is being run by none other than her husband's sister, Sarah. Excuse her language, but Sarah can be quite insipid. Sanctimonious to boot. A horrid combination. But the evening is for a wonderful cause, after all, and Peg knows how to conceal her true feelings, despite everyone believing she wears them on her sleeve.

Josephine

Oh, the gossip that's transpired surrounding this one. The twentysomething daughter of a billionaire businessman and politician, Josephine Bamford is one of the country's most elite botanists—with a keen interest in plant toxicology. It's said she was expelled from a boarding school in England due to a daffodil-poison incident. Thanks to Daddy, very few details are known about the event. And soon after, Josephine was whisked away to the United States. One must wonder if the poisoning was accidental or intentional. Courtney, pen at the ready, is keen to get to the bottom of it.

Marie

One could debate—and wonder—how a woman south of thirty could have the time and mental endurance to bury three husbands. Marie Morgan's fourth should sleep with one eye open or, at the very least, insist on retiring to his own suite each evening. There's enough suspicion for her to have earned the nickname of Murderess Marie. At least husband number four will have the night off as Marie dazzles in the whist drive. She's said to be a distinguished and strategic card player.

Sarah

The evening's fundraising host, Sarah Cudahy, is one of those women who, try as they may, inadvertently get a person's dander up. A fair warning, dear reader. It's best not to get attached to Sarah Cudahy.

Chapter One

GINEVRA

Snow, in October. Unusual this early in the season, but not completely unheard of for Chicago. I run a gloved hand down the arm of my coat, the few snowflakes brushing off the fur easily.

As I approach the Bellevue House, a smattering of footprints means I'm likely the last to arrive. Sarah will shoot daggers at me as I walk in.

Though I wager they won't be as sharp as the ones my husband threw at me before I left the house this evening. He spat, "I thought I told you to remove that man from your life?"

I gritted my teeth together. He meant F. Scott Fitzgerald, my former lover and a current novelist. "I did ages ago." Bill and I married in 1918, nearly a decade ago. Shortly after, I stopped seeing Scott. I crossed my arms. "You're making something out of nothing."

"All of town is comparing you to his Daisy Buchanan."

All of town? Hardly. Bill can be so tiresome. Still, I retorted, "Then you and the rest of society are creating similarities where there are none. Frankly, it's ridiculous and beneath you, Bill."

In fact, I wouldn't be surprised if the individual who was beneath him at the time was the sole perpetrator of telling Bill that I'm Scott's muse. But why have this pillow talk with him now, when Scott's book came out an entire year ago?

My dear husband was not done, saying, "What's ridiculous is how you've put yourself—and me—in this situation."

"That's rich, coming from you." As if he had any clue how difficult it was to play the perfect bride to his perfect family. "That's *especially* rich considering who you were with when you came by this false information."

"I don't know what you're talking about," he said absently.

Lies.

I warned, "You'll ruin everything—for us both—if people find out about her."

"Don't worry. The situation is handled."

"What's that supposed to mean? What did you say to her?"

"I said not to worry about it, Ginevra."

At that, I was dismissed, Bill turning his attention elsewhere. I stormed out, the clacking of my kitten heels punctuating my anger. Now I mind each footfall up the snow-covered steps to the Bellevue.

The invitation for tonight's charity event, a whist drive, listed eight o'clock as the start time. It's nearly quarter past. I could beg off. I almost declined with regrets when the invite first came in; I often choose to avoid functions with Sarah "the Snake" Cudahy. Alas, here I am, an unyielding supporter of good causes and an even greater advocate of spending an evening with my Big Four ladies, especially after a preposterous row with Bill. It's been some time since I've seen the girls, Edith having been on a golf tour, Courtney splitting her time between Chicago and the nation's capital, and Peg a homebody like no other. Oh, the delicious gossip we're about to fall into—God willing, about people other than me.

I step into the portico lights and shimmy off any remaining precipitation. Thankfully, my cloche hat has protected my curls. I make quick use of the lion-head knocker, though tonight's attendant is not as quick to open.

A gust of horrifically cold wind travels down the collar of my coat. Taking matters into my own hands, I try the knob, effectively letting myself in. I've been invited, after all.

The attendant startles at my sudden appearance, mere steps away in the foyer, his caterpillar eyebrows shooting toward the coffered ceiling. He's mid-conversation with another guest, lifting his hand from her arm and gesturing her toward the ballroom.

"I do apologize for the wait, Mrs. King Mitchell," he says to me in an accented voice. I *do* love how the British speak.

"Nonsense," I say, stepping deeper into the Georgian-inspired building. Warmth from the fireplace off the foyer immediately greets me.

"May I take your coat and gloves?" the attendant asks with a friendly smile, two dimples forming.

I turn, allowing him to slide off my fur, revealing my scarlet dress, silk and dripping with beadwork. I slip free my winter gloves and hand them over. My clutch remains with me. I wouldn't want it falling into the wrong hands.

"The other guests have already gathered in the ballroom," he says with a subtle peek toward the grandfather clock.

"I know the way," I assure him. Then I pause, collecting myself for whatever scathing glances Sarah is about to throw at me. As I cross the threshold, I instinctively look to the raised platform—a stage for any women's talks or performances the Civic Daughters puts on—at the far side of the grand room, where twenty or so bodies separate me from Sarah, tonight's host. I'm correct about the scathing glance. Hers says, *How dare you parade in here late*. Mine says, *How dare you put those rumors into my husband's head*. Though neither of us actually utters a word. Manners. Saving face. Call it what you will.

I'd like to call it being the winner. That is, if Bill wasn't trying to pull the wool over my eyes and actually ended things with her earlier.

Shoulders back, I waltz deeper into the room, every quick interaction I'm about to have a way to further endear myself to these women. It's a tightrope of charm and calculation that I'd like to think I've perfected after debuting ten or so years ago. I begin with the woman closest to the door. "Hello, Marie, looking as lovely as ever in white."

Never mind the fact she's on husband number four.

She smiles innocently. "And you, a vixen in red."

I laugh freely, then raise a brow at her quip before nodding toward Sarah. "I do believe that title's already been claimed."

It never hurts to add some wit, as long as it's not laced with too much rancor.

Marie, eyes shadowed in a dark blue that gives them a smoky look, follows my gaze to Sarah, then lifts her eyebrows in an "oh" manner. I'm testing fate. But also, I'm testing the waters, gauging if Sarah's transgressions with my husband have seeped into society or if I'm in the clear. There's a chance their dalliances may not have reached public consumption. And I'd rather it stay that way, not for my marriage's sake but for my reputation's. I relish being at the center of gossip but not the subject of it.

I continue my megawatt entrance. "How lovely you look," I say to Elizabeth Field. "Let me help you with that," I offer to Cynthia McCormick, dipping to retrieve the linen she's dropped. Mouth full, she mumbles what I assume to be a thank-you behind her hand.

I'm about to move on when she stops me. "I suppose," Cynthia says, swallowing, "Sarah has seated me at the lowest table for tonight's games. It's becoming tradition, after all."

I touch her arm. "I'm certain you can fight your way up."

I'm actually not certain of that at all. But I'm on to the next hello. "Is that really you?" I gently touch another arm, Josephine Bamford's. She jumps. I chuckle, saying, "Apologies. I didn't mean to startle you. It's been some time since I've seen you out and about."

Josephine's expression pinches ever so slightly, and I notice Sarah watching me. Watching us. "I'll be honest," she says, "it's been some time since I've received an invitation. Sarah asking me to come was very . . . generous."

"Oh, I'm sorry—"

"No need for that. I haven't taken offense."

I smile. "What a relief. Also a relief to hear you haven't been avoiding us." I follow the pleasantry with a wink.

She laughs lightly. "Of course not. I've been busy in the lab, working with something volatile and unstable. It'll make my head spin if I'm not careful."

"Ah, occupational hazard of being one of the best. Let's chat more later. I have a fern in my parlor that unfortunately appears to be on its last leg."

Then I'm off again, offering greetings to the Swifts, then the Armours. The Breuers are deep in conversation, so I bypass them.

Finally, I reach Courtney and Peg. I throw my arms around them both. We part, giggling, all eyes on us, the Big Four. Though it appears we're missing one. "Where is Edi—"

She makes her entrance, stealing the spotlight, an even later arrival than my own. I grin as my dearest friend sashays into the room in a mustard-colored dress and matching cloche hat. With her strawberry blond hair, it'd clash on anyone else. But Edith's gray eyes very effectively complement the color combination, and she pulls off the look, holding a golf club no less.

She stops, makes a show of swinging her club. Half the room is scandalized, the other enamored with her confidence.

"There you are," I say, enveloping her in a hug, then link our arms, claiming her and proclaiming to the ballroom, "Edith is my whist partner for the evening."

A tight-jawed Sarah looks none too pleased to see Edith's late arrival. I wager she also won't be pleased if I take control of the room. I clap sharply. "Go on, everyone, hurry and find your own partner. We'll run out of time to play otherwise."

On the stage, Sarah presses her lips together. She claps twice. "Yes, now that all our guests have graced us with their presence, we can begin." She clambers down the small set of steps. "After you've secured your partner, please take a seat at one of the tables."

There are five in total. Chandeliers, dripping with oval crystals, hang over the tops of each.

Edith and I make for table one, the top table, where we plan to reign all evening. Others will advance up a table if they win. They'll be relegated to a lower table if they lose. When Edith and I win the final round, we'll be declared tonight's victors. It's all in good fun. Mostly. I'm actually quite surprised Cynthia McCormick has shown her face after last summer's devastating performance, as she herself noted, spending the entirety of the evening at the lowest table. A glutton for punishment, clearly. My eyes meet hers, offering her a smile that communicates "Bless your heart."

"Bill acting up?" Edith whispers as she settles in the chair across from mine, removing her cloche hat and tossing it onto the table.

"Is it that obvious?" I sigh, doing my best to smooth the tension between my brows.

"Only to me," she says.

A young woman sits down between us at our round table.

I mouth, "I'll tell you later."

Then, imperceptibly so, as I've practiced how to be discreet in the mirror, I cock my head at the woman. I cannot recall her name or if we've met before. But as Mrs. Burton Kingsland says in her etiquette manual: *A woman secure in her social position is never afraid to meet strangers, to bow or speak first, nor to show herself gracious and friendly to anyone.*

"And who might you be?" I ask the mystery woman, younger, closer to twenty. "I don't believe I've ever had the pleasure of making your acquaintance." Though it appears I am not the only woman with bold moves, as she's unknown to me and claiming a seat at the most coveted table.

"This is Greta," Sarah says, putting a teacup in front of herself and another in front of Greta, then taking the final seat. "You could say I've taken dear Greta under my wing. Teaching her the dos and don'ts."

Is that so? Maybe I'll have to see about taking this new fledgling from Sarah and putting her under my own tutelage.

I smile politely.

"Greta was the first to arrive this evening," Sarah praises her. She raises her eyebrows at Edith, last to arrive. Then coos, "And she has such a pretty name, don't you agree?" Sarah scooches in her chair, adjusts her plum-colored dress, and reaches across the table to pat Greta's hand, saying, "But imagine if you'd been born the other Greta. Garbo, that is. I read about her in the papers only yesterday, a star on the rise. What a bright future you'd have ahead of you in that case."

And what a peculiar thing to say. Peculiar but not strange or uncommon. Sarah, along with being as slimy as an eel, is the queen of the backhanded compliment. A real way with words, that one. Who will she insult next? I could make a game of it. Though odds are it'll be either Edith or me.

Mrs. Burton Kingsland has also decreed: *The best way to be rid of an embarrassing acquaintanceship is to strangle it in its birth.*

I wasn't able to do this with Sarah. She is Peg's sister-in-law, so we are forever stuck together. I currently have a silent auction with her next month in my diary.

I'd like to groan, but instead—head, hands, hips, arms, and knees—I arrange myself as a well-bred woman should. I note that Greta hasn't taken Sarah's bait and given her a response. Very admirable. Instead, she takes a measured sip of her tea. Smart girl. I say, "Well, it is lovely to meet you, Greta. Are you new to Chicago? There's so much I could show—"

Sarah's voice overpowers mine, instructing each table to designate their dealer and begin play. All the while, she gestures demonstratively with her left hand, where a diamond now sparkles. "Greta, darling," she says to our table alone, "why don't you lead us off as our dealer, given that you and I are partners." Sarah bookends her dictation with a smile.

Greta returns the polite expression and palms the deck of cards with her white elbow-length gloves. Like Marie's, her dress is white, as is the feather in her headpiece.

As she's shuffling, she loses control, the cards flying every which direction. At once, I bend to pick up the cards on the floor as she profusely apologizes. The poor girl must be nervous attending her first event with us all.

After I straighten and pass Greta the cards I collected, I immediately think to focus attention elsewhere. I reach across the table to grasp Edith's hand. "How was your latest victory on the links?"

"Dull," she says, a hint of something in her voice I can't quite read.

"However so? You won, didn't you?"

"I did."

"And?"

"And nothing. Being on the links has lost some of its appeal, I suppose."

"It has?" I'm utterly flabbergasted. Edith loves golf. She even forces me to play from time to time. While I grew up at the same club, playing tennis and golf, there are no expectations for me like there are for Edith. She's a professional. That is her identity, and that is all she's supposed to be. God forbid she ever try to get serious with a man. Their mothers immediately dismiss her as a sportswoman and direct their sons elsewhere. Which is where my shock comes in. Does she want to pull back on golf so she can attempt to become something else? I'd like to press her, to peel back whatever layer she's put up, but a room full of people is not the place for that.

Greta deals the final card to herself, doing so face up for us all to memorize the suit. A diamond, a woman's best friend.

Edith focuses on the card. My attention is drawn there as well. Neither of us likes to lose. Mentally, I crack my knuckles, something I may have done in private a time or two. It's one of those nasty habits where after you do it once, you feel ashamed, yet compelled to do it again. But never in public.

Greta adds the card to her pile.

Each of us picks up our stack of thirteen cards. I fan them out the best I can, holding them in one hand.

The play begins clockwise—to me. I play the highest-value card I have: a ten.

Sarah sips on her tea while searching for something higher, eventually playing a jack.

Edith's eyes narrow mischievously. If she has a club, she must play it, even if it's lower than what's already been put down. In the end, whoever has the highest card will win. But chances are, my endlessly competitive friend does not have the queen, king, or ace of clubs to beat Sarah. Nor does she want to play a card that is lower.

We make eye contact. Now I'm laughing on the inside. I know her. I know she indeed has a club—and doesn't wish to play it because we'll lose the first trick. And now she's debating how fairly to play this game. She could play this round's trump suit, which will beat whatever is already on the table, and pretend she has no club.

But if she plays a club in a later round, will Sarah or Greta remember this moment and call her out for being a cheat? That is what is currently running through Edith's pretty little head.

She throws down an eight of diamonds.

Oh, Edith.

Greta plays a three of clubs.

That makes us the "winners" of the first trick, as far as the table knows. Edith sweeps the four cards from the tabletop and lays them face down in front of her. She quickly plucks another card from her hand, beginning the next round.

When the play is to me, I am thumbing through my cards when, face void of emotion, Sarah addresses me. "Your turn, Daisy."

That name immobilizes me, a shock to my ears. A stab to my heart. "Daisy?"

"Oh, silly me." Sarah giggles, running a dainty finger over the lip of her teacup. "An honest slip of the tongue, Ginevra."

In this moment I must do my darndest to remember everything Mrs. Burton Kingsland has put into her book, when all I want to do is twist in my chair toward Sarah, wrap my hands around her neck, and throttle her. That was no slip of the tongue. No slip at all. I can all but hear her poisoning Bill with blather about me.

Ginevra is his Daisy.

It's plain for anyone with eyes.

She must still be seeing him behind your back.

But to what end is Sarah saying such things? What is it she hopes to achieve by slandering me to her lover?

Unless she threw these words at him after he ended things?

And now she's throwing the name Daisy at me—for the whole room to overhear. If only she knew the true significance of that name. Not that I'd reveal such a thing to her. Only my closest and truest friends know a lick about my time with Scott.

Heart beating in my ears, I meet Edith's steady gaze, pleading silently, *Help me!*

Chapter Two

Edith

I stare back into Ginevra's green eyes, panic building behind them with every barely there breath, knowing my best friend is thinking, *Edith, help.*

I'm catapulted to the summer months, back to a conversation we had, a private telephone call.

"Hello," I began, "this is the Cummings residence. Edith speak—"

"E," Gin cut in, that single syllable, her common nickname for me, infused with a sense of panic. "He'll ruin me."

"Who? Slow down."

"Scott."

I wrinkled my brows. "You've seen him?"

"No. You know it's been years."

My grip on the phone was fierce. "Then what's happened?"

"He published another book last year. I've learned of it only now. Saw it on a shelf at Bennett's. There's a character in it—her name is Jordan Baker. I think it's you, Edith. It's you."

"Me?"

"She's a professional golfer, a socialite, mostly unattached. Ring any bells, E?"

I was alone, which allowed me the privacy to react however I damn well pleased. "For the love of Mike, Gin, that could be any old gal. Why pin it on me?"

"Because Jordan is best friends with Daisy, who some may believe to be me."

"Why?" I paused, then said to Ginevra, "Are you pacing?"

"I am. I'm in distress."

Instinctively, I wrapped my pinkie finger around the cord, as if Gin could feel my grip and it'd bring her comfort.

She let out a sharp breath and said, "You know I once wrote Scott a letter. Well, I wrote him many letters when I was younger and completely besotted with him. This particular letter must've been around 1916. I said something along the lines of how it'd be slick to have him write a story about me, though I feared I'd be a dry subject. Could I have been wrong? Hear me out. This Daisy's storyline is nearly identical to a story I made up one morning during a perfect hour where Scott and I lay in bed. A woman trapped in a loveless marriage with a wealthy man, yet she desires someone else. That someone else makes a name for himself, so the young woman is willing to be with him. In the end, the man attains enough money to take her away from her adulterous husband. It was a fairy tale."

Poor Ginevra. She's always sought comfort over love. It's how she was raised, her father once telling her that poor boys shouldn't think about marrying rich girls. But that was beside the point. I asked her, "And that's what happens in his new novel?"

"Yes. No. More or less, except for the happy ending and the fact his Daisy Buchanan is a murderer. She's beautiful yet shallow. Charming yet fickle. Careless. Snobbishly materialistic. Am I those things?" She sighed, and her tone became more exacting. "She's a mother, Edith."

Which Gin undoubtedly is. She's *all* those things, perfectly imperfect, even if she didn't want to admit it. I swung the phone as if it were a club, releasing the emotions bubbling inside me, then brought the receiver to my ear again. "All right, say it is us—who'd be clever enough to clock it? What's he got me doing, rolling my eyes and lighting cigarettes?"

Ginevra laughed, but there was no humor in it. "Aloof, cynical, self-centered."

I said dryly, "Sounds like me, sure—but between the two of us, I'm the one who'd bump someone off and make it look like a party trick."

"It's not the time for humor, E. This is serious."

Who said I was being funny? I refocused. "But what can be done? Is his book popular? I haven't yet heard of it."

"I can't be sure. But I fear it'll pick up steam. I called Scribner's offices. His print run was 20,870 copies."

"That's very specific. Is it a good amount?"

"I don't know. I've heard that Hemingway's first book had only three hundred copies printed. But they were printed specifically for a storefront in Paris. If twenty thousand is large, let's hope Scott's sales are nothing spectacular. His last novel underperformed. Still, Scott's ego is out of this world. He likely believes this new book to be the best American novel ever written. The one saving grace is that he dedicates the book to her."

"To Zelda?"

"Yes. It says 'Once again to Zelda.'"

"Then, voilà, Zelda's Daisy. That's our line if anyone starts flapping their gums."

"And Jordan Baker?" She groaned. "Or worse, Tom Buchanan."

"Who is that?"

"Tom is Bill. My Bill, with no discretion when it comes to women."

Ah, so that was what this was about. "Gin, are you more upset about people thinking you've inspired Daisy or everyone realizing who is modeled after Bill?"

It put a chink in her carefully polished armor. Ginevra King—now King Mitchell—gives off an air of perfection. Perfect home. Perfect children. Perfect marriage. Except that last one is a load of bull, and Gin doesn't want a soul to know it.

She scoffed. "I caught them, I'll have you know. At the Summer Soiree. Bill denies it, but who needs to use a coatroom in the middle of summer. *And* needs assistance checking an imaginary coat."

In truth, I was avoiding Sarah for my own reasons, but yes, I saw the three of them return to the ballroom one after another. Ginevra somehow kept the red from her cheeks and her head held high as she waltzed in, pretending that nothing was amiss. She likely sold it like snake oil. Only, I knew. Ginevra's jaw was the slightest bit too tight. Her laugh an octave higher than usual. She spent more time on Bill's arm, when I knew she'd rather converse with me and the other women.

Of course, I told Ginevra not to sweat it. "Scott's novel will remain in obscurity," I said. And that would've been true, if not for Sarah.

Now, as I lock eyes with my best friend across the whist table, it's clear a cat got her tongue. Either that or Gin is fighting for dear life to maintain control of her words and keep up her carefully manicured appearances.

"Truly, Ginevra," Sarah says, sweet as sugar and twice as fake. "I didn't mean to call you Daisy. I've been dizzy all day. My engagement was announced in the paper only this morning, and it's been such a whirlwind. Did you all happen to see it?"

Says the woman who's been stepping out with Ginevra's husband, and I fight the urge to narrow my eyes.

"I saw it," the newcomer, Greta, says, and I almost tell her Sarah is not worth flattering.

Sarah offers Greta a smile; then she sets her lying eyes on Ginevra again. "Please accept my apologies. I assure you it was a slip of the tongue to call you Daisy Buchanan."

And I'll eat my cloche if that was accidental. She says this so-called apology loudly enough for the entire ballroom to overhear. Courtney and Peg turn fully, and, judging by Court's pressed lips, my dear friend is a hairbreadth away from also stepping in to protect Gin. Murderess Marie and Josephine also tick toward our table, trying for discreetness.

Greta apparently has not mastered the art of subtlety, her face balled up with confusion as she asks, "Who is Daisy?"

Ginevra finds composure in the form of a small, tight smile. She places a hand over Greta's gloved one. "A character in a silly book, my dear." Gin speaks loud enough for the other four tables to overhear, yet she speaks to Greta. "Years ago, I dated a man who has now published a book. Because of our connection, those that once knew of our romance assume this Daisy is me. However"—she pauses and gives a small shake of her head, as if all this is beneath her—"the book is dedicated to the author's wife. Her name is Zelda. She's a southern belle, a socialite, a young woman who lives a very comfortable life. It's his wife who he's drawn inspiration from. Maybe she's even murdered a woman in secret." Gin winks, and the room appropriately chuckles. "Now, whose turn is it? Oh yes, mine. Here we are. I'll play the seven."

Without missing a beat, Sarah responds by throwing down a trump card, in the form of a queen of clubs. Trying to make a statement, is she?

Tension laces through the room, tightening. Outside, the wind howls.

I chuckle. "Ah, I cannot beat that. Sarah wins."

At that, the room's chatter continues as the others finally return to their games.

Ours continues as well. We play, round after around. And we'll continue to do so until we're out of cards. Mathematics tells me I'll need to play a club at some point, even though by playing a trump card earlier I broadcast I didn't have any clubs. My mistake . . .

I've been a sap. Sloppy. But I got caught up in the game's beginning. Anyone who knows me knows I'll do anything to win. In fact, I've only just won this last trick, honestly this go-around. This win means I'm to start off the next suit.

I decide to play my club, to try to sneak it in and hope Greta will play her turn without skipping a beat. She hasn't said much all game. She seems unsure of herself, almost a fish out of water. After we break for refreshments and she's more settled in, I'll pester her for more of her story. If I have to guess, Ginevra will take her in like a lost puppy. She's the type of person who prides herself on—and feels good about herself for—coming to the aid of others, especially when everyone else witnesses her good deed. Conscious giving, I call it. I don't necessarily think it's a bad thing. Ginevra has helped every woman in this room in some way.

But back to the game. I nonchalantly play my two of clubs, keeping my expression neutral.

Sarah's head snaps to me.

"You cheat."

The words are said from between Sarah's teeth.

"I cheat?" I say, giving her a look that could slice champagne. "Careful, darling. You're the one blowing smoke in a room full of matches."

Although she's not wrong. I am a sham in this exact moment, but how disappointing of her to call it out like that. Sarah has very little self-control.

"You're a cheat," she insists, louder this time, all other commotion in the room going still, only the sound of the howling wind outside remaining. And if looks could kill, I'd be a goner.

Chapter Three

GINEVRA

With a slight curl to my lips, I say, "Now, now, Sarah, let's not cause a scene." I lower my voice. "Remember Joyce Mullins?"

"Who?" Sarah barks.

"Exactly," I say. A low blow, but she asked for it.

The wind shrieks, quite the violent sound, and some of the women momentarily shift their attention to the three sets of glass doors, where snow patters against the panes.

"This is for charity," Sarah insists, forcing attention back to herself. "And Edith is making a mockery of that."

She goes to sip from her tea, finds her cup empty, and clunks it back onto the table, clearly frustrated and flustered.

Edith saved me only moments ago during that Daisy nonsense by throwing the hand to Sarah; now I shall do the same for her. I push back my chair and stand. Addressing the room, I say, "Why don't we break for more refreshments?" I motion toward the walnut sideboard tables. Illuminated beneath wall sconces, there are tea, finger sandwiches, small cakes, and such. Pretty flowers accent the refreshments. "Then," I say, going on, "we can return to the game in better spirits." I set my gaze on Sarah. "Yes?"

She's red in the face. Mrs. Burton Kingsland would be disappointed that Sarah has let her anger show.

Edith retrieves something from beneath the white-clothed table—the golf club she walked in with. "Speaking of charity, I brought the club I used while I won the Women's Amateur. Unless you'd no longer like to include it for next month's silent auction?"

Edith's question is directed at Sarah.

Sour Sarah, who clearly wishes to decline the offer but can't without looking petulant.

This is such an Edith thing to do. Instead of apologizing, she pivots.

And I, being the loyal friend I am, will fall in line. I reach for the clasp at the back of my neck. "You may have my pearls as well. An offer too good to refuse, no?"

It's actually one I almost refused to offer. I don't actually wish to donate my pearls. I like them enough to even have had them restrung, after one of my sons accidentally tore them from my neck. There are five strings and, at the front, a large cluster of diamonds and pearls. That's what must've caught William's mischievous eye.

But I'll hand them over to mollify her. I'd rather she not bring up Daisy again or, God forbid, become truly reckless and mention her familiarity with Bill. Though doing so would be her own sabotage as much as mine. I'm certain her fiancé wouldn't be pleased to know about her canoodling with my husband.

Sarah sighs and stands, a bit wobbly on her feet. "As you wish. I'll put these with the other donations in the parlor."

Edith pushes back her chair. "I'll join you."

I smother a laugh. Classic Edith—bold as brass.

Sarah would likely rather a *Tyrannosaurus rex* join her than Edith. Although the beast probably has a less ferocious bite.

The three of us are the only women standing. I glance at Courtney and Peg. They quickly stand. "Refreshments sound wonderful," Courtney says.

"Indeed," Peg agrees, repositioning her larger-than-necessary evening bag over her arm.

Quickly, a chatter builds in the ballroom. Edith leaves, club in hand, Sarah following. Chairs are pushed back. Women begin to mingle, some heading toward the food, others also wandering off, likely to use the facilities. I hightail it toward Courtney and Peg, Henrietta Swift stopping me on the way.

"That was good of you," she says under her breath.

"Always pleased to put an end to wayward talk or defuse a tense situation, whichever you were referring to."

She raises a brow. "Yes, that. You've always been so good with people. However, I meant putting Sarah in her place."

I stifle a laugh at her forwardness, and then she crosses the room toward her daughter. I continue toward Peg and Court, the two of them dazzling, one in an emerald-green gown and the other in a deep blue. I appear between them and link an arm with each of theirs. "Sarah's in a mood, and we've only just begun."

Peg dry laughs. "That's to be expected. One thing or another is persistently ruffling her feathers."

"Tonight," Courtney says, "it appears to be Gin and Edith."

Peg pokes me with her elbow. "You know Sarah cannot handle herself when you're cheeky with her."

I smile coyly. "She's brought it upon herself. Bill and I got into a row earlier because of how she squawked into his ear about Scott's new novel."

"He's still seeing her?" Courtney whispers.

"He makes poor decisions. *We* know this. Though he claims he's put an end to it. Sarah's only fortunate I'm not one to make a scene." I arch a suggestive brow. "Unlike Edith. Not to worry—when we resume playing, E and I will beat her, and she'll become your problem when she moves down a table." I look to said table, but no one is there any longer, everyone on their feet, conversing, sipping, eating. I murmur, "Remind me, who are you playing?"

Courtney leans in, lowering her voice. "My newest muse."

I must admit, I hope this one sticks. Courtney has struggled to find "her thing." Whereas Edith is pigeonholed as an athlete, Courtney's place in society has always been centered on her looks. She's beautiful, yet I can't blame her for wanting more than that. Lately, it has been her aspiration to put pen to paper. And I will support her through and through. I chuckle, encouraging the idea. Though: "You may need to be more specific about who this muse is."

"Josephine Bamford."

I raise a well-manicured eyebrow. "The botanist."

The jumpy botanist, I correct in my head.

"The very one," Courtney says.

Peg is lost, evident by the fact she's not chiming in. Though Peg *can* be quiet, the most demure and easily scandalized out of the four of us. Many in our circles see her as docile and sweet natured. But we know the true Peg: cunning and calculating. I very much love that about her. Tonight, however, she also appears to be distracted, with something else on her mind. I touch her arm. "Remember, Josephine began at the Westover School the year before we left."

Courtney cuts in with a laugh. "Darling, you were the only one who was expelled. The rest of us graduated."

I harrumph. "It was worth it. Anyway," I say, keeping my voice low, "she began in '17 after being expelled from *her* boarding school in England."

"After 'the incident,'" Courtney adds with a waggle of her brows. "Which is why she'd make the perfect subject if I decide to write a mystery. I could pen her as the Poisoning Posy."

"How do I not recall her from Westover?" Peg asks, scouring the room for her, giving up, and returning her focus to us.

Funny, I can't spot Josephine either.

"It was a long time ago," I say, edging us toward the refreshments. I remove my arm from Peg's so I can retrieve the clutch beneath my arm. "I brought something to make Sarah more bearable. Prohibition smohibition."

"Above the law, are we?" Peg asks coyly.

"Always. Gin for Gin," Courtney quips, already pouring tea into bone china for us.

"None for me," Peg says.

I tease, "Surely you're not going to be a wet blanket now of all nights?"

"No. Fine. I had planned to tell you all later in the evening." She looks around. "And Edith isn't with us at the moment."

"Tell us what?" I prod.

"Well, you know how Eddie and I married after only eighteen days."

"Oh yes," Courtney says. "All of Chicago was talking about how you already had a bun in the oven."

Deep lines form between Peg's eyes. "*That* I did not know. Anyway, ironically, it's having a child that's escaped us all these years."

I squeeze her hand. "I'm sorry. I've wondered, of course, but haven't wanted to ask."

"Well, ask away, because it appears my oven is officially in service. And all is finally right as rain, as far as society is concerned."

In unison, Courtney and I squeal like schoolgirls.

"Shh," Peg says, chuckling. "I don't wish for the whole of Bellevue House to know yet. Like I said, it's still early." She runs a hand down her green dress, her stomach flat beneath.

"I'll have you know," Courtney says, "you're not the only one with news."

"Oh?" I ask.

The other season, Courtney's second marriage to millionaire explorer John Borden was quite the affair. The newspapers buzzed that her marriage came with, and I quote, "a house on Astor Street, a Rolls-Royce, magnificent jewelry, and a trust fund for her children from a previous marriage."

I say, "Don't tell me you're expecting too."

"Oh heavens, no." Courtney says. "There will be no more children. It appears I have been named one of the top twelve most beautiful women in the country."

I narrow an eye, knowing this is the response she wants from me. I even throw in a deadpan joke. "Twelve? Why not ten?"

"Ginevra," Peg scolds.

"Courtney knows I am forever in her corner. Who has given you this honor?"

"Does it matter?" Court says. "Ginevra's tone was exactly right. I've been called beautiful all my life. It's losing its luster. Besides, Peg's news has completely upstaged me."

We all laugh, and it's so good to be with them all again. I wish this portion of the evening could go on forever. And also that Edith would return so she could join in the fun.

"Speaking of my news," Peg says, "I promised Eddie I'd call again at intervals. I wasn't feeling quite myself this morning."

"Go," I say, finally retrieving a small heirloom flask from my clutch.

Courtney angles her body to cover me from prying eyes. "More for us," she says simply.

Indeed. I add a dash of illicit spirits—then a little more—to my tea to enhance the evening. Sarah will be back any moment, hollering about us all returning to our seats. Games will resume, and it'll be some time until I'm with my ladies again. God willing, Courtney and Peg will win and join E and me at our table for the next round of the tournament.

I add another pour for good measure.

Marie Morgan and Cynthia McCormick reenter the room, pulling my attention. Cynthia beelines it for the sandwich table, whereas Marie begins chatting with the first person she sees, Elizabeth Field. Marie's dress may truly be the brightest white I've ever seen. And the rock on her finger suggests that husband number four has been kind to her. Seeing her sparks my memory. I ask Courtney, "Is Marie not at your table too? I'm shocked she's not lighting up your brain with book ideas. A murder mystery perhaps?"

All Marie's former husbands are dead. Either it's tragic or she's brilliant at burying the past—quite literally.

Courtney has opened her mouth to respond when the five grand chandeliers flicker. All heads turn toward the finicky and admittedly eerie-feeling light fixtures. "Sure feels like the start to a murder mystery."

Then the entire room is plunged into darkness, the only light filtering in from the foyer's fireplace.

"What's happened?" I ask, instinctively taking a step closer to the light.

Around the large room, the women echo my question.

"The storm," someone says. I can't match the voice to the person. Nor can I see anything. Has the snow taken out the electricity?

Hand in hand with Courtney, I fumble closer to the foyer.

Suddenly, a deep, accented voice says, "Ladies." It's the Bellevue's attendant, the only male here this evening. "Please stay as you are. I will light some candles before sorting out this inconvenience."

There's so much electricity in the room from the excitement of the lights going out that I'd hardly be surprised if they gleamed back on. But no, we're left with only the sounds of harried breathing, the rhythmic drumming of snow against the glass, and the attendant moving about, his presence indicated only by the small beam of light from his handheld flashlight.

Soon, dots of light illuminate the room, placed on each of the five tables and the sideboard, and a few along the stage. I cross to the first glass door and cup my hands around my eyes to try to see out. I cannot. The wind has tossed the snow, completely covering the panes. Had I known the storm would be so fierce, I'd have stayed in tonight. Bill mentioned having someplace to be. I would have had the house to myself, minus the children.

I sigh, take a long sip of my gin-enhanced tea, and then turn to rejoin the room. "Sarah," I call out. "Shall we postpone and all head home for the evening? The weather seems to have taken a nasty turn."

No answer comes.

"Sarah?"

In the glow of candlelight, the twenty or so heads twist in an attempt to locate our host. My gaze travels the room. Edith is back, her face shadowed as we lock eyes. She shrugs a shoulder.

"Sarah?" I try again, anger bubbling. "Where is she?"

I don't wait for an answer, instead grabbing a candle from the sideboard table. I make toward the foyer, taking care not to spill my drink. My heels thud against the rug, then click-clack against the marble flooring. Others follow, the lot of us making a cacophony of noise with our hurried heels and our concerned chattering, many debating if we should leave this very second before the storm worsens. The sleet is already thudding against the doors.

"Sarah!"

The parlor is off the foyer, next to the main entrance. I turn in, the other women trailing. A fireplace on the left lights up the middle portion of the room. The glow of light catches on the tea table at the parlor's center, the head of Edith's club brightening and darkening to match the dancing flames. Other items are beside it. My pearls, for one. Beyond the low table, mahogany settees stretch into the darkness.

I take another step into the room and look to my right. I let out a breath. In the corner is a lady's chair. And the outline of a woman, sitting upright, completely statuary. Sarah. "There you are. Did you not hear us calling your name? This house is gargantuan but not large enough for your ears to fail you. And the lights have gone out, if you haven't noticed. Shall we call it for the evening?"

Silence meets me and the others who have sidled up beside, around, and behind me, a few having brought candles as well. Someone steps closer, her halo of light extending to Sarah. There's a scream, a screech.

I twist, hand to my chest, nearly sloshing my tea onto my dress, trying to locate whoever is responsible for such an obnoxious sound. "What is the meaning—"

"She's dead!" Rose Pullman calls out. "I think she's dead!"

I take a sip of my doctored tea. It burns my throat. Dead? Surely not. Not here. Not tonight.

Chapter Four

Edith

I, Edith Cummings, know one thing for certain. This isn't how I'd choose to take my final bow.

A roomful of too many women, everyone too dazed to say a thing. No tears. No sobs. Just blanched faces staring at a lifeless body. Until there's a thud. Mrs. Pullman has fainted, and her daughter immediately begins fanning her mother's face.

The other women spring to life, fanning their own faces, covering their mouths, knitting their brows.

After the shock comes the disbelief, the questioning.

There is no blood. Sarah's purple dress is intact. Not a single strand of styled brunette hair is out of place.

It's the vacant, wide-eyed stare, the stillness of her chest, how her mouth is slightly ajar, and the modest tilt to her head that are a dead giveaway to the fact she's, well, dead.

I half expect her to spring to life and chastise us for being out of the ballroom while we still have whist to play. I assume Gin is beside me. I turn to tell her this very thing but realize it's Cynthia McCormick to my right, with a sandwich sticking out of her mouth, hand unmoving. The woman is scared stiff. If she keels over, we'll have ourselves a double feature. I lower her hand, removing the smoked salmon with cream cheese from between her lips. Good deed complete, I relocate to Ginevra. The parlor isn't large, and with so many of us packed in here, elbow room is a luxury.

"How did this happen?" Ginevra *thinks* she whispers to me, only the whole room hears her question.

"She was so young."

"Healthy."

"From good breeding."

"Perfectly fine just a moment ago."

"Could it be foul play?"

The statements are murmured throughout the room, the last question asked by Cynthia, who does a very poor job of not looking at Josephine—Josephine who was involved in a poisoning incident.

The words *foul play* run through my head again. No one has ventured close to Sarah's body. But even in the shadowed corner, I see no overt signs of death.

One could assume she passed naturally.

But as Cynthia suggested, there could be something untoward at play. After all, the dead can no longer blackmail or threaten to reveal secrets, and Sarah has them on all of us, myself included.

There's a rustling of fabric, and someone maneuvers in front of Sarah. It's Murderess Marie. "I can't . . ." she stammers. "It's dark in here, but I can't . . ." At that, she holds up the white cloth napkin she's carried in from the ballroom and drapes it over Sarah's face and head.

And now . . . the top portion of her resembles a ghost. And dear God, I'm forced to stifle a laugh. It's wrong of me. Some say I have a problem with serious situations, in that I don't take them seriously. Others call me a cynic, considering I hardly ever show when I'm ruffled. I say, why let people see what I'm really thinking or feeling? I like to keep them guessing. And hey, at least I'm self-aware.

Case in point, I've known for ages I don't like Sarah. Though it's become crystal clear after all she's put me through the past six months.

But now she's dead. Dead. And I should feel remorse.

What I do feel is relief that Marie has successfully sliced the tension in the room in half. Without Sarah staring blankly at us, people begin murmuring, hypothesizing, questioning. Pearls are clutched. Mouths are covered. Heads absently move side to side. Cynthia resumes eating her sandwich.

"I'm leaving!" someone proclaims.

Who said that?

Josephine Bamford. With her black dress, shoulder-length black hair, and dark features, she appears utterly ghastly in the glow of candlelight. "My daddy won't be pleased to have me caught up in another scandal."

"We're leaving as well."

The second woman who wishes to flee the scene is either Jasmine or Cordelia, the Breuer mother or daughter. Their voices are near identical.

"Sarah has died," Gin says, voice even. "Nobody is leaving. We must telephone the police. Greta, is that you closest to the door? Can you please call? Where is the attendant?"

Greta agrees.

No one knows where the attendant is.

Greta returns, cheeks rosy with exertion. "The telephone isn't working."

"Wonderful," Gin says with a sigh. "Now what?" She drinks from her teacup. Is that gin I smell? I help myself to a few sips. If ever there was a time to drink . . .

"I'm taking this back," Murderess Marie says as she bends over the tea table, retrieving a piece of jewelry.

"You shouldn't do that," Elizabeth Field admonishes.

Marie lets out a soft laugh that sounds like it's half stuck in her throat. "Whyever not? This brooch is an heirloom from my second husband's grandmother, God rest their souls. I didn't want to donate it to the silent auction to begin with." The gemstone scrapes as she plucks it from the wooden table.

Well, color me bamboozled. Didn't see that coming down the fairway. And as a golfer who is always thinking one hole ahead, I wonder if I should also fetch my club to safeguard myself. The idea of foul play has already been floated, and my gut is telling me that Sarah didn't die of natural causes.

"We should go," Gin says.

"As I've said," Josephine all but whines.

"No, we should all go back to the ballroom." She makes a clucking sound. "Let's regroup there . . . where Sarah isn't. It wouldn't be right to simply leave the scene of a crime, no?"

There's a pause.

But then it's as if a silent consensus is made. Not to stay, but to leave.

Josephine, Marie, the Pullmans, and a blur of hair and dresses make toward the coatroom. The door is yanked open, only for the attendant to be standing there, palms raised, his expression panicked, feeble looking in his advanced age.

He's brave to say, "Mrs. King Mitchell is correct. We cannot leave. This is a crime scene. Proceed to the ballroom, and I'll go in search of a police officer."

His words fall on deaf ears. To my surprise, that includes Ginevra, who charges past the other women, a dangerous act while she holds a flame, and to the front door. I follow at her heels, saying, "No, wait, what are you doing?" Wasn't she the one to suggest no one leave?

Chaos ensues in the parlor. Some demanding their coats. Others up in arms at Ginevra's exodus. The attendant's regal accent feels entirely too posh within all the high-pitched voices and mayhem.

Ginevra yanks open the main door, her gaze falling toward the ground in front of her, which is blanketed with a surprising amount of snow. She slams the door closed. Ginevra turns on her heel, nearly running into me. She sidesteps the Pullmans and Josephine.

The attendant continues to demand everyone return to the ballroom. Courtney and Peg begin ushering people that way, while I remain close behind Ginevra as she darts across the foyer, into the ballroom, and goes straight to the first set of glass doors. Gin hands me her candle and fumbles with the locks. The door sticks. No, it's not that. Ginevra slams her shoulder and body weight against it, the door pushing against the foot or so of snowdrift that's accumulated on the other side. She peers out, yanks it closed. There are two more sets of double doors. She repeats the process two additional times.

By this time, I think everyone has reached the ballroom. Which leaves nearly twenty perplexed women looking at her, us, questions flying about what on earth Ginevra is doing.

She's breathless, but manages to ask, "Are there any more exits?"

I answer, "I assume the kitchen."

Her head jolts up, and she looks to the far wall, where there is an entrance to that room. She takes off. I follow. The women trail us with questions as to what on earth Ginevra is doing. Once more, Peg and Courtney are like captains, instructing everyone to stay calm and take a seat.

In the kitchen, Ginevra walks at a clip around the room's perimeter.

"Windows," she says. "No exterior doors. Only windows."

I stop her manic movements. "What is it, Ginevra?"

"There were footprints when I arrived," she says.

"I'm not following, Gin."

"There aren't any now."

"It's snowing. They'd be covered."

"Yes," Ginevra says. "Only, Sarah *just* died. If someone killed her and fled, footprints would be leading away from the house. There are none."

"You think that someone killed her?"

"I do. Sarah is entirely too stubborn and controlling to die of natural causes."

She makes a valid point. But the real point I think she's trying to make . . . "You believe whoever is responsible is still in the building."

"Yes," she says, green eyes wild. "That is exactly what I'm saying."

I shudder a breath.

Ginevra doesn't blink, asking me, "Was it you?"

Chapter Five

I wait for Edith to answer, my body humming with adrenaline and fear, feeling as if I'm high on a tightrope and I could topple at any moment. I lower my candle to the kitchen counter, afraid I'll drop it. Edith's expression is stoic and faraway. "Edith! I've just accused you of murder."

In the glow of her own candle, she visibly returns to the present, her gaze refocusing on me, her expression seemingly more alarmed at my outburst than the turn of events. Finally, Edith says, "It could have been anyone who killed her."

"Anyone? I know *I* didn't do it. What happened in the parlor, Edith? When you were in there with her, what went on?"

Her brows crease. "You think I had something to do with this?"

I throw up my hand but say, "No, of course not. But it doesn't look good that you were one of the last people to see her alive. Ten minutes ago Sarah was living and breathing. Now she's growing colder by the second beneath fancy linen. And if anyone were to have a motive, it'd be me."

God forgive me, but part of me is relieved. A dead woman cannot speak ill of me to my husband, call me Daisy Buchanan to get under my skin, or ruin my reputation in society.

Edith grabs my flailing hands and holds them tight. She links her pinkie with mine. I need this. I need her. She's the only one who I let myself fall apart around. "I'm sorry. I shouldn't have—"

"Gin, she was alive when I left the parlor. I only went with Sarah to keep her in her place. I gave her the club and that was that."

I blow out a breath, loud and unladylike—and genuine. "Did you see anyone on your way back to the ballroom?"

"I was distracted, thinking about golf and what's next for me. I could have bounced off someone and I'm not sure I'd remember who it was."

"What do you mean what's next for you?"

Edith shakes her head. "Not the matter at hand."

"You're right. I wonder—should we sneak in and check Sarah for signs of how she was killed? No, strike that. What a horrendous notion."

I shiver, but Edith presses on. "We *could* investigate. The kitchen must also connect to the dining room. Which then leads to the foyer. We could get to Sarah in the parlor undetected."

"Maybe," I say, the word holding very little conviction. And Edith's expression is hard to read, only half her face illuminated. Does she truly have the gall to go back into that room?

I pick up my candle again, thinking I'd rather discuss Sarah from this greater distance. "The parlor was lacking light . . . but she could have been strangled? There could've been marks we didn't see. Or what if she was struck in the back of the head?" I touch the crown of my own head. It's tender. It wouldn't take much. I blow out another breath. "Or there is always poisoning. I've read how people foam at the mouth, but does that happen in every instance? Josephine would likely know. We could talk to her. Unless she's the one who's done it." I rub my brow.

"Ginevra, it's okay."

What she's not saying is . . . *Calm down. Get ahold of yourself.*

E is taller than me, and she dips slightly to my eye level. "If it'd help to have a look, I could go alone. But I'd need to hurry before anyone comes looking for—"

Her suggestion is cut off with a scream—from the ballroom. We run at a clip in that direction, Edith's flame going out.

I've been in the ballroom on many occasions and for many functions as a longtime member of the Civic Daughters. This room, this setting, should be familiar to me. But without the usual brightness of the chandeliers bouncing off the light walls, I've already forgotten the details. I could say the same for remembering who else is in the room. Let me think.

My two dear friends, of course. Then there are Marie Morgan, Josephine Bamford, Cynthia McCormick. The three most suspicious to me.

But then there are the others from the Armour, Swift, Field, Breuer, Pullman, and Morgan families.

Who appear to have lost their minds. Who has released that bloodcurdling scream? And why?

In the ballroom, the glow of candlelight shows there are women sitting. But not nearly enough to account for everyone. The attendant is hollering for women to return.

To stop fleeing.

Either they haven't given up on the idea of escaping or they've come to the same conclusion as me about a killer being among us.

And you know what? I may've been the first to insist we cannot leave, but I'm going to join them.

"Where's Court and Peg?" I say to Edith, having already progressed a few paces toward the closest exit. "We need to get out of here."

"But you said—"

To hell with that. "I've changed my mind. What if whoever went after Sarah isn't done?"

That must be all the convincing E needs. She's at my side, then a step ahead. Damn the fact she's always been quicker than me. A candle's glow catches on a green gown. Peg is wearing green. I call her name. She twists, her already-large eyes like saucers. I open my mouth—to say what, I'm not entirely sure—when there's a loud yell that could only have come from a man, although Ruth Armour could double as a bass singer in the opera.

Suddenly, I'm taking steps backward and not by choice. We're a herd of livestock—startled, skittish, and all moving as one.

"Back, back!" the man calls. A man without an accent. A man who is *not* the attendant.

I bump into a chair, momentum forcing my back end into a seat. On my way down, my candle catches on someone's curls. I blow a puff of air in her direction. No true damage done, I hope.

"All of you, find a seat. Sit down!"

It's this new man again, commandeering.

Well, I'm already sitting.

"E, Court, Peg!" I call into the room. "Over here."

The herd is no more. It's as if we've moved on to a game of musical chairs. Edith's perfume wafts beside me. I grasp her arm. "Here," I say, and I relight her candle. Once Peg and Courtney are seated, a dancing dot of light in front of each of us, I ask them, "Who is it that's telling us what to do?"

"A detective," Courtney provides. "Josephine opened the front door, and there he stood brandishing a badge."

"But the telephones are dead," I point out, forced to raise my voice over the frenetic noise of the room. "How did he know to come?"

Peg says, "The attendant was going to go out, but didn't have a chance."

I can't imagine anyone is walking about in such a storm, and no one has an answer to my question, though I'd struggle to hear them if they did.

"Quiet!" the detective yells. "You're acting like animals."

If he means to insult us into compliance, it works. The room falls silent.

"That's better. Now can someone tell me what in the hell is going on here?"

"Not until you tell us who you are, sir," Elizabeth Field demands. "It's not as if you're in uniform."

He fishes a badge from his pocket and flips it open. "Detective Davis. We wear plain clothes. Any other questions?"

What a foolhardy thing to ask. Has he never spoken to a room full of women before? I see a number of them are staring at the holstered gun beneath his suit jacket. I stand, drawing the room's attention, saving him, my shoulders squared. "It appears there's been an accident here this evening."

"What kind of accident?" he asks.

"Well," I begin, only for Elizabeth Field to interject, "There's been a murder."

"Yes, that," I say.

It's only the backlit glow from the foyer's fireplace that gives the detective any shape, and I miss his reaction. Though his voice is gruff as he questions, "And you were all trying to leave?"

I try for calm. "We are but nervous women," I say, my fingers instinctively reaching for the pearls no longer around my neck.

"Where is the body?"

"In the parlor."

"Why are the lights out?"

I scrunch my brows. "I can assure you, sir, we're not playing blind-man's buff. The storm . . ." But I trail off. As I speak, I instinctively look toward the outside. Before, when I opened and closed the exterior doors, my haste knocked the snow from the glass panes. And now I see the windows lit up on the building adjacent to ours. "Only our electricity is out?"

How can that be?

Detective Davis demands, "No one move. Stay exactly as you are."

Truth be told, I'm too startled and off kilter to take a single step. But I do move. I sit down, not trusting my knees.

Trusting hardly anyone in this room . . . because now I'm realizing that someone not only murdered Sarah but also purposely cut our electricity in the aftermath of her death.

Chapter Six

EDITH

The grandfather clock chimes. It begins to gong the first of nine. I ask myself, *Edith, how have we only been here an hour? And not an eternity?*

And now that the brass has arrived, we'll likely be here for many more hours until this whole thing is resolved. This is not how I planned for the night to go.

"Nobody move an inch," the detective barks to the room. To the attendant: "Come with me."

The two men leave the ballroom, I assume to see to getting the lights back on.

With Detective Davis gone, the room immediately erupts, with women talking over one another. It's an odd sensation, hearing but not being able to see everyone fully. It makes our Big Four table feel intimate and private, just how I like it.

Along with the chatter, I also expect a mad dash toward a door. Yet there's no movement or sounds of movement, only a low murmur from Ginevra as she says, "Somewhere, I put down my teacup and my clutch. I could really use more 'tea' to get ahold of myself."

"I'd share, but . . ." Courtney turns her cup upside down, not a drop falling out.

At the other tables, the women all fall into hushed conversations.

"What an evening," Gin says to our foursome, then palms Peg's hand. "Are you okay? Even if you weren't Sarah's biggest fan, she was still your sister-in-law. And Eddie, he'll be upset."

"He'll be upset about the family name being in the paper again, I suspect," Peg says, her voice deadpan, as if in shock. Usually, Peg is the most emotive of us. I worry she's been broken.

Quite a few years ago, before she ever met Eddie, when Eddie was only a boy, he was kidnapped. A ransom was demanded. Eddie's father, also an Eddie, paid it. Many vilified the family's decision to do so, believing that paying the criminal set precedent for future kidnappers being paid off.

The man who did the deed, Pat Crowe, also went on to publish a book from prison about his wrongdoings. It put him on the map. It made him a bestseller, in fact. Considering we're stuck here, it gives me an idea. I lean across the table, careful not to singe the beading along my mustard-colored dress, and speak so only my three friends can hear. "Court, you could write about tonight's events. A catalyst for finding your thing." Not a question, but a statement. A suggestion. I add, "We could help you gather information."

I wouldn't mind having a hand in what she writes.

Courtney's head cocks. "Imagine if this is how I make my mark. Murder is even bigger than unearthing the story behind Josephine being the Poisoning Posy. Unless, of course, Josephine is behind this too. Poisonings are quite common in murder mysteries. I can think of four stories from Agatha Christie alone that involve cyanide, strychnine, or some other life-ending substances."

Gin chuckles. "Your face is lighting up, my dear. Perhaps downplay your enthusiasm, or you will be the first person this detective questions."

Courtney matches her laugh. "I may be the one asking him questions. Or better yet, why should he have all the fun?"

"Fun?" Peg asks.

"Merely a turn of phrase," Courtney says. "What I was going to say is—what if *we* solve Sarah's murder?"

Now that's an idea.

Peg frowns. "Isn't that unsavory?" Her expression turns sheepish. "Though I was going to suggest we continue our whist drive to pass the time, and that's not much better. In either scenario, Sarah is dead and we're trying to amuse ourselves."

"Not solely amusement," Ginevra says, "but also self-preservation. The murderer is still among us. The sooner we find the culprit, the sooner we'll be out of her clutches. I don't know about you, but I don't want to be added to the body count."

"You think . . ." Peg's bottom lip trembles. "You think the murderer will strike again?"

"That's the jam," I say, as Gin covers Peg's hand. "We don't know anything at all. I like this plan of donning our own detective caps. The four of us doing it together."

Ginevra reaches across the table, lifting up her pinkie finger and with it her rose gold ring. All four of us link up. It's been our thing for years, ever since we debuted and began wearing identical rings with *The Big Four* inscribed on the inner bands. Other women have tried to finagle their way into our foursome over the past decade to no avail.

"So we're going to truly do this?" Ginevra asks. "I won't lie—it's very exciting. Where do we begin?"

Courtney smiles. "With the queen of murder mysteries. I suggest we take a page out of Agatha Christie's book. Edith, you'd like one of her recent novels. It takes place on a golf course."

I release a very throaty noise, one that startles my friends.

"What on God's green earth was that sound?" Gin questions. "Please tell me you haven't been poisoned."

"It's golf," I say, thinking on my feet. "I'm growing bored of it. Well, maybe 'bored' isn't the correct word. But I may be ready to move on."

I never imagined I'd have these thoughts, but being on a golf course has been soured for me. I still play weekly and in competitions—it's what's expected of me—but every time I step onto the sixth hole, bone-chilling memories flood me.

Courtney lifts her candle, shadows dancing over her face. "Perchance you want to move on to murder?"

I barely hold in a choking sound, the idea of murder and golf hitting too close to home.

"Stop that," Peg says, gently pushing Courtney's wrist, and the candle, back down. "Don't make light of death. Especially Sarah's. She's bound to begin haunting us this very moment."

Ginevra looks utterly appalled. "Anything but that. Courtney, tell us about this Christie novel. How does she go about solving the murder?"

"Well," Courtney begins, the four of us in our own halo of combined light, darkness beyond, "the novel starts with Christie's detective receiving a pressing letter inviting him some place or another because the letter writer fears for his life. But by the time the detective arrives, the man is already dead. Found stabbed in the back on a golf course."

Ah, a knife as a murder weapon. Or at the very least something sharp and piercing. I pose a question: "We've speculated about poison, but we don't actually know our cause of death. None of you saw anything while you were in the parlor that could explain how Sarah died?"

No one speaks.

"No," Courtney finally says. "So I suppose we could skip directly to the whodunit portion. If memory serves me, the man's wife claims several men, maybe two, broke into their home and abducted him. Clues are found, such as the remains of a check in the fireplace and a footprint by the body. The man also had a heated argument with his son prior to his death. The father—the now-dead man—didn't approve of the son's paramour."

"Love, money, and revenge," Ginevra says, shaking her head in jest. "Isn't that always the case?"

I raise a brow. "Should we ask Murderess Marie her take on those particular motives?"

Courtney laughs. "Quiet, she'll hear you."

I scoff. "I'm not buying that angelic act of hers."

We all exchange a shared expression, agreeing.

"And next?" Gin asks, ever the ringleader keeping us on target. "What's next to happen in Christie's mystery?"

"The paramour is also killed."

"A second murder," Peg all but gasps.

"Yes. After the second death the detective digs into everyone's past and their connections. It all becomes very complex. In fact, Ginevra, it reminds me a bit of your Scott's *Gatsby* novel."

"First of all," Ginevra retorts, "he is not *my* Scott. Not anymore. Second of all, you didn't tell me you read that thing. How did you even hear about it? I thought it was mostly Sarah spouting that nonsense."

There's hurt in Gin's voice.

Courtney's eyes flick to me.

Oh, horsefeathers and halibut.

"Edith," Ginevra more than snaps. "You told her about Scott's novel?"

"It's a nationally published novel," I say in defense. "It's only a matter of time before more people read it. It's his fourth book. He's not a nobody."

Gin pouts, her expression sinister looking in the candlelight.

"I'm sorry," I add, truly hating that she believes I've betrayed her. I didn't think telling Courtney, an aspiring author, about another writer's published work was grounds for getting iced out.

"Forgiven," Gin says, gripping my hand tightly. "Now, Courtney, what was your point in bringing up Scott?"

"Only that in his novel almost all the characters are connected to the murder in their own ways. It adds to the complexity of the death and the paths that led to the death."

Peg's lips are more pursed than ever. "For Eddie's sake. For our sake. I hope this isn't complex."

"Agreed," Ginevra says, "It could make for a very late evening for us. But we could hurry it along and put an end to this ghastly evening. Who knows, maybe I'll single-handedly identify the culprit."

I raise a brow.

Ginevra chuckles, as if she was trying to get that exact rise out of me. Then she questions, "In the Christie book, how does the detective's sleuthing continue?"

All eyes are on Courtney. "Truths are revealed. The murderer is identified. A motive is established."

I say, "The good stuff. How did it play out—"

The chandeliers flash on, blindingly so.

I scrunch my eyes, palming them for a beat. But when I remove my hand, a chill runs down my spine. Murderess Marie is staring directly at our table. Directly at me. There's nothing angelic about her expression. And I wonder how much she's overheard.

Chapter Seven

Ginevra

The lights are back on. It's disorienting. It's alarming. Cards are strewn about on the round tables. Something, I'm not entirely sure what, triggers me to count heads. Nineteen of us. Twenty with the attendant. Twenty-one with the detective, as the two men saunter back into the room. We are all accounted for. Minus Sarah. Though I suppose she's technically still in the building . . .

Sarah "the Snake" Cudahy. If she could entangle herself with another woman's husband so effortlessly, what other lines might she have crossed without blinking? Who else could she have rubbed the wrong way? Honestly, I'm curious to uncover who has murdered her. But not only that, my involvement in this mystery allows me to control the narrative.

And Edith isn't wrong. If Courtney were to write a tell-all of a prominent Chicago woman who hails from a family known for scandal, her work would fly off the shelves. Much better than Scott's. She'd overshadow him in bookstores, maybe even push his novel more toward obscurity. Now there's a lovely thought.

If I solve this, I come out on top. A simple equation. I pause from my thinking and primp my curls, sensing eyes focused in my direction. Marie's. She notices me noticing her, her expression morphing from hard lines to something softer. What a peculiar girl. Gorgeous. Even more innocent looking than Peg. It's intriguing yet startling that she's on husband number four in so few years.

And that's something coming from me, who was expelled from the Westover School for being—and I quote—"a bold, bad hussy." Such colorful language from my former headmistress. But as I said to Scott at the time: I know I am a flirt and I can't stop it.

Though I have tempered that behavior. Mostly. My marriage to Bill was arranged, as many are. It makes me wonder again . . . if I'm claimed to be Daisy Buchanan, is Bill meant to be Tom Buchanan? One could argue there are similarities there. An avid polo player. A cruel body. Enormous power. Arrogant in every way. Racist politics. Limitless superiority. Adulterous behavior.

Daisy could have chosen Gatsby.

I could have chosen Scott.

"Whose is this?"

The question bursts through my reverie. The detective is holding a mustard-colored cloche hat in his fist.

It's clearly not mine. My red dress would clash. And it obviously doesn't belong to Courtney, who is wearing a complementary color. Blue should only be used judiciously. Nor can the hat be Peg's, whose green dress is a saturated color and would be too overwhelming a choice to accompany a yellowish-brown accessory.

Those with neutral tones—Marie, Greta, Josephine—could pull off the garment the detective is dangling.

But truly, the hat can only be Edith's. It's the exact mustard color of her dress.

I ask the sensible question: "Why do you have Edith's hat?"

The detective's gaze jumps around the room, as if he's trying to single out E and place who she is.

Eyes are scrunched at his lack of common sense.

Ruth Armour states, "The woman in mustard."

Everyone's gaze, last but not least the detective's, now falls on Edith. She stands from her chair, impossibly tall, a picture of poise, yet her forehead wrinkles. She repeats my question. "Why do you have my hat?"

He clears his throat, still holding the accessory in question above his head. "I found it next to the electrical box."

"That's impossible," she says, a chuckle to her voice.

"Ma'am—" he begins to say, but I cut in, also standing. "Hello, I'm Ginevra King Mitchell." I palm my chest and wait for recognition to bloom on his face. It does not, though I suppose we run in vastly different circles. "I can assure you Edith was nowhere near the power box." I actually cannot guarantee him such a thing, but the next part is true. "None of us even know where an electrical box can be found."

This is met with general agreement from the other ladies.

"So," I go on, "there must be some sort of misunderstanding."

The detective finally lowers his arm. A steely gaze emerges on his face. "I intend to get to the very bottom of it."

"Splendid," I say. "I can speak for all of us when I say we'd like answers for what's transpired here this evening with poor Sarah. And, of course, with Edith's hat too."

The detective locks eyes with me. "I'll speak with you first."

"Very well," I say casually. Bill has tried this intimidation approach with me. It never takes.

The detective adds, in a voice I presume he thinks sounds authoritative, "I'll be interviewing everyone, so the rest of you are to remain in this room."

I sneak a peek at my girls. Edith's wrinkles have smoothed, and her countenance seems more perturbed than anything that her name has been mixed up in tonight's unsavory events. She meets my eyes. Where the detective tried for toughness, Edith's expression holds a glimmer of something mischievous. She mouths "Good luck" to me.

A silly thing to say, considering I didn't have a hand in Sarah's demise. I take a step in the detective's direction, then pause. I look back at E. She's smiling, casually taking her seat again. I narrow my eyes, knowing that grin. I've seen it before, whenever we are matched head-to-head on anything.

Tonight, Courtney has proposed we solve this mystery. I've proclaimed myself capable of finding the culprit. And that antagonistic expression from Edith suggests she has thrown down the metaphorical gauntlet. Edith has just made finding Sarah's murderer—and the truth regarding her hat—a competition, one she believes she'll complete first.

In actuality, it shall be me who wins.

I return her smile.

She nods.

I nod.

As Sherlock would say, "The game is afoot." And I'll be a step ahead, the first to speak with the detective.

I begin to follow on his heels, but someone snags my elbow.

"Oh, Peg. Why are you frowning at me? You'll give yourself lines."

She presses on the skin by her mouth, stretching it taut, then refocuses. "Are you truly making this unfortunate situation into a game?"

She knows me . . . us . . . too well. Still, I argue, "Edith was first to suggest . . ." I trail off; it's not the answer Peg is looking for. So I amend, saying, "I know how it sounds, Peg. But let's think of it as a friendly competition to help pass the time?" I hold up a finger. "Or better yet, a contest to see how quickly I can bring Sarah's murderer to justice. Wouldn't you rather I solved this quickly, before anyone else gets hurt?"

"Ginevra . . ."

"He's getting away, Peg. I must go."

As soon as the detective and I are in the foyer, my gaze lands in the parlor. There's no door to the room, but a receiving table that was once against a foyer wall has been moved in front of the entryway. Fortunately—or maybe unfortunately for sleuthing purposes—Sarah is positioned out of sight, her chair in a corner, and the detective and I pass the main entrance and go toward the dining room. It has the most stunning pocket doors, gold in color with beautiful millwork. I pass through, expecting the equally beautiful room I've previously dined in.

It immediately becomes clear it's been redecorated, along with the fact the gentleman of the house, Mr. Larson, is a gamesman and that his wife is very tolerant. It's the only explanation for why a giant elk head is positioned as the focal point of the room. At least it's a tasteful mount and doesn't clash with the aesthetics, which are, in fact, rustic. An earthy color palette. A large cast-iron chandelier. Two wooden beams across the room. All that remains from before is a long centuries-old table. Some say it was once owned by Henry VIII, an avid hunter. Who was also known to take heads.

If that table could talk . . .

"Please have a seat, Ms. King Mitchell."

I wish to correct him and say "Mrs.," but I only arrange my face pleasantly.

He gestures to a seat, which he does not pull out for me. I can do it on my own, of course, but have manners also perished this evening? His lack of etiquette is a shame. He's handsome, with a strong jawline accented by a beard, and with flecks of auburn in his long brown hair, swept to one side. It's his snazzy plum-colored suit jacket that makes him a dead ringer for a sophisticated-looking headmaster. Or at least someone in line to become one, as I surmise him to be in his twenties.

Head positioned just so, hands on my lap, I once again arrange myself as a well-bred woman should. "I must ask," I say, speaking first, admittedly not as a woman should, "was the electricity tampered with? You seem to have had no problem getting the lights back on. I must thank you, by the way."

"It was a simple fix."

And a simple answer that does nothing to address my question. Another springs to mind. "How did you know to call on us? One of the women said she tried to telephone, but the lines were down."

The detective removes a small notebook from his breast pocket. "Who is the woman who tried to call the police?"

I have to think a moment, staring at the grass cloth wallpaper as I do. I'm momentarily distracted, thinking the wallpaper was different last time I dined in this room. Yes, it was floral. I refocus; it's important that I provide him a woman's name. I help him. He helps me. Ah. "Greta. She was closest to the door, so I assigned the task to her."

"What is Greta's surname?"

That I do not know. Sarah didn't include it in our introductions, which isn't uncommon. Many of the families in attendance have been in acquaintance for generations, and it's assumed we know who is who. If I had to speculate, Greta's features could very likely put her in the Breuer family tree with Jasmine and Cordelia. I detect a hint of German in her voice. I could say as much, but I want to be seen as a trustworthy source who doesn't speculate.

The detective likely recognizes I don't know the answer, as he asks me a new question. "How did you become the woman dishing out assignments?"

I chuckle. But his expression is serious. In my lap, I thumb my pinkie ring. My slight laugh morphs into a demure smile, a little pompous. Intentionally. "It's expected of me to take on a leadership role. I'm sure you can relate as a detective in such a large city."

He blows past my flattery. "Yet Miss Sarah Cudahy was tonight's host."

"How do you know . . . Oh yes, our attendant for the evening. You've spoken with him, I assume." The detective is silent, but I've been married eight long years. I know the ploy of omission equaling truth. "This particular event is run biannually. This time, Sarah was named the host."

"Who ran the previous event?"

"I did."

He jots in his little notebook. I let him. A guilty woman would add more and talk herself into a corner. Me explaining that it's time consuming to work with the kitchen staff ahead of time, then see to everything after the staff leave, will mean nothing to him. Besides, I'd rather ask him the questions. "Forgive me for the nature of my question, but is Sarah still in the parlor?"

He looks up at me from his writing. "The medical examiner has not yet arrived. On account of the storm, I don't expect him until the morning."

How ghastly, to think Sarah will remain sitting upright, a cloth napkin over her head, for hours still.

Hours that I will use to solve the mystery of this unfortunate turn of events. Not only do I wish to win, but we also can't have a murderer running around freely. "What questions do you have for me, Detective? I wish to be nothing but helpful."

He proceeds to ask me a slew of them: where I was when the lights went out, any interactions Sarah had with guests prior to leaving the ballroom, who else was missing from the ballroom, who was still with me in the room.

I answer honestly. I interacted the most with Sarah upon my arrival, the first hand of whist beginning only moments later. I was speaking with Courtney when the lights went out. Peg left the room. Edith returned to the room. Same with Marie. I can't recall particulars on the others. There were many of us in the darkened space.

"The two women—Edith and Marie—returned from where?"

"I can't speak for Marie, nor would I ever speculate and do you a disservice, Detective. I'll be candid that Edith had been with Sarah in the parlor."

I'm only so cavalier, casting suspicion on my best friend, because she's already told me she left Sarah in the parlor *alive*. Though I don't say as much to him. He'll ask her himself, and I'll use that time to continue my own investigation and get a leg up on her.

He finishes jotting information on his pad, then claps it closed. He's about to dismiss me, but I haven't gleaned anything from him yet, nor has he answered my original question of how he came to be here.

I'm about to ask him again when he frowns, then says, "I have to admit, I expected someone of your standing to have more to tell me."

Rude.

I search my mind for something to say, to ask, to offer. I also don't want to leave this room without a clue to continue to explore.

I'm not about to tell him Peg is related to Sarah and thrust suspicion on her. Edith can hold her own; Peg I'm unsure about. And the others, it's them I'm leery of. Now that I think about it—and as much as it chagrins me—it's possible some of the ladies here know about Sarah's indiscretion with Bill. They may try to paint a picture of me as a scorned wife. I'm sure the elk, marble eyes locked on me, would've liked a say in things.

I find it best to derail any gossip. When that can't happen, I like to get ahead of it. So I tell him in this private setting, to which his brows rise. He replies, "Some would say adultery is an excellent motive for murder."

I clear my throat. "Perhaps, if I cared much about my husband's infidelity. I do not. I want for nothing. I have two sons. And as far as I know, my reputation has gone unscathed. I'm respected in society. Some would say an essential cog in the wheel. Bill's dalliances—plural—aren't worth killing anyone over, that I can assure you."

"Huh," the detective says, though I struggle to ascertain if it's a positive or negative response. "But what if the perception of you would begin to falter?"

Like if I were called the muse of a fickle, careless character in some book?

A sharp and quick pinging noise jerks my attention toward the two large windows. "My goodness," I say, "now that doesn't sound good."

"The storm is a nasty one. A combination of sleet and snow by the sounds of it."

"It's so violent."

Speaking of violence, a thought comes to me. "I apologize for the nature of my question, but I'm curious—does poison always result in foaming in the mouth? Or is that something the silent films portray for the sake of being dramatic?"

One would think my question would catch him off guard, but he simply says, "There is not always foaming."

"I see. It's just that when I discovered Sarah, I can't recall any outward signs of death. But if I'm understanding correctly, you're saying she could have been poisoned without detection."

"Do you think Miss Cudahy was poisoned?"

"Like I said, I saw no signs of a bludgeoning." Do I mention Josephine at this point and her past expulsion due to a poisoning incident? No, I'll let the detective do his job. "But perhaps you could tell me—what are some common flowers that could, let's say, kill a person quickly?"

Is that amusement I see in his eyes? And he'll humor me with an answer? "We commonly see lilies, orange blossoms, hyacinth, oleander, and daffodils as being toxic, in varying degrees, to humans."

Impressive. He spouted those off without a moment's thought. But also, terrifying. "You've just named every flower I have in a bouquet at home."

Not to mention some of the very blooms that are in the ballroom on the refreshment table. I decide to keep this information to myself as well. He has eyes and will soon see for himself.

But then I stiffen. Sarah was drinking tea. Could it have been tampered with? The very same tea that I drank, that Courtney drank, that a number of the other woman drank?

"Ms. King Mitchell, are you all right?"

"Yes." I mentally inspect my own welfare for any nausea, stomach pains, or . . . what are the initial signs of poisoning? And how long until symptoms begin? Within minutes? Hours? Or perhaps even longer. Years ago, a story spread of a woman who had been poisoning her husband for an extended period of time before he finally succumbed to death. "Forgive me, it's all setting in that Sarah is actually gone and that someone here has had a hand in it. Do you think the rest of us are safe all in the same room? Maybe we should be split up. There are many rooms in the residence."

"I'll see to it," he says, "if that'll make you feel safer."

"Yes, thank you."

"Of course, Ms. King Mitchell. Also, I may want to ask you more questions later, as you seem to have a finger on the pulse of all matters and people within the building."

I smile warmly. "Why don't my close friends and I cordon ourselves off in the library? I trust Edith, Peg, and Courtney implicitly. Should you need me, I'll be there."

"Very well. I'll see to situating the other women. Could you ask Miss Edith . . ."

"Cummings," I provide.

"Could you ask Miss Cummings to wait for me in here?"

"Absolutely, and if you need anything—a refreshment, perhaps—please don't hesitate to call on me."

I begin to leave the room, then pause, realizing he never answered my question as to how he came to know a murder had been committed here this evening.

Chapter Eight

EDITH

Ginevra returns to the ballroom, looking equal parts accomplished and unsettled. That's a lot for her to put on display. Squared shoulders and a confident walk, yet a crease between her brows.

As she passes the table we sat at earlier with Sarah, she discreetly swipes a stray teacup, saying "Hello, ladies" to the women who now sit there.

She slides into a seat with us and tilts on her elbows toward the table's center, which has the effect of making Courtney, Peg, and me lean closer too. She says, scanning each of our faces, "Who all drank the tea? Have you, Peg?"

Peg shakes her head no. "Why?"

"Thank goodness. Don't. Let's take extra precaution for you and the baby."

The what? I wonder. "Peg?"

"I'm so sorry, Edith," she says. "Ginevra and Courtney got it out of me right before we found out that Sarah . . ."

I congratulate her while being simultaneously frightened for her and how she'll navigate children. Peg's sweet disposition and curtain climbers seem in complete opposition to one another.

Gin asks, "Anyone else drink the tea? I know Courtney did. How do you feel? Woozy? Any pain?"

Court cocks her head but answers, "No."

What is Ginevra going on about?

"Splendid," she says, "I feel fine as well. I'll explain."

Finally.

"But first, I appoint Courtney our scribe, the Keeper of Clues." She clanks the teacup against the tabletop. "And I just may have our first lead. Sarah drank from this. I nabbed it from where she sat earlier. Is there a way we can test it for poison?"

"What did you say?" Peg questions, eyes wide.

"You know what, not here," Ginevra says. "Come with me to the library. I've chosen that room for us. Conrad will be separating us into small groups and putting us in various rooms."

"Who?" I question.

Ginevra chuckles. "The detective. We know his surname to be Davis, but I've decided he looks like a Conrad."

"Like the film star?" Peg asks.

"Which one?" Ginevra twists her lips.

"Nagel?" I offer.

"Veidt," Peg says.

Gin bobs her head. "Yes, the second one. From *The Cabinet of Dr. Caligari.*"

I ask, "The horror film? You barely kept your eyes open during it."

She laughs. "Yes, not my cup of tea, but it must be why the name Conrad sprang to mind. Similar long hair, but less ghoulish looking and with a beard. Anyway, the detective will now forever be Conrad to me."

Renaming someone is such a Ginevra thing to do. As if on cue, this Conrad enters the ballroom, announcing the very thing Gin just shared about us being assigned rooms while he conducts his interviews and investigation.

Immediately, there are high-pitched voices and commotion, and the detective tries to herd the women as if we're cats.

Gin speaks into my ear: "Conrad wishes to speak with you next in the interrogation room."

"Where?" I ask.

"The dining room. But trust me, he won't be serving you any delicacies in there. While you do that, I plan to get one step closer to a victory by scouring the library for any helpful information on poisons." She wiggles her fingers at me in a cheeky wave. I wrinkle my nose. She thinks she's already won, gathering clues while I'm talking with the detective. Well, game on; I intend to gather clues directly from him. In fact, why don't we up the ante. "Shall we set a wager?"

Gin's eyes light up. "For example?"

"If I win, you cannot update your wardrobe for an entire year."

A gleam enters her eyes. "And if I win, you must give William a golf lesson."

That's low, and she knows it. Children and I go together like gin and gravy. And her older son has the athletic ability of a tree stump.

But I have no intention of losing. "Deal."

She lifts her chin. "Deal."

We go our separate ways, Gin toward the library and me toward the so-called interrogation room. As I make my way, I notice a receiving table's been moved in front of the parlor's entrance. I can very easily climb over it and get inside if I need to, when the time is right. I'm not sure if Ginevra has the gall to go back inside that room, but I do.

I position myself in the interrogation room so that I can see the detective as he walks in. In the meantime, it's only me and a large six-point bull. When the detective enters, sliding the doors closed behind him, I plaster on a distressed expression that's unmissable in the well-lit room. "Please tell me, Detective, that you have an idea of who murdered Sarah."

He takes his good old time pulling out his seat, sitting down, removing a notebook from his breast pocket, arranging his pen. "Be reassured, I won't rest until I find the person responsible. You're Miss Cummings?"

"I am."

"Ms. King Mitchell was forthcoming that you were in the parlor with Sarah prior to her death."

Was she now? And look at Detective Davis, teeing off like Glenna Collett-Vare with something to prove. I play ball right back. "There is a strong likelihood I am one of the last people to have seen Sarah alive."

"How did she seem to you?"

"Ill-tempered. Though that's par for the course. Ginevra had gotten under her skin. Well, in truth, Sarah had gotten under Ginevra's first."

"About what?"

"A past love. A current love. Painting Ginevra in a bad light. Common weaponry for women in our station."

He raises a single eyebrow. "Ruthless."

"We can be, yes."

"Ms. King Mitchell claims she wasn't in the parlor with Miss Cudahy at all."

"That's correct."

"But you were."

All I do is smile. We've established that.

He licks his lips. "What were you and Miss Cudahy doing in the parlor together?"

"Sarah is—well, was—running a silent auction next month. I was bringing one of my golf clubs to the parlor to add to the donations some of the other ladies brought this evening."

I see the question in his eyes. Shall we see what happens when I create suspicions and stir the pot? I begin, "Marie Morgan brought a family heirloom. A brooch. Josephine Bamford donated a pressed flower. It must be rare to be worth anything, though I don't know the flower's name." I raise a finger theatrically. "Though I know it's not a daffodil. Josephine's history with that particular flower is less than charmed, especially after she nearly poisoned her lab mate, both believed to be fighting for the same TA position. This happened in England and didn't make the papers here in Chicago, most likely on account of her billionaire-politician daddy. He likes flashy vintage sports cars. Not flashy daughters. I attended boarding school with Josephine after it all happened, but unfortunately, her past followed her across the pond. A shame. Josephine likes to keep to herself. The quiet, reclusive type. But you'll see for yourself when you interview her."

Do I feel guilty for casting so much suspicion on Josephine? Yes and no. If not me, someone else here tonight is sure to share her story with the detective. At least this way I can remove a bit of his scrutiny from me.

As it is, he studies me. Then he thumbs backward in his notebook. "I don't recall seeing a brooch in the room."

So he's astute. He's also either not taking my bait about Josephine or not broadcasting his next move.

"Marie took back the brooch after we discovered Sarah no longer with us." I place a hand over my heart. "Something about never wanting to donate it in the first place."

My own statement sparks a question. Then why did she offer the brooch? There's more to that story, and I intend to unearth Murderess Marie's motive. Could it be blackmail? Blackmail that'd cause Marie to not only donate something precious to her but also kill? It makes a girl wonder.

"Ms. King Mitchell didn't bring a donation." He is really stuck on Ginevra, isn't he? He's correct that she didn't, though she did end up giving her pearls. I won't correct him, mainly because he goes on, "She also says she didn't see any signs of death. Did you?"

"No, not that I can recall. Though as you know, the lights were off at the time. We only had the light of the fireplace and candles. Can I be candid?"

"Please."

"Sarah often put on a facade. We all do at times, but Sarah more than most. When she delivers barbs, she does so congenially. With me, in the parlor, it was as if she dropped the act. She was agitated, aggressive, even. It's no fun to spar with someone in that condition. So I left."

"So you exchanged words?"

"It was mostly Sarah. We dated the same man. We all have over the years, truth be told. Though not many of us are still unmarried."

"But you are?"

I offer him a tight smile.

"Society doesn't know what to do with a woman who doesn't fit neatly into a hope chest or a housewife's apron. Anyway, Sarah was informing me how I'd never get a man down the middle aisle. Not like her. She recently became engaged to Thomas Winchester II," I say, using a hoity-toity voice for his name.

"Did the two of you date?"

"Of course we did. He's a dish. But Tommy is old news."

"Hmm," he says, "he wasn't old news for everyone."

I'm not sure what he means by this. But I move on, shifting my hands from my lap to the tabletop, folding them casually in front of myself. "When I left the room, Sarah had worked herself into a tizzy, but she was very much alive."

The detective taps his pen.

What? What is he thinking?

He clears his throat. "I'll also be candid, Miss Cummings. In such a scenario, the medical examiner could deem Miss Cudahy's death a result of cardiac arrest upon agitation."

My blood freezes. His tone. The slower cadence of his voice. The words themselves. Him making this accusation—I don't like it. I don't like it one bit. Where did I go astray with our conversation? It's as if I hit myself straight into a sand trap.

He eyes me, eventually saying, "Did you know, Miss Cummings, that there is something called homicide by heart attack?"

I tighten one hand into the other, heat breaking out over every inch of my skin. Yes, I've heard that phrase before. Maybe not those exact words, but that precise idea—that someone can be deemed a murderer by inducing heart failure. I have no response, no adequate rebuttal, too taken aback. But it's no matter; he continues to do all the talking. "Causing cardiac arrest through severe emotional distress can lead to criminal charges."

I hate that he sees me swallow roughly. The light above my head feels too bright, as if he can see every minute twitch of my face. The unblinking elk over the detective's head suddenly feels unnerving, a second interrogator watching my every move. I don't like being rattled—on the back nine or in a room where I've just been cast as the leading lady in a murder investigation. "Do you have any further questions for me, Detective?"

He smiles. His facade is even better than Sarah's. "I'd tell you not to go anywhere; I may have more questions for you later, but the blizzard should take care of keeping you close by."

I stand to leave, unable to get out of the shrinking dining room fast enough. I've only just closed the heavy double doors when movement catches my eye. A brunette in a scarlet dress, heels dangling from her fingertips, is just beginning to tiptoe up the staircase to the Bellevue's second level.

"Ginevra," I whisper.

Chapter Nine

GINEVRA

I nearly topple over at the sound of my name. Swinging my occupied hands for balance, I steady myself, raising a heel.

"Oh, it's you," I say to Edith.

She huffs, voice barely above a whisper as she nears the staircase, her heels clanking against the marble flooring, and says, "You knew I was speaking with the detective in there." Edith removes her left shoe, then her right, then soundlessly steps onto the stairs' runner. "What are we doing?"

"Well, I'm apparently trying not to break my neck when people surprise me from behind."

Edith glances toward the parlor (and Sarah) and makes a soft, sympathetic clucking sound. "A broken neck, perhaps?"

"That'd be a gruesome way to go." I shimmy as a shiver comes over me. "Come on, let's get out of sight before Conrad goes looking for his next woman to question."

We pad up the steps at a clip I'd usually never entertain. By the landing, my breath is growing labored. There's a simple wooden chair here. I can see why. Without delay, Edith rounds toward the next flight of stairs. I let out a soft groan, determined to keep up.

At the top, we pause. She whispers, "Now what? Why are we sneaking around?"

I'd rather not work in tandem on this clue, but E will never let me shake her now. I acquiesce. "I had planned to scour the library for a book on poisons—"

"Let me guess—not a one."

"No, toxins do not appear to be an encouraged topic in this house. Anyway, there aren't any other rooms on the main floor, so Josephine must be up here somewhere." I raise my left hand, in which I hold not only one of my shoes but also Sarah's teacup. "My plan is to ask for her help."

"Your plan is to ask a potential murderer about the potential murder weapon? Murder accessory? I don't know how to refer to it."

I press my lips together, like I do when one of my sons talks back to me, then say, "It's what could have been *inside* the teacup I'm interested in." At the top of the stairwell, I let out a breath as I survey the double doors in front of us, which lead to a hallway and various rooms. Or we could continue up to the third level. "Do you know how many rooms are above us?"

Edith shakes her head.

"Me neither," I say. "I've only ever used the lavatory on this level, but I believe there are multiple rooms."

A cough sounds nearby.

Behind us.

Down the stairs.

A manly cough.

Can a cough have an accent? I detect none. In any case, it's either Conrad or the attendant. I haven't seen the latter since we all scattered to various rooms. No matter who it is, I don't want him to catch us snooping around. I grab Edith's hand and drag her through the double doors and toward the lavatory. On the way, we pass a closet and detour inside. The space is without a door, but it's large, and we're able to tuck out of sight.

Footsteps bound up the stairs, not bothering to be discreet. It's Conrad, then. The attendant would never dare thump around like a brontosaurus.

My gaze jumps left and right, falling on linens and things, listening intently.

Conrad passes through the double doors. I hold my breath. Depending on which room he enters, he could spot us. I hear no knock, but the sound of his footsteps stops. "Did he go inside a room?" I whisper to Edith.

She's arguably braver than me. Not that I'd admit such a thing to her. But that means she should be the one looking to see if the coast is clear. However, E's expression, even within the darkened closet, is clear. She's frightened.

"What is it?" I ask her. "We've dodged him."

She closes her eyes and sucks in a steadying breath before she can speak. "I made a mess of things."

We're speaking at a whisper.

"How so?"

"I thought I had a handle on things with the detective, but instead I think I've made myself a verifiable suspect."

"You did what?"

"Don't gloat."

"Truly, E." I take her hand. "I'm merely surprised you'd let that happen. What on earth would your motive even be?"

"Thomas."

I shake my head, trying to keep up. "Thomas Nelson?"

"No."

"Philips?"

"No."

"Crawford?"

"Please, stop. No. Thomas Winchester."

I ask, "But why?" But then I remember, and answer myself: "He's Sarah's betrothed."

I'd forgotten. No, that's a lie. I ignored how she flashed around her ring and the mention of her engagement announcement. I didn't want to give her the satisfaction.

I question Edith: "But did you want to marry Thomas? I thought you dined with him a single time."

"Twice, and dessert."

I scrunch my brows. "As I recall, not serious between the two of you?"

"Not at all."

"Society couldn't have handled it," I say flatly. "But regardless, I'm confused, E."

She rubs her temples. I've seen her do something similar on the golf course after flanking a shot. She says, "The detective likely believes I was jealous of Sarah marrying him. I told him she was ill-tempered with me. She spat at me how I'd never marry."

"Why would you tell him such a thing?"

"I was trying for honesty."

"Oh, Edith, have I taught you nothing? But let's focus. Love. Money. Revenge. We know those are the reasons people kill." I tap my lip. "Speaking of which, perhaps we should try to determine the motives of the other women. Wait, pretend I never said that." This is a competition, lest I forget that.

Edith rolls her eyes and is about to say something when there's a noise. A door opening? Or closing? Voices. Conrad's. And a woman's I can't place. Another guess: He's bringing someone to his interrogation room.

I do hope it's not Josephine. I have my own questioning to do.

The sounds dissipate.

"Coast clear?" I mouth to Edith.

She nods.

I whisper, "Which room should we try first?"

The second room is directly across from us. No place like the present. I slink into the hallway, then press my ear against the door. "Nothing."

Edith gestures for me to go in.

And okay, why not? If Josephine is not within the room, I can utter an apology and go on my way. First, I may as well peer through the keyhole. I do, but the side of the fireplace blocks much of my view. I can only discern the corner of a four-poster bed.

I twist the knob, the hinges barely reacting to the swing of the door.

I nearly burst out laughing.

Josephine is indeed in the room . . . with her ear pressed against a door on the opposite side of the fireplace.

I say, "If I had to guess, you're not eavesdropping on a linen closet."

Josephine looks truly abashed, her cheeks growing a rosy shade of pink.

I stifle a second laugh. In the far corner of the room, tucked between the wardrobe and the wall, and as far from Josephine as possible, sit—on the floor—Mrs. Pullman and her daughter. I want to ask them what on earth they're doing, but it feels insensitive. So instead I simply question, "Rose?"

My mind blanks on her daughter's name. She only just debuted. Daisy, maybe? Though just thinking the name causes aggravation.

If I had to guess, the Pullman women know of Josephine's reputation, thus their sequestering themselves in the corner. Though, to think—Josephine's stain occurred years ago. These misgivings are hard to overcome, and as far as my unfortunate situation, I'm hopeful any inkling of Bill's affair has died with Sarah.

Edith and I walk into the bedroom and close the door.

Rose never did answer me, but maybe it's because I've turned my full attention back to Josephine.

A grin appears on E's face. "Hear anything juicy, Josephine?"

"I wasn't—"

"You were," I say. "But I won't judge you for snooping. Who is in the adjoining room?"

Josephine answers in a small voice. "Marie Morgan and Elizabeth Field, if I've distinguished their voices correctly."

I file away this information and gesture to a trio of chairs. This room, in comparison with the interrogation room, is much more feminine, with blush pinks, pale lavenders, and mint greens.

The three of us sit, and I present the teacup as if we're about to embark on an innocent tea party. Unfortunately, our topic of conversation is much more serious. "I won't insult your intelligence, Josephine," I begin, my gaze momentarily straying to the frazzled Pullmans in the corner. "We all know of your knowledge of toxins."

At that, the elder Pullman begins to fan herself. The younger one eyes the shoes we're still holding, no doubt doing the math that we've removed them to better skulk around the house.

Does it make us appear suspicious? Yes, yes it does.

Beside me, Edith sets her heels down on the oriental rug, as if that'll defuse the tension. I wager it can't hurt to do the same.

I focus again on Josephine. "Could you examine this teacup? Tell me if its contents were toxic?"

She hesitates. Josephine is beautiful. Her hair, dress, eyes, even the feather in her hair, all matching. A raven black. It's all very dark, but the look appeals to me in a polished sort of way.

Josephine takes the cup from me and brings it to her nose. She angles and tilts the vessel toward the light, sconces for reading lining the walls. She runs a finger along the inside, then brings her fingers to her lips.

"Should you do that?" I ask.

Josephine smiles, a cunningness behind her timid demeanor. "I thought you said you wouldn't insult my intelligence."

I like her. "Please, carry on."

She does, finally handing the cup back to me. "I've had the tea tonight. Something has been added to Sarah's."

Mrs. Pullman may need smelling salts. As it is, my heart pounds wildly; I wasn't expecting Josephine to confirm that Sarah's tea had been tampered with. "Do you know with what?"

She licks her lips, ultimately shaking her head. "No, sorry. I was one of the first to arrive tonight. I saw nothing peculiar. Nor anybody acting strange."

Every ounce of me wishes to let out an egregious sigh. I glance at Edith, her lips twisted. "We should go," she says.

"Wait!" Josephine says, causing me to jump.

"What is it?" I ask her. "Is something the matter?"

"It's just that . . ." She takes in Edith with a quick look.

"What?" Edith questions.

It's as if I can see Josephine counting down in her head, convincing herself to say it. Then she does. "I overheard you and Sarah in the parlor."

My mouth drops open.

Edith's is the opposite, jaw tight.

"And," I prod.

No one answers.

"What is it you're implying, Josephine? What did you overhear?" I insist.

"Later," Edith says. Just that single word.

"Excuse me?" I say.

"I'll tell you later."

"You'll do no such thing. Josephine—"

Edith starts toward the door. "Fine, stay if you want, but if the detective goes to the library and finds us missing, it won't look good."

She has a point.

I give Josephine a final fleeting look. She's wringing her hands together. Quite a different response from Edith's, who is coming off agitated and guilty as sin.

"Thank you, Josephine." I turn to leave, offering the Pullmans a smile as I do. The daughter . . . Daisy . . . has scratches along her neck. Defense wounds? Could she and Sarah have gotten into an altercation? Could Daisy have had a hand in Sarah's death?

Despite the threat of Conrad discovering us missing, I must find out. "Dear Daisy," I say, hoping I haven't gotten her name wrong. "You've been injured. No doubt as we were running around like banshees in the dark."

Rose, still clearly rattled, her voice shaky, speaks up. "Oh, no, they're from me. My own fault during a moment of panic."

My mind is cruel to me, instantly making a comparison with Scott's novel, where someone covers up Daisy's act of murder. Could that be the case here? Protecting someone under the pretense of love?

Edith offers, "I could get you some tea to calm your nerves."

Rose's mouth falls agape.

"Of the nontoxic variety," I assure her.

Still, she declines.

Very well.

As soon as I close the door behind me, Edith whispers into my ear. "She's lying."

Chapter Ten

Ginevra huffs out a dry laugh. "No kidding. The question is, which one of them is trying to fool us? Should I include you in that list? What is it you're keeping from me?"

"It's nothing pertaining to tonight."

"Then what *does* it pertain to? Since when do we keep secrets from each other?"

I puff out my cheeks, letting the air whoosh out. "We don't. I'm just not ready to talk about it yet. Please, Gin. When I'm ready . . ."

She twists her lips, and I know it's incredibly difficult for her to stand down on this. She's not happy. She'll likely continue to make offhand comments on the topic. But for now, she'll let it go; she proves me right when she says, "I think all three of them are lying."

"I tend to agree."

Gin dangles the teacup in front of my face. "Even if Josephine— one of the country's most elite botanists—claims not to know the toxin, I believe she's telling the truth about there being a toxin."

I nod. Now access and motive, the next two questions to be answered. I don't need to say this out loud. I know Gin is thinking the very same thing.

We slink down the stairs and into the foyer, again passing the parlor—with its lights off. Which means someone has been in there since the electricity came back on.

In the library, we find Courtney and Peg huddled by the fireplace. Above it is a portrait of a woman in a black dress with black hair. Her expression looks a touch downtrodden. She reminds me of Josephine.

"There you both are," Peg says, a protective hand over her stomach. "This is all too much. You know my grandmother had a weak heart. When the attendant came by to check on our fireplace, he had suspicion written all over his face at the two of you missing."

So he knows we've left the room. It feels like one of those scenarios where I must read the putt before my next turn. I ask, "Only the attendant? Not the detective?"

"Correct," Peg says.

Gin asks, "Did he say anything of note?"

Courtney shakes her head.

To which I snap my fingers. Trying to glean something from his words goes out the window. But if I've learned anything from an "incident" on the links six months ago—I can't help glancing at Gin just thinking about it—it's that the truth is in the details. But also that those details must be protected at all costs.

"What is it?" Gin asks me. "You've got your thinking face on."

Do I? "Nothing of note from me either," I lie. "But," I say, addressing Courtney and Peg, "we've learned something."

We settle into the two remaining chairs. Four in total, in a semicircle around the hearth. It's as if this room was meant for the Big Four to come together and solve tonight's misadventure.

Ginevra fills them in on our conversation upstairs, leaving out the juiciest tidbit about how Josephine overheard me with Sarah before she died. Gin didn't need to omit that. She could have pressed, and I likely would have folded and spilled my guts. I know my girls will forever have my back, even if I am staring down a murder.

Court, the Keeper of Clues, writes our first clue in her notebook.

Poison.

She underlines it and adds: *Possible cause of death?*

Possible, indeed.

She also adds: *Josephine lying?*

I'd bet my life on it.

Ginevra taps a manicured finger to the page. "Court, why don't you put my initials next to our first entry."

I widen my eyes at Ginevra.

"What?" she says innocently. "You assisted, but I was already on my way upstairs when you came along, so I should get credit. And just so you know, William is a horrible putter."

"Information that does not concern me," I retort. "I have no plans of losing—certainly not to your short game."

Peg and Courtney exchange confused expressions. I explain our bet, and that I'll let Ginevra have this one. I have bigger fish to fry. In fact, I'd love a longer peek at the parlor, at Sarah, at any other information I can gather.

I stand, my gaze giving away exactly where I'm headed: the door that connects our Big Four room with the parlor.

Peg gasps. "Tell me you're not going in there?"

I cross my arms confidently. "I intend for the next entry in our clue book to be mine. Ginevra, I hope you like that gown. You'll be wearing it all next year."

She rolls her eyes. Then, she glances at the parlor door, giving a shake and shimmy as if she's just walked straight into a spider's web and is trying to get the thing off.

I say to her, "It's okay. You don't have to come."

I'd prefer if she didn't. If none of my friends did. Though Peg is clearly not interested in joining me, and Courtney looks all too pleased to be sitting in a floral wingback chair, toasty by the fire, while scribbling in her notebook. I see *MOTIVES* at the top of a clean page.

"Splendid," Ginevra says. "While you go poking around, be a dear and fetch my clutch, would you? I think I left it in there.

Meanwhile, I'll go examine the refreshment area for any evidence." She holds up the teacup as if in cheers. Our Big Four room is conveniently attached to the ballroom as well. No wonder Gin declared the four of us would hole up in this room, giving us access to two additional rooms undetected. Mostly. Once I enter the parlor, anyone walking by can catch me in the act, even with the wall sconces turned off.

I tip an imaginary hat, then inch toward my connecting door. I pause, ear to the paneled wood, to ensure that Detective Davis isn't on the other side. All's clear. As I turn the knob, a gusty sensation rolls down my spine. I fight the urge to shiver, and I step inside, closing the door behind me.

I've no time to lose.

The fireplace is mostly embers, giving off only a soft glow.

Instantly, I shake out my arms, much like I do before I tee off to loosen up and relax. Much like I had to do last summer on the course after all hell broke loose. Back then, on the sixth hole, I had to tell myself to avoid looking at the deceased. I failed then, I fail now. Sarah, in the shadowed corner, is exactly where my gaze lands.

She's untouched, upright in a chair, feet crossed at her ankles, hands very demure in the lap of her plum-colored dress. Her posture appears posed. The linen still covers her head and face. That will remain untouched. For now.

From my position, standing just within the door, in the farthest corner from Sarah, I realize a shadow also does a decent job of obscuring me. Releasing a pent-up breath, I scour the remainder of the room. Much like in our Big Four room, the walls are a soft cream, but with thick wood moldings around the ceiling and door that are painted white. The slight flicker of the fireplace plays off the white ceiling, with a filigree that takes up much of the space. My parents' parlor is similar, including an oversize mirror that makes the room appear twice as large—and reflects myself back at me.

I have no desire to stare myself down just now. I'm afraid of what I might see—and worse, what I might admit.

Instead, I focus on the table of donations. On my golf club. You never know when I may need it, in a mansion full of women who may begin to act out of character. Or rather, in character.

Quickly, yet as quietly as possible against the marble flooring, I take the few steps needed until I'm at the table.

Gin did leave her clutch in here. I tuck it beneath my arm. Though, *curious*, I think. Ginevra's pearls are very much missing. But it's not only that curiosity that almost has me rushing back to Courtney to log a new clue with my initials beside it. It's the fact that the pressed flower appears to have been tampered with. The purple flower is in a glass frame, which brings to my attention a smudge of sorts. I tuck my club under my arm and lift the frame from where it sits atop a newspaper and extend it the best I can toward the light of the fire.

And yes, I see it clearly now. The petals are a vibrant purple, overlapping along a long stem. It looks similar to something in my parents' garden and at the club. A type of honeysuckle, if I'm not mistaken. Though I don't think it's rare. Josephine would know. Josephine brought the flower this evening. Josephine may have lied about this very flower. Because just there, if I look closely between the overlapping blooms, is the faintest of outlines—a portion that looks smudged against the glass. Meaning: Petals have been carefully removed.

And used in Sarah's tea?

Is honeysuckle toxic? Or is this not honeysuckle at all?

And the most haunting question: What would the effects of poison look like on a person?

I step toward Sarah's corner.

I'll use my club.

I'll flick off the linen from a safe distance.

I'll examine her, again from a safe distance.

I'll return to Courtney and Peg flush with evidence to mark with an *EC*. But I won't get ahead of myself. As a golfer, I never write down my scores until I arrive at the next hole.

And first, I must get through this.

My hand trembles, causing my club to shake as I stretch out my arm. I grow angry with myself that this very scenario has happened before. I quivered when I tried to prod him with my club that day.

Stop it, Edith, I silently chastise myself.

I reach and reach, my club only inches from Sarah, ready to reveal her face.

A scream slices through the silence, clean and sharp as a nine iron on a windless green.

I gasp, turning toward the sound. Close. In the foyer?

Another scream, this one stretching.

Without thinking, golf club in one hand, clutch still under my arm, I hurdle the table that blocks entry into the parlor and skid into the foyer. Detective Davis emerges from the interrogation room. His gaze passes over me before flicking to the left, toward a short hallway that leads to the coat closet.

Did he see me come out of the parlor?

I don't think so.

If he did, it won't help my case. Something else to make me look guilty as hell. But if he did, he also doesn't let on. Instead, he goes through the door. I follow. Murderess Marie, virginal in all white, blocks entry to the coat closet, which is actually more room than closet. A hand is at her mouth. "He's . . ." Shock's written all over her face as she turns to face the detective—and me. "I think he's dead."

"Stand back," the detective demands.

I do no such thing, instead inching forward, needing to get a look at our second victim of the night.

On the ground, only his black pants and polished black shoes show. The remainder of him is tucked behind our many hanging coats.

It's the attendant.

The only other male in attendance.

Detective Davis tries to separate the coats to get to him, but there's little room to adjust our thick furs and wools. He gives up, taking hold of the attendant's feet and yanking.

Little by little, with some resistance, the attendant is revealed.

With Ginevra's pearls wound tightly around his blue-tinted neck.

Chapter Eleven

At the sound of an earsplitting screech, I go completely still on my hands and knees beneath the sideboard table, where I've regrettably found no further poison-related clues. Not beneath, not on top of, not anywhere.

Quickly, I crawl backward, careful not to bang my head, and immediately run out of the ballroom.

I don't recognize the screamer's voice.

I nearly crash into Peg and Courtney in the foyer, staring in the direction of the coatroom. "What's happened? Who screamed? Where's Edith?"

My heart's pounding too fiercely to give them a moment to respond. I brush past them and down the short hallway, where I collide with E.

She's peering over Conrad's shoulder. Marie is here too.

"What is it?" I say to whoever is willing to answer.

Edith grabs my arm, her club knocking me in the hip, and switches our positions. She's taller than I am. Ignoring the dull pain from Edith's whack, I roll onto my toes, trying to gain every inch possible to look where the detective and Marie are gawking . . . inside the coat closet.

Then I see it.

I see him.

I see . . . "My pearls!"

Wrapped around the attendant's neck, the cluster of diamond and pearls tight against his Adam's apple.

I wail, "I'll never be able to wear them again now!"

I realize the insensitivity of my proclamation immediately. The detective's swift turn toward me and sour expression punctuate my disregard for the poor man.

A man whose neck and face are the same light shade of blue as my boudoir draperies. The similarity is off putting, and I make a mental note to order a new pair to be made. *Stop that,* I chastise myself. A man is dead, one whose name I didn't even know but who did a fine job at his, well, job. A man who was living and breathing not long ago, having gone by to check on Peg and Courtney.

How alarming to think the end can come so quickly.

So unexpectedly?

"Gin," Edith whispers, once again directing me, this time away from our newest crime scene and back into the foyer, which is now full of women. Cynthia; Greta; Elizabeth Field; Daisy and Rose Pullman; Henrietta, Rebecca, and Marjorie Swift; Jasmine and Cordelia Breuer; Ruth Armour and her twins—they're all here.

Courtney and Peg pounce. "What is it?" Courtney asks.

Edith is the one who answers, loudly enough for all to hear. "There's been a second murder."

That sends the foyer into a frenzy.

Cynthia calls out, "Who?"

Rose makes for the door, dragging Daisy behind her. At least she's on her feet instead of lying unconscious on the ground. This time it's Ruth Armour who looks as if she could topple like a redwood cut down. I motion to Elizabeth Field to steady the poor woman.

In a blink, Conrad is beside and then ahead of the Pullman mother-daughter duo, thrusting a hand against the door to keep it closed. "No one leaves!" His steely eyes jump from woman to woman. When his gaze passes over mine, I do my very best to straighten my spine. He growls, "Have some respect. This building is an active crime scene."

"Exactly, we're *all* in danger," Rose Pullman cries.

"You're *all* suspects," the detective corrects.

"I think you mean hostages," Greta seethes.

And she may have a point. We're all sitting ducks.

Conrad singles out Greta, pinning her with a look that causes me to take a step closer to her. "Shut your mouth."

He says the three words slowly, aggressively.

My next step is larger, bringing me to Greta's side. I put an arm around her shoulder. "You will not speak to her that way. She's afraid. We're *all* afraid."

"How's this?" he says, sneering at me. The tone of his voice softens, yet the feel of it is overwhelmingly condescending. "No one is to leave this building until I say so. Not only has the storm shut down the city, but it should also go without saying that anyone who tries to flee will be charged with obstruction of justice."

Elizabeth Field, her shoulders back, begins to say, "My husband—"

"I don't give a flying rat's ass who your husband is."

Such language. Bill is currently an investment broker of sorts. But there are some powerful husbands connected to these women that Conrad *should* care about. Mr. Field, for one, owns one of the nation's most influential wholesale and retail merchandising firms. This'll come back to bite Conrad in *his* ass.

Elizabeth Field squares her shoulders. "My husband is someone who will begin to worry if he does not hear from me. At least let us call home to let our loved ones know we are safe."

Without missing a beat, the detective takes three steps to a small table in the foyer that houses the telephone. He grabs it. He yanks the cord from the wall jack. He focuses again on Elizabeth as he nudges aside his jacket to reveal a gun within his cross-body holster. "I won't have you women creating any further hysteria. The coroner and whoever else is needed will arrive as soon as the storm allows."

This display of masculinity and authority feels completely heavy handed. I'd shake my head in disdain if I weren't feeling prickles of unease up and down my spine and if I didn't have a young woman currently trembling beneath my arm.

Slowly, the detective breaks his gaze from Elizabeth and scans the rest of us. "All of you, return to your rooms until I've had the opportunity to question you all."

The grandfather clock gongs the half hour.

We all jump at the sudden noise.

I recover quickly. I know it won't do me or my friends a lick of good to defy an officer of the law. "Will you be okay?" I say to Greta. She nods solemnly, then begins following the trail of women up the stairs. "Let's go," I say to my Big Four, ushering them toward our room.

Let's conspire.

Am I scared?

Naturally—a second person is dead, and there's no telling if my friends and I could be next.

But has Conrad's treatment of us lit a fire in me stronger than before to solve this? To beat him to an accusation?

Absolutely.

As soon as the door is closed and it's just the four of us again, I say, "So what do we know?"

Peg shakes her head solemnly. "That someone else is dead. And . . . and . . . that Elizabeth Field isn't wrong. Our husbands will begin to worry."

"Mine won't," I say flatly. Bill is likely sound asleep, not a single one of his indiscretions giving him pause. "But Eddie, yes, I can see that."

Edith shrugs. "I don't have a husband."

I sour at that. She could.

Peg wrings her hands. "Eddie will expect me to check in again soon. I've been experiencing sickness in the morning and night. He's overly protective."

I ask, "How are you feeling now?"

"Well enough."

Good. "And you were able to speak with Eddie earlier before the electricity cut off?"

"Yes." Peg nods. "Then the lights went out. I told him I'd let him know once they were back on, but I never got the chance."

I sigh. "He's surely worried. Maybe he'll come and help push this investigation along. Now, back to the second murder. It was—"

"The attendant, strangled with Ginevra's pearls," Edith provides. "I noticed them missing when I was in the parlor."

"And I notice my clutch."

I slip it out from where it's tucked beneath E's arm, promptly open it, pull out the crystal-studded flask, uncap it, and tilt it to my lips. It's been quite the evening.

"Wait, what?" Courtney says.

"I know," I say, "not very ladylike, but would you also like some?"

"Yes." She wiggles her fingers for the flask. "But that's not what I meant. Can we back up to your pearls?"

"Well, it's quite simple," I say. "My pearls appear to be the murder weapon. Write it down." I point to the notebook, then begin to pace over the floral carpeting. I retrieve my flask from Courtney, take another sip, then consider. "What is the connection between Sarah and the attendant? Are the two deaths related?"

I watch as Courtney jots down my questions.

"Oh Lord," Peg says. "Wouldn't it be horrible if the attendant was simply in the wrong place at the wrong time? He could have nothing to do with Sarah at all. He seemed very kind to me."

"Maybe," Courtney says. At first I think she's validating Peg's concern, but as she goes on, I see she has her own theory. "Maybe the attendant killed Sarah, and then someone killed him so he wouldn't talk?"

I ask, "You mean if he murdered Sarah on someone's behalf?"

"Exactly."

I pat her arm. "You may make it as a mystery writer yet, my dear."

Courtney's lips turn up into a small smile as she continues to scribble. I, on the other hand, continue to pace, once again kicking off my kitten heels. "Did you discover anything else in the parlor, E?"

She waggles her brows.

"Out with it," I say. "This is murder. Stop acting so smug."

Edith snorts, then reveals that she believes Sarah's body was posed.

Peg, as if finally realizing she's been standing all this time, lowers herself into a chair. "You believe someone killed her and staged her body? How disturbing."

Edith nods. "Can't you picture her—"

"I want to do no such thing," Peg insists. Her chest rises with a deep breath before she opens her oversize evening bag. From it, she pulls out a half-done crochet project.

"I'm with you, dear," I say, eyeing her hands as Peg begins to busy them with hook and yarn. But still, I go on. "Edith, you're saying she's sitting as if Mrs. Burton Kingsland herself is judging her etiquette. As important as perception is to me, I can't fathom that my dying breath would be wasted on ensuring my feet are crossed at the ankles."

"That may be tonight's biggest twist yet," E jokes.

I ignore her and continue to pace, glancing at my own feet—and the floral carpet, which reminds me . . . "The poison. Edith, if you are done with your quips, which we all know are a defense mechanism"—I pause to widen my eyes at her—"perhaps you could share if you found anything that could be related to the poison?"

"Did you?" Edith counters, taking a seat across from Peg.

I frown. Or as much as I'm willing to frown without getting wrinkles. "No. No petals seem to be missing from any of the flowers. Nothing was out of the ordinary about the refreshment station in general. But I take it you found something?"

She smiles, eerily reminiscent of the Cheshire Cat.

I pin her with a look I often use on my boys.

Edith reveals, "As a matter of fact, I think I've discovered *the* flower that poisoned Sarah."

She shares her finding and directs Courtney to mark it with her initials, bringing us to a tie. I hate to admit it, but the discovery that petals have been removed from the frame and were used as our toxin is a good one. What's more, I believe her to be correct.

Courtney asks, "Josephine brought the pressed flower?"

I nod.

The question is, did she do so for nefarious reasons?

Courtney has started a new column labeled *MURDER WEAPONS*.

So far, it includes the pressed flower and my pearls.

But wait . . .

"There's no way my pearls killed anyone."

Peg puts down her hook to wrap a hand around her throat, utterly distraught.

Courtney taps her pen against her lip.

Edith is the one who actually asks the question: "Why do you say that?"

"I've had to restring my pearls on account of William. We were playing together after luncheon, and he gave them a yank. Sent pearls scattering everywhere. If they snapped under the force of a toddler, there's no way they'd be strong enough to strangle a grown man."

"You have a point," Edith says.

I smile.

Courtney asks, "So what does this mean? Someone strangled the attendant, then made it appear as if Ginevra's pearls were used to do the deed?"

"Oh, Gin," Peg sputters, "Do you think someone used your pearls to suggest that you murdered the attendant? I can understand why someone could believe you killed Sarah. But the attendant . . . why insinuate you had a hand in his death too?"

Even asking the questions seems to have overwhelmed her. I cross the room and lay a hand on her shoulder. "We're all a bit wound up. I can assure you and whoever else needs to hear it that I've had no hand in either death." I release a long breath. "Two murders. I can't say I was expecting that. But we'll be okay."

I say it as much to comfort myself as to reassure the others, even if it is an empty statement. What's stopping the killer from killing again?

"Why stop at two?" Edith asks, echoing my exact sentiment.

"Edith!" I whisper-yell and nod toward a ghostlike Peg. No need to further upset her.

"Sorry," Edith says, standing. "I'm on edge."

She grabs the golf club propped against her chair and performs a perfect practice swing.

My attention catches on her—and that club . . . that I am only now realizing was with her in the foyer. I point. "Conrad saw you with that thing. If he has a brain, he'll know where you got it."

"I forgot I even had it with me," she admits. "When Marie screamed, I was using it at the time to . . ." She trails off. "Never mind."

I let it go, for the sake of Peg's fragility. "You better hope Marie's impressive lung capacity fully distracted him. Or if not, that he didn't remember seeing your club in the parlor with Sarah. He'll know you were in there poking around."

Courtney shakes her head. "Should I make a new column for suspects with your two names at the top?"

I palm my face. Take one last sip. What a mess. "We need to get to the bottom of this. And quickly. We're averaging a death an hour at this point. The only true lead we have is the pressed flower."

Edith nods. "Josephine. She has the answers, at least to do with the flower."

I assert, "And this time she's going to spill them."

"I'll go," Edith says.

I raise my chin. "Me too."

Edith opens her mouth, no doubt to object.

I put a defiant hand on my hip. "You tagged along with me last time. This time I'm coming with you."

Chapter Twelve

"Fine, but I'm bringing my club."

I didn't tell the girls, but the detective definitely saw me holding it in the foyer. Whether he does have a brain is to be determined. In any case, the damage has been done. All I can do at this point is make sure neither Ginevra nor I become the fall guy for this murder.

I crack my knuckles.

Ginevra gives me a look like I just lit a cigarette in church, then shrugs—because she knows I'm right.

I kick off my shoes and say, "If the detective sees us, we can claim our dogs ache. It's not as if he knows what it's like to wear heels."

Gin says, "How about he doesn't catch us." She passes her flask to Courtney. "Save some for me." Then, to me, she says, "Shall we?"

Her voice isn't necessarily carefree, but it's upbeat. It's also completely put on. Ginevra is a woman who relishes being in control. Not a woman who is often told no. Now she's trapped in an environment where she's being told what to do *and* where she wants to keep Sarah's affair with Bill under wraps. I'm surprised she only took three swigs of gin.

This night will be one for the Ginevra King Mitchell history books.

"If we don't return," I say, "tell Daddy he can buy that yacht he's been mooning over. He always said if I hit thirty unwed, he'd trade my dowry for a mainsail."

Gin retorts, "The least he could do is name it after you."

Peg rolls her eyes. Already whatever she's stitching is a few rows in length. "Why do the two of you insist on making such offhand comments?"

I say, not unkindly, "For the same reason you're stitching up a storm."

Peg reaches out her hand, wiggling her fingers. I take them, squeeze them. We understand each other. "Be safe," she says. "Both of you."

At the door, Ginevra and I pause to listen. I haven't eavesdropped this much since I was a child and my parents were throwing a dinner party I wasn't invited to.

Gin nods.

I nod back.

Then I turn the knob.

The foyer is empty.

The doors to the interrogation room are closed, hopefully with a less ill-tempered Detective Davis inside.

The receiving table is still in front of the murder room.

The telephone is sitting directly on the floor. The table it used to be on is nowhere to be seen, marooning a matching mirror on the wall. If I had to guess, the table now blocks the door into the coatroom, the second murder room.

We begin to creep toward the staircase.

The wind wails like a saxophone solo, covering the faint swish of fringe and beads as our flapper frocks shimmy through the dark.

Ginevra whispers, "How horrifying and sad to be standing between two dead bodies. It's not something I thought would ever be on my bingo board. Bingo. You know, that would've been more entertaining than whist. I have to admit I was nervous to play Marie Morgan tonight."

I cock my head. "Murderess Marie."

"That's right. We've played against her before, remember? She's quite—"

"No, it's not that," I say, pressing on. "Murderess Marie is the one who found the attendant. But why was she in the coatroom to begin with?"

Gin clucks. "Excellent question, my dear Watson. Shall we find out? She's in the room next to Josephine. We'll do a quick detour. Marie first. Josephine sec . . ."

There's a loud creak above us.

My heart beats wildly.

I don't think Ginevra and I are the only ones skulking around.

Could whoever is causing the noise be after us?

Going up the main staircase feels too risky. The detective could also emerge from the interrogation room and use the main stairs at any moment. But there's got to be . . . "A back staircase," I mouth to Gin.

Usually, such a thing would be accessed through the kitchen. We start that way.

"I have to use the ladies' room," Ginevra whispers.

"Now?"

"Yes," she says, an edge to her voice. "There's one just there."

On the other side of the ballroom's stage, inside a changing room, I know. "Just hurry."

She shoots me a look that says not to rush her, but I have to laugh as she prances, quite unathletically, onto the stage.

Now that I'm alone in this large room, I'm even more unnerved, gripping and regripping my club. The best way to describe the ballroom is *broken*. Abandoned games of whist, chairs toppled, teacups overturned, tea stains on the white tablecloths. I've sat in this room many times before, the street and building lights filtering in through the three glass double doors helping to light up the room. Tonight, with the doors once again completely blanketed with snow, it's as if the Bellevue has been buried alive. The chandeliers provide the only illumination, casting halos of light and giving off an ominous feel.

I'm pulling at the neckline of my dress, a second away from fanning myself, when Ginevra returns, face aglow.

"Edith," she whisper-shouts.

"What?" I say, meeting her.

"A door. I'd completely forgotten the changing room has an outside exit. We could leave." She backpedals, pointing. "We could get the girls and get out of here right this second. With Peg in her condition, I hate to think of her here."

"The snow will have created a barricade."

She shakes her head. "I remember there being an overhang. Maybe the snow's not as deep and we could shove open the door."

Now I shake my head. As dangerous and as suffocating as this house is becoming, I can't leave . . . because of what happened on the sixth hole. Because of what I did.

I have a strong feeling that someone else in attendance this evening knows about what happened that morning. And I worry I could be targeted next. But if someone is after me, I'd rather face it here and now when I know it could be coming.

Ginevra is waiting for me to reply, so I say, "We can't leave, not until this is over."

She narrows an eye. "Because of what Josephine overheard?"

I'm still not ready to bare my soul. Instead, I provoke her: "If you want to go because you don't think you can beat me in our clue game, just say so."

Her mouth drops. "It's not that at all."

"If you say so."

She squares her shoulders. "Never mind—let's get upstairs." Ginevra marches toward the kitchen, mumbling to herself, "Thanks to my darling husband, I have a secret to protect too."

I blow out a silent breath.

As suspected, we find a staircase behind an interior door. There are steps leading up . . . and down. Both are shrouded in darkness.

Gin mutters, "I didn't realize there was a cellar in this building. I have no desire to ever go down there."

I'm not too big to admit, "Me neither."

In unison, we lift our chins to gaze up the staircase. Even that feels creepy. It's not well lit. But we don't have any more time to waste. Detective Davis could come looking for us, especially me, at any moment. He could confiscate Courtney's notebook. None of that would look good for us.

Gin loops her arm through mine.

The first step creaks under our weight.

I pray no one heard it, the sound seemingly reverberating through the otherwise quiet house. We're tucked away, and the sounds of the storm feel far off. It'd be easy to hide here.

While on the greens of a course, it's best to keep the pace moving. So I forge ahead, bringing Ginevra along with me, squeaks be damned.

At the top, there are additional stairs to go to the third level. Before we go any farther onto the second floor, I proactively raise my golf club. I expect Ginevra to gawk at me. Instead, she taps her head, as if saying *smart thinking*.

We continue on. I peek my head into the first room we come to, the door ajar. The hallway light filters in, making the shapes of a faucet and cabinets recognizable. A butler's kitchen.

Ginevra points to another door within the small kitchen and mouths, "Another room?"

As in an adjoining room for future eavesdropping? I raise my eyebrows and bob my head in agreement.

From here, we'll have to pass by the main staircase. In retrospect, it would've been easier to simply use that one.

Or not.

Voices.

We scramble to tuck ourselves around a corner, back the way we came, shoulder blades pressed against a wall.

It's Detective Davis on the move again. And once more with a woman.

If only I could make out what they're saying. Or who the woman is.

Their footsteps move toward the stairs.

I have my club at the ready. "We would've been caught," I mouth to Gin.

She shakes her head, her expression truly exasperated.

Once we can no longer hear them, we pad past the staircase and down the hallway. We pass the room that connects to the butler's kitchen. The next door is the bedroom where Josephine and the Pullmans are holing up, undoubtedly at opposite corners of the room.

We're coming for you next, Josephine, I think.

But first the final door is where we head.

To Murderess Marie.

The john flushes. The lavatory is to our left.

We quicken our pace.

I try the doorknob on Marie's room, but it doesn't budge. Strange—the keyhole is empty. I crouch, peering through. A chair has been propped against it.

"They've blockaded the door," I whisper to Ginevra.

She sighs. "This is getting ridiculous. It shouldn't be this difficult to get to where we need to go." Ginevra raps her knuckles lightly against the door. "Marie," she whispers into the keyhole, "Please let us in. We're not the murderers."

I chuckle. "That's exactly what a murderer would say."

Silence.

I try, "Marie, it's Edith. Please let us in."

Will my name make her more or less willing to open the door? I curse, realizing my being here may hurt us, remembering the way Murderess Marie was glaring at me after the lights turned back on. If she *does* let us in, I make a mental note to drop the *murderess* portion of her name. That certainly won't win me any favor.

Whoever is in the lavatory is now washing their hands.

"Hurry," I say as Ginevra taps her foot impatiently, head on a swivel between the doorknob of Marie's room and the knob to the restroom. I try, "I think we know who the murderer is, and we could use your help."

That does it.

The chair against the door is pulled away.

Whoever is in the lavatory could emerge any second. That person may not be a fan of Gin and me leading our own investigation. Or we could be walking into the lion's den as soon as Murderess Marie lets us in.

But in golf, I have to be ready to play when I step up to the tee.

Or in this case, to Murderess Marie's door.

Which finally opens.

We stumble through, nearly clobbering Marie with my golf club in the process. It's a good thing we're not wearing shoes, our ivory-colored stockings making no noise on the hardwood. "So sorry," I say, as Ginevra twists to quickly yet quietly press the door shut. It looks practiced, as if she's closed a nursery door in this same manner a number of times so as not to wake her sons.

"Well," Murderess Marie says in a soft voice, her smoky eyes wide, "who is trying to kill us?"

She crosses to a vanity table and stool and sits, her back to us, examining herself, as if to make sure the evening's events aren't aging her. Then she peers at us in the gilded mirror.

Her late husband's brooch catches the light, pinned over her heart.

Ginevra couples her hands in front of her middle and says in an earnest voice, "We lied. We don't yet know. But we're determined to crack this case open."

Crack this case open?

I stifle a laugh.

Gin shoots me a look. "Anyway, you are the one who found the attendant, so we wanted to ask you some questions."

Marie is quick to say "I didn't kill him." She blows out a breath. "Please, sit. Let's hash this out further."

With Marie at the vanity, that leaves only a valet chair and a bench. Gin and I squeeze onto the bench together. The walls are adorned with photographs of the Larsons, who allow the Civic Daughters and other groups to use their former home for social gatherings. For a fee, of course. I doubt we'll ever be invited back now.

"Wait," Ginevra says, "we thought Elizabeth Field was in here with you?"

That's right—or did Josephine lie about that as well?

"She was originally," Marie answers, adjusting her headpiece.

Never mind; not a lie.

"But," Marie continues, looking quite at home in someone else's dressing room, now leaning closer to the mirror to assess her eye makeup. "Elizabeth decided to go to another room where she felt more comfortable."

I narrow an eye. "Because of the rumors about you."

Marie laughs, though it lacks humor. "Probably. Ever since my third husband died—"

But I don't hear the rest.

I'm transported back to the golf course.

To an argument.

To Thomas Winchester's face growing brighter by the second.

To Sarah glaring at me.

Only three of us walked off the golf course that day.

Marie's third husband was not one of them.

Chapter Thirteen

GINEVRA

"Edith," I say, shaking her arm. "Are you all right?"

It's as if her head has disconnected from her body.

Suddenly, her muddled expression clears. "Sorry," Edith mutters, then immediately averts her eyes from Marie's steady gaze, reflecting back from the mirror. "What were we saying?"

"Marie was saying how the attendant never made it to their room to light the fireplace."

Currently, the flames blaze only feet away, the orange hues reflecting on the embellishments of Marie's white dress. Slowly, she twists on the stool, facing us. "The detective ended up lighting it for us after . . . well, you know what happened. I initially went to the coatroom to get Elizabeth's and my coats so we wouldn't freeze to death. That's when I found h-him."

"You poor thing," I coo.

Wits once again belonging to Edith, she asks, "You didn't see anyone on your way there?"

"No one. I already felt like I was breaking the rules by being out of this room, so I went as quickly as I could."

"So you heard nothing either?" I ask, leaning closer on the bench.

"Not that I can recall."

I slump back.

Marie rips the feathered headpiece from her hair. "I don't know why I'm wearing this stupid thing." She closes her eyes, as if refocusing. "But no, when I was out of my room, I truly felt like a horse with blinders on."

"Do you ride?" I ask, head cocked slightly.

Edith says, "Perhaps we should stay on topic?"

I smooth out my scarlet dress. "I'm merely curious."

Though I do want to try to help Marie feel more relaxed. She is sitting on the edge of the stool, seemingly ready to hop up at a moment's notice.

So I ask her, "How long have you ridden?"

Marie smiles sweetly, two dimples forming. "All my life. A life I'm not ready to have cut short. So if you ladies are trying to find the person responsible for this horrendous evening, then I'd like to help."

Edith and I are both silent.

Is she truly offering to be helpful? Or is she trying to wring us for information to see if we're getting close to the killer's identity?

How bizarre to spend so much time with a group of women I actually hardly know, our conversations only ever going surface deep at these types of gatherings.

Talk about strangulation and poisoning to breathe life into an event.

I respond first. "I do have a question that's been bothering me. How did my pearls come to be around the attendant's neck?"

Marie gawks at me as if my sense has gone on holiday. "Someone wrapped them around his neck, of course."

I chuckle. "Of course, but this didn't occur until after his death." As soon as the words are out of my mouth, I study Marie's reaction.

She gasps. "Whatever do you mean?"

Her fingers idly tousle the headpiece she's holding.

Her long neck holds tension.

Her pupils expand.

I know the third to be a sign of a) fear or excitement, on account of William and Charles, or b) lying, on account of Bill's all-too-frequent infidelity.

Damn, I truly am like Daisy Buchanan in that regard.

Edith cuts in. "Ginevra means that the pearls weren't used to murder the poor man, but to perhaps frame someone else."

"Who?" Marie says, nearly breathless.

An odd question, considering I've claimed the pearls. But I'll play along. "As luck has it, they were mine. Who do you know that'd want to pin the murder on me?"

Marie's lips circle. Her pupils remain dilated. Ever so slightly, her head rocks. "Cynthia."

"Cynthia?" I parrot. I could be mistaken, but I've always taken Marie and Cynthia to be close.

Marie presses her lips together. "I feel awful saying as much, but she doesn't like you."

What is this, grade school? Still, I have to know: "Whyever not?"

"You ran the whist drive last summer, right? I couldn't attend. It was shortly after my poor Thomas's funeral, and I wasn't feeling up for gaiety."

Beside me, Edith stiffens.

I glance at her. She forces a smile. Marie continues in a low voice, "A few weeks later, I was having afternoon tea with Cynthia. That's normal for us, you see."

She waves around her hand with a truly egregious-size ring from husband number four. I can't help myself—I wonder if this one will last longer. The first died in his sleep. He was older, but in my opinion, not in the "never wake up again" stage of life. The second grew mysteriously ill after a dinner at which it was just him and Marie. The third suffered a heart attack.

Husband number four is brave. Or maybe it's more that Marie is beautiful and charming.

"Anyway," Marie goes on, "Cynthia told me how you insisted on her presence that evening at the whist drive."

"We needed an even number," I say simply. "I didn't realize she'd take up residence at the lowest table."

And there I was, lying to her earlier about how she was perfectly capable of clawing her way to a higher table, all so I could feel good about our quick exchange before I moved on to the next person. I'm lousy.

Marie says, "I'll have you know, Cynthia's not as helpless as she seems. Don't let her wide-eyed demeanor fool you. Though she would be mortified if she knew that I told you this next bit. She suffers from a condition that's often called word blindness, but in Cynthia's case it causes her trouble with visual processing and symbol recognition. All necessary when playing cards."

Edith scrunches her eyes. "So why is she here tonight?"

Marie scratches at the embroidery on her dress. "I asked her to come. I thought she'd beg off with an excuse with a million holes. To my surprise, she didn't. I'd be lying if I didn't say I suspected Sarah had a hand in Cynthia saying yes." She leans closer and whispers, "Maybe Cynthia was blackmailed."

And now Sarah is dead, and Cynthia is trying to pin it on me because she dislikes me?

My children have come up with more persuasive arguments.

Though it's curious to me how this conversation ended up here, Marie so graciously laying breadcrumbs before making a rather presumptuous conclusion.

I say, "You've given us much to think about. Why don't we continue to poke around, and we'll sneak back to see you. We'll do a special knock. The opening to "Sweet Georgia Brown." How about that?"

Marie inches farther onto the edge of her stool, risking toppling over. She leans forward and places a hand on each of ours. "Thank you."

I notice the attached door, the one to the bedroom and Josephine, where Marie has also lodged a chair against the doorknob. Is this an act of a scared damsel trying to keep people out? Or a skilled assassin trying to make herself appear frightened so she can get away with murder?

As I said earlier, the game is afoot. And Marie has shown herself to be an able-minded player, one we must stay a step ahead of. Our lives may depend on it. And Josephine may have the answers that we need. Speaking with her was our initial reason for risking a second trip upstairs. Why did Josephine lie before? And how did the flower she brought this evening come to be tampered with?

I stand, shaking the wrinkles from my dress. After dislodging the chair from beneath the doorknob, Edith and I lock eyes, as if we're the police about to surprise a criminal.

Three, two, one.

We throw open the door to the bedroom, and I step in first, Edith on my heels.

I look from place to place around the room. The Pullmans are no longer huddled in the corner, both mother and daughter more comfortable on the bed. Their eyes shoot wide at our sudden entry.

I go deeper into the small room, turning a circle. Once more, I try to clutch my pearls, only they're no longer around my neck.

I go so far as to peek inside the wardrobe, knowing only a small child would be able to hide in such a place.

No one else is here.

Josephine is missing.

Chapter Fourteen

Now, this is an interesting development. Josephine has left the room. I should march down to the interrogation room and tell Detective Davis this very minute.

There's your suspect, I'd proclaim. Her, not me.

Means: *Poison.*

Opportunity: *She brought the plant.*

Motive:

Well, there's where the record scratches. Still, I'd bet my best cloche Sarah rubbed Josephine the wrong way at some soiree or supper club. It's Sarah's way.

Ginevra straightens after looking behind each of the chairs, as if this is a game of hide-and-seek. She locks eyes with the Pullman women. They're propped side by side against the headboard, as if waiting for someone to bring them breakfast in bed and a newspaper. Their expressions remain frightened, but in a much more comfortable state of being alarmed. Of course, it could be all for show. I ask them, "Where'd she go?"

No answer.

I try, "How long ago did Josephine leave?"

Still no answer. Again, are they truly fearful, and a murder mystery is not their cup of tea? Or are they merely adept at appearing as such?

Gin prods softly, "Daisy? Rose?"

We're getting nowhere. I've taken Ginevra's arm to leave when Daisy finally speaks up. "Why are we being kept here?"

I refrain from cocking my head at them, but my answer is plain and simple. "Because one of us has blood on her hands."

"Not us," Mrs. Pullman insists, suddenly with a firm bottom lip.

Ginevra perches herself on the edge of the bed. "Of course not. Nor did we intend to come in here and get everyone all worked up. Why don't we play a game?"

I shoot her a look, as if to say, "Another one?"

She goes on, "Tensions are high. But we're all intelligent women. We can get to the bottom of who killed Sarah, thus allowing us all to safely go home. But in order to do so, we need to get to the bottom of Sarah." Gin offers the Pullmans a sympathetic look. "Sarah has likely wronged every one of us in this house tonight. Any one of us could have reason to kill her. We wouldn't all act on it, but yes, countless reasons. She's insulted me more times than I can count. Now, your turn, Daisy. How has Sarah wronged you?"

I hold up a hand before she can answer, cutting in. "Mrs. Pullman, if I had to guess, your reason would be to protect your daughter. Be an accomplice to her actions, even. But back to you, Daisy—what is it Sarah has done to you that'd drive you to murder?"

I've rendered both mother and daughter speechless. In the silence, the wind howls and batters icy snow against the window.

"A protective mother," Ginevra says, raising her voice over the raging storm. "I can understand such a thing. But yes, go on, Daisy."

Only it's Mrs. Pullman who lets out a disgruntled sound and talks for her daughter. "You both already know."

Do we?

Ginevra's eyes are narrowed. Then they widen. "I do remember. What was it, two seasons ago? Daisy almost didn't debut."

"Because," Mrs. Pullman says bitterly, "Sarah insisted that Daisy had been going all over the city unchaperoned. She made some very unsavory claims."

"It was a lie," Daisy says vehemently, though the welling of tears in her eyes and the twisting of her hands say otherwise.

It's clear this is a wound that she'd prefer to stay under wraps. And here we are, bringing it to the surface once more, Ginevra even pushing the issue, overlooking the girl's obvious discomfort, asking, "But you debuted, did you not?"

Her mother answers. "She did, after we agreed that Sarah would be invited to any and all dinners, balls, teas, engagements, et cetera, my household threw until the end of time."

Gin says, "How horrid."

Both women nod in sync, before Daisy insists, "But we didn't kill her."

I say, "Someone else solved your problem for you."

Their slightly ashamed expressions telegraph that they're not sorry about it either.

"Okay, then," I say, "I think we've dredged up enough bad memories for one evening."

As soon as Ginevra and I are in the quiet hallway, she throws up a hand and whispers, "They could very easily be lying."

"Wouldn't be the first fib of the evening."

"And as for Josephine's whereabouts—those two were about as helpful as a corset at a dance marathon."

"The opposite," I say. "There's something about the Pullmans that's unsettling. I once played against a woman who proclaimed she couldn't drive off the tee. She could. Exemplary, in fact. It put me on my back foot. The Pullmans could be doing something similar." I cluck my tongue and whisper, "Though I believe them that they don't know where Josephine could be. I can see Josephine slipping off, without a word."

Ginevra nods. "She does seem wily like that. And," she says, holding up her pointer finger, "quite jumpy when I first arrived. Maybe it's connected. Maybe she wanted to distance herself from the Pullmans. What if she's simply in another room?"

There are four in total on this second level. The butler's kitchen, Murderess Marie's room, the Pullmans in the bedroom, and . . . one last one we haven't checked. But when we do, it's empty. In more ways than one. Not only is there no woman to speak of, but the green-wallpapered room is nothing but furniture covered in sheets. On what is likely the outline of a desk sits a green-shaded lamp. Turned on.

"Whoever was in here is probably in with the detective," I surmise.

Gin points upward, to the third and final level of the house. We creep up the stairs, pausing at any creaking floorboards, though the violent storm eclipses the noise.

On the third floor, we get our bearings. The layout is similar, with a long hallway, though there are many more doors. Where the butler's kitchen is below us, we find a small room and lavatory. Empty.

We proceed to the next room.

I grip the doorknob, prepared to go straight in, but Ginevra stops my hand. "We should knock, no?"

She does, gently. When there's no answer, I give more oomph.

"Who's there?" we hear.

"It's Ginevra," she says sweetly.

I press my ear to the door, hearing a mishmash of voices.

Gin tries, "Could you open the door, please?" She sighs. "I assure you, I had no hand in the attendant's death."

I snort. "Because you've never told a lie."

She pins me with a glare. "How is that helpful?"

To my surprise, the door opens, though it almost closes again when Mrs. Swift sees me beside Ginevra. I'm insulted. I've been nothing but nice to the Swifts. I even let her son—and Mrs. Swift—down gently, after they assumed I'd give up golf and settle down. Besides, he's now married to one of the women in the room, Marjorie.

"Hello, ladies," I say, forcing Mrs. Swift, along with her daughter, Rebecca, to acknowledge me.

"Yes, hello," Ginevra says. "May we sit?"

The room is a similar shape to the rooms beneath it, with a curved far wall and with two large windows. A single soft light dangles over a cigar table, a carved wooden humidor atop. My club has a similar smoking room, not that I frequent it often, with nearly identical leather armchairs and a chesterfield sofa.

Once settled at the table, I cut to the chase. "Has anyone seen Josephine Bamford?"

Mrs. Swift's eyes widen. "Why is the question one of consequence?"

I smile warmly, ignoring the lingering aroma of cigars in the air. A gentleman's club used the Bellevue earlier in the week. Gin mentioned Bill had attended. I clear my throat. "Ginevra and I are trying to get to the bottom of Sarah's death, to get us all home more quickly. We haven't been able to find Josephine."

Marjorie speaks up. "She's not with us. We haven't seen her since Detective Davis split up everyone."

Rebecca adds, "I didn't see her in the lobby after—"

"The attendant's death," Ginevra finishes for her. "How unfortunate. Can you ladies think of anyone who would want to hurt him? *And*"— Ginevra palms her chest—"do something as horrid as frame me for it?"

"Because," I add, "Ginevra assures you she had nothing to do with it."

My friend's restraint at my friendly jab is admirable.

Rebecca shakes her head. "This is the first time I've attended an event with him at the door."

Marjorie chews on her bottom lip. "Me as well. I can't place him."

"I've been coming to Civic Daughter events for years," Mrs. Swift says, talking to Ginevra over me. "I remember a Mr. Benjamin, a Mr. Monroe. I didn't get our attendant's name this evening, nor can I recall having seen him before."

Come to think of it, this was the first I've seen this particular attendant too. What poor luck he has.

"How interesting," Ginevra concludes. "He was extremely cordial to me when I arrived, even if he did leave me on the doorstep for a bit. I can't see why anyone would want him killed. Or why anyone would then try to frame—"

I lay a hand over Ginevra's. Do I believe my friend murdered the attendant? No. But do I think there is something to the saying *The lady doth protest too much*? Absolutely. And Gin's insistence on portraying herself in a certain way is only making her appear guilty. I stand. "We're going to continue our search for Josephine."

"Whatever for?" Mrs. Swift says. "Do you think she killed Sarah because of that evening at the club?"

I stiffen. "What club? Mine?"

As she does before, she focuses on Ginevra, as if she's the one who asked the question. "No, the Chicago Club. My Henry was there, as he is most evenings, and he saw Edward Cudahy, Thomas Winchester, Jagger McCormick, and Marcus Bamford all having a very clandestine meeting at a table in the corner. Then, money exchanged hands."

Slowly, I sit again. "Between who exactly?"

"Between who exactly?" Gin has to repeat.

"Edward and Marcus."

Sarah's daddy. Josephine's daddy.

Ginevra and I exchange looks, but for one of the first times, I'm not entirely sure what's behind her eyes. Does she speculate something? Know something she's not letting on?

Gin asks, "When was this?"

"Quite some months ago, at some point over the summer."

"You've been most helpful," Ginevra says as she stands.

I follow her right out of the room, then whisper, "I'm confused."

Gin blows out a breath. "About her dislike of you? It can't be all because of Jacob, can it?"

"I wasn't referring to Jacob," I say flatly. "What was the meaning of the look you gave me back there?"

"Oh." She licks her lips. "Isn't it obvious? Edward, Thomas, Jagger, Marcus. Sarah, Marie, Cynthia, Josephine. Four women who are—were—here this evening. Coincidence, I think not. Shall we try the next room while we let that marinate in our heads?"

Instead of knocking and going through the same song and dance we did with Marie and the Swifts, I simply open the door. The room is not much larger than a closet, the width only slightly larger than that of the single window. There's an unlit fireplace. "Doesn't look like anyone is using this room."

"Excellent deduction, E," Gin says. "Next room?"

I barge into this one too.

And immediately freeze in place.

It's an ordinary game room with a billiards table, a card table, and two rifles showcased above the fireplace. The taxidermy on the walls is proof they work.

What's not ordinary is the woman hanging halfway out one of the two windows, only wearing a single shoe, the other lying on the parquet floor. I can't tell who it is by only her backside—a backside I'm at risk of seeing entirely too much of if her dress creeps any higher. But Mrs. Field and Mrs. Armour are each holding a stockinged leg. One of the Armour twins is standing by, her back to us.

"Ahem," Ginevra says.

Chaos ensues. One of the twins—I've never been able to tell them apart—turns and muffles a scream. Elizabeth Field nearly loses her grip on the left leg of the dangling girl, who I assume is twin number two. Mrs. Armour throws her entire body onto her daughter, lest she completely fall out the window.

And here I am, thinking I've put myself into some tough predicaments. This almost takes the cake.

With some help from Gin and me, they're able to get the shoeless twin back inside the room, the window closed, and everyone seated around the fireplace to warm up.

"That was some excitement," Ginevra says. "Would you care to explain what you were doing?"

Mrs. Field and Mrs. Armour exchange a look but say nothing.

"Very well," Ginevra says. "I suppose we all have our secrets."

This time, the twins are the ones to exchange glances.

There's entirely too much of that going on.

"Listen," I say. "If you were trying to flee, I don't blame you. Though I must applaud your attempt from a third-story window. We're looking for Josephine, who also may have fled."

I purposely say this, wanting to see their reactions. They're all surprised: dropped jaws, jerking heads, and the twin with icicles in her hair asking, "How?" and her tone giving off a feeling that she'd love to follow suit.

"That's what we're trying to figure out," Ginevra says, "along with who is responsible for Sarah's death."

I tag on, "Do any of you know of someone here tonight who benefits from Sarah's death?"

"Rose Pullman," Mrs. Armour says, sharing a knowing look with Mrs. Field.

"Ah, yes," I say, "Mrs. Pullman has only just reminded us about Sarah's blackmail. Killing her to end that open invitation would have been a rather calculated decision. Even if it does feel extreme."

Then one of the twins says, "Peg."

Peg benefits? Really?

And now that all shoes are back on all feet and the snow has been shaken off, I've lost my only way to tell the two women apart, both wearing identical champagne-colored dresses and their hair pulled back in exactly the same manner. But I'd like to know which twin in particular has suggested such a far-fetched thing.

Her mother swats her. "Why would you say her? She's in the Big Four with these two."

"No, no, it's fine," Ginevra says calmly. "Why *would* you say her?"

The other twin answers. "Peg doesn't have any children."

Ginevra and I are not about to give up Peg's happy little secret. I ask, "What does that have to do with anything?"

Mrs. Armour answers, "The first grandchild is important, as you know, Ginevra."

I raise a brow. I guess someone like me—unmarried and childless—would be unable to grasp such a thing.

Mrs. Armour either doesn't notice the slight or doesn't care. "And as Sarah has been so vocal about, she's soon to be married. That could put her in the position of having the first Cudahy heir."

"But Ruth," Mrs. Field says, "if Peg was going to have children, wouldn't she have already? They've been married for nearing on ten years if I'm not mistaken."

"Completely unfair," I say, unable to stop myself this time. "That's like saying if I were to marry, I would have done so by now."

I'm met with blank stares from the four women. It's only Ginevra who squeezes my arm, and says, "There's certainly a reality where Edith can marry, should she wish. And plenty of time for Peg to have children."

One of the twins pipes up: "Definitely plenty of time for Peg now that Sarah is out of the picture."

"Now that's downright slander," Ginevra says, color rising to her cheeks. "To paint a woman in such a light all because of some inheritance. Are we not better than that, ladies?"

Mrs. Armour sighs. "Ginevra, sweetheart, a woman is dead. Clearly one of us has her reasons for doing such a thing. It could even be you."

"Me?" Ginevra gasps. "But what would I even kill her over? I'm paralyzed with happiness in all areas of my life."

Mrs. Field covers Ginevra's hand. "Oh, darling, you work so hard on that facade of yours, but we all know what's happening between you and Sarah. And I mean more than Sarah comparing you to the woman in F. Scott Fitzgerald's novel."

"We all?" Ginevra says, a note of panic in her voice. "You all know?"

Mrs. Armour and her daughters are each nodding, faces laced with sympathy that's shy of being fully sincere. "Well, maybe not everyone," Marjorie says. "But Sarah told Rebecca and—"

Ginevra removes her hand from beneath Mrs. Field's and clasps both her hands in her lap. "I don't know what you're talking about."

Chapter Fifteen

Six months ago
King–Mitchell residence

I hang up the phone with Edith and lean against the wall to gather my composure. We concluded that should anyone compare me to Daisy or Tom to Bill or Edith to Jordan, we'll deny it and pivot to a new discussion topic.

Alas, there's always that one woman who is known to sink her teeth into things like a dog on a bone. If that dog were also smiling, giggling, and pretending not to be a total hag.

That woman is Sarah.

It's always Sarah.

Sarah, who debuted five years after me in a dress that looked remarkably similar to my own but with a "splash of something extra." Her words, not mine.

Sarah, who "joked" to everyone at the Christmas Gala that I overindulged on the eggnog, while I actually left early because my younger son Charles had a fever.

Sarah, who I later caught with my husband in the coat closet at the Summer Soiree.

Having just told Edith about that particular instance during our telephone conversation has riled my blood once more.

This has to stop.

I purse my lips, check my wristwatch, then decide it's the perfect time for a row with my dear husband. His morning meetings are over, yet he hasn't poured his prelunch scotch. He'll be in his home office for another hour still.

I head in that direction.

Our housekeeper dips her head as I pass. Usually Ingrid would ask me if I need anything, but I'm a woman on a mission.

My heels click-clack against the marble flooring as I cross the foyer. At Bill's closed door, I primp my hair. It's lost some of its bounce from my pacing and determined walk across the house.

I don't knock.

I enter.

"Bill."

He lowers the stack of papers he was reading in the dimly lit room. Why he keeps the curtains drawn is a mystery to me. "Ginevra?"

Funny how he's shocked to see me in our own home.

"Are the children all right?" he asks.

At least he cares about them.

A steadying breath—then I say, "Yes, they are fine. What's not fine is your behavior at the Summer Soiree."

His brow wrinkles. There was a time I found him unbearably debonair with his blond hair, blue eyes, impressive height, easy remarks, and handsomeness in his aviator uniform. I was fresh out of school. My parents decidedly dangled something pretty and fancy and rich in front of me so I'd give up Scott, who my parents deemed an outsider with financial instability. The promise of wealth and convenience and an address on Astor Street won me over.

I accepted society's position of the perfect wife and, God willing, the perfect mother.

Bill and I agreed to *till death do us part.*

We spoke the words about forsaking all others.

While I gave up Scott shortly thereafter, a decision that still haunts me to this day, Bill only spoke his vows as a formality.

And that's been mostly fine. We have an agreement. Bill's not to bring any of his dalliances into our home. I'm not to see his unfaithfulness. Nor can he parade his infidelity around for others to bear witness to. And yet . . . I found Bill and Sarah in a coat closet, a room into which there was no need to venture, especially during the summer months. It's precisely why they chose the location.

It's no wonder I once lay in bed with Scott, tracing a finger down his bare chest, and questioned if the best thing a girl could be in this world was a beautiful little fool, one who wanted to believe in a fairy tale. Of a wealthy woman trapped in a loveless marriage. Where she ached to be with another man, as soon as he made a name for himself. In the end, he does. Our heroine runs off with her hero, leaving behind a man who never loved her.

Now, years later, I'd revise. I'd also have to take my children with me.

I breathe in through my nose, my blood pumping at the memory, at how Scott has used *my* fairy tale for his own gain, and also at how Bill is currently looking at me, as if I'm an inconvenience that he's hoping will vanish.

I will not.

He finally says, "The Summer Soiree was three weeks ago."

I stand taller. "It does not alter the fact that you were with Sarah only a room away from all our friends. It was irresponsible and careless of you, William."

"Do not speak to me like I'm one of the children."

I have a retort. But I hold it in. Instead I say, "What will people think?"

"No one saw us."

"I did. And I had to cover it up afterward."

"Which you did a marvelous job of."

At that, he picks up his stack of papers.

"I shouldn't have to do a marvelous job. That behavior can't continue."

I can't tell him that he's Tom Buchanan. Even the slightest mention of Scott's name sends him into a tailspin. Yet tongues will wag if two and two are put together.

Bill pouts like a toddler. "I see no reason why our agreement needs to be altered."

I briefly close my eyes. "Sarah Cudahy of all people, Bill. Enough with her, at least."

"Truth be told, I've tired of her."

"Splendid," I say, exasperated.

"It would be if I could quit her. But it's best I carry on. I don't know that Sarah would let me go so easily."

It feels as if my eyeballs bobble around in my sockets. "What does that even mean?" I fight to keep the shrill from my voice. "Just end things, Bill. And before anyone finds out."

He lowers his papers and leans back in his chair. The start of a smile appears on his face, and I have the urge to take the copper mallard from the bookcase and throw it at his handsome head.

"It's quite comical, Ginevra. You are so caught up in appearances. Yet how you are perceived isn't in your control the slightest bit."

My mouth drops open before I can stop the reaction.

He snorts a laugh, pushes back from his chair, and pours himself a drink from the bar cart.

I regain my composure and say, "There's no need for you to attend the Pullmans' dinner this evening."

He quirks an eyebrow. "But what will people say?"

I smile tightly. "I'll say you've come down with a cold."

He throws back his drink. "I think I'd like to attend."

Because Sarah will be there. He's doing this to get under my skin. He's doing this to assert that control he's only just mentioned.

But that night, I do not let him succeed. Rose is kind enough to discreetly swap Bill's seat with Tommy Winchester's under the guise that my husband requested to chat business with Jagger McCormick. That puts Tommy next to Sarah instead. It also puts Bill at the far end of the table, a complete godsend when Sarah plasters a fictitious smile on her face and says, "Ginevra, I read the most arresting novel recently. And—*oh*—I believe it's by a man you once knew intimately."

Chapter Sixteen

Mrs. Armour's little bombshell about Ginevra, Sarah, and Bill might've cracked my best friend like a fine bone china teacup at a jazz brunch. She's gone catatonic. I give our goodbyes and lead Gin from the room.

"It's okay," I tell her in the hallway, linking our pinkies. "No one thinks any less of you."

Ginevra closes her eyes, breathes in deeply through her nose, then sets her pretty green eyes on me. "We should check the other rooms for Josephine. We find her. We put an end to this evening. We put an end to any prattling about my personal life."

I know better than to press the issue, so we do as she suggests, finding a linen closet, a lavatory, an empty room, and the Breuers and Cynthia in what's made up to be a screening room. The three of them are sitting in the near dark, yet not watching a thing. Though the oddest bit of all is that Cynthia is with Mrs. Breuer and Cordelia Breuer and not with Murderess Marie.

I keep my inquiries focused on Josephine. No one has seen her.

Ginevra, however, veers off into her own line of vague questioning. "Have you ladies heard any interesting information about any of the women in the house?"

Even if they had, there's no way they'd admit it to Ginevra's face. She leaves their room tight as a drum.

Once back in the hallway, Ginevra asks, "Do we think Josephine could've left the building entirely?" Her head ticks toward the stairs. Her question isn't meant for me to answer. Any second now, she'll seek that answer on her own, taking off to once again check the building's exits. The proof will be in the pudding. Or rather, in the footprints. Either they'll show Josephine leaving the house from one of the exits or they'll prove that she's still inside—where Ginevra will no doubt endeavor to pin Sarah's murder on her, not only to beat me in our increasingly silly game, but also to put an end to this increasingly dangerous evening, which could end up with her killed or socially ruined.

Well, I'm determined too. For my own reasons. Josephine must know much more than I've realized. Information that could be disastrously incriminating. Against me. It's me who must find her first.

And at that, both Ginevra and I are all shoulders as we jockey for which one of us will reach the stairwell first—and have the advantage in finding Josephine.

I press my lips together, keeping in a grunt when Ginevra's bony elbow catches me in the ribs. I allow myself a smile when I begin descending first. The interrogation room door is closed. Good. I go left across the foyer, leaving Ginevra a choice. Follow me or go her own way.

She pads forward, toward the main door.

I pick up the pace, doing my best to sprint on tiptoes toward the ballroom. The three double sets of doors are blanketed white. Still, I turn the knobs and lean a shoulder into each, none of them budging.

The door off the changing room, then . . .

I run toward the stage to try that exit next. I turn the knob and throw my body into the door, and it flies open, colliding with a bank of snow that's formed at the end of the overhang.

What I don't see is a single footprint.

But there could be . . . if I'm the one to leave. With the way the detective is narrowing his eyeballs at me, Josephine may not be the one to damn me. Fleeing would be the intelligent decision to distance myself from this place. Though the blizzard whirling only feet away would eat me alive. The conditions are near whiteout. There'll be no taxis. I'd have to foot it all the way home. And then what? Continue to flee to save my own hide? It's completely impractical.

Closing the door, I curse under my breath.

Alas, I must find Josephine before it's too late.

This isn't unlike hitting a bogey on the back nine when my score needs to stay at par for me to be victorious. If Josephine didn't leave via a door, and is desperate enough to risk hypothermia, perhaps she left through a window? Lord knows I disappeared through one a time or two in my youth.

I make toward the kitchen, choosing to remain in the dark once I enter the room. There are four windows. Each locked. Letting out a soft growl, I lean against the counter to think, saying in a singsong voice, "Where are you, Josephine?"

A scuffing noise in the staircase brings me back to a stand, muscles taunt. "Ginevra?" I whisper. "Is that you?"

No one responds.

Nor can I be caught lurking around.

Quietly, I push through the kitchen door into the ballroom, then dash toward our Big Four room and burst through one of the connecting entrances.

Peg's hand flies to her chest. "Can neither of you enter a room in the proper manner?" She groans in a low voice. "I'll need to redo this row now."

I begin to cock my head until I see Ginevra. On her tippy-toes. Grunting as she holds the top window frame in place and tries to push up the bottom sash.

If I had to guess, she burst into the room only seconds before I did.

"Gin," I say flatly.

"What?" she says without turning, still heaving to no avail.

I point out, "No one could have left from that window."

"It leads directly to the portico. No drop at all."

I bite back a laugh. "The window is clearly locked, from the inside."

Gin drops her hands.

"But also," I say, "don't you think Peg and Courtney would've witnessed Josephine escaping through a window in the very room they are in? Wait . . . where's Courtney?"

"Talking with the detective," Peg offers, her composure returning.

I stiffen. "Tell me he didn't come here to fetch her."

Peg harrumphs. "And find the two of you missing. Yes, that's exactly what happened. But we covered for you. Edith, you have your monthly courses, and Ginevra accompanied you to the ladies' room."

Ginevra palms her chest. "Thank you. That was quick thinking." She flops into a chair and puffs a breath at a stray wisp of hair. "Look at me," she says. "I'm like a shark who's gotten the taste of blood and has lost all senses. Peg, be a peach and pass my flask."

Peg looks at the flask on the small table beside her, then back at Ginevra.

"No," I say, "she's only self-medicating."

"Who is doing what?" Courtney says, like an apparition. Yet Peg doesn't jump at her reentrance into the room.

"My drama can wait," Gin says to Courtney. "You were speaking with Conrad?"

"Nothing that can help us, I'm afraid. Of course I didn't tell him I've an interest in tonight so I can write the next bestseller. With me living in DC, though, I don't have the same connections to Sarah as the rest of you. Our chat was quite abbreviated. Now," Courtney says, "what is this drama?"

Ginevra palms her face. She's among friends. Friends who would never judge her. I give her the chance to share her frustrations. She sighs. "Everyone knows."

Peg's hand flies to her chest, nearly stabbing herself with her hook. "Who's killed Sarah?"

Another sigh from Ginevra. "No, about Sarah and Bill. Or at least the Armours and Elizabeth Field know. I could kill Sarah." She squints an eye. "If she weren't already dead."

"Don't say such things," Peg chastises her.

"Sorry, too late. Too late for Sarah. Likely too late for me." She extends a droopy arm toward Courtney for her flask.

"Gin," I deadpan.

She closes her eyes. "I apologize. This evening is getting to me. If only we could find Josephine."

Court doesn't acquiesce to passing Gin her gin, but she does ask, "Josephine has escaped?"

"Not exactly," I say, taking a chair, mine next to Peg. I squeeze her arm, thinking she's making either a blanket or a scarf. Perhaps a table runner. Time will tell. Anyway, I say, "Josephine's still here. Somewhere. Only, we don't know where."

"What's worse," Gin says, "is we didn't have the opportunity to question her."

Court drums her fingers atop our notebook. "So we know nothing more?"

Ginevra sits straighter, as if the life has been breathed back into her. "Au contraire." She looks at me, and I know what's awoken her from her self-pity; she remembers that Josephine said she overheard me talking with Sarah. I subtly shake my head and hold my breath. Gin presses her lips together. One, two, three seconds pass. Then she says, "We know Josephine is involved. Why else would she make herself scarce?"

I slowly release the dwindling air in my lungs as Peg asks, "Could she have been in with Detective Davis before he came for Courtney? Or in the lavatory?"

I say, "We did hear someone leaving the restroom, but if it was Josephine, she didn't return to her room."

Gin adds, "And we've checked all the others."

"So she's not only hiding, but she's also really good at it," Courtney concludes.

I sigh, standing. Finding Josephine feels like a dead end. But I wonder if the detective has a new victim in his lair. I poke my head out the door and eye the dining room door. As luck has it, he's escorting someone to the interrogation room at this very moment. Murderess Marie.

I scrunch an eye, returning to the ladies. "We also learned Mrs. Field switched rooms because she doesn't trust Murderess Marie."

Gin sips from her flask. It appears she's taken matters into her own hands as far as retrieving her illicit alcohol. She swallows, then says, "I second that distrust. Imagine if Josephine and Marie are in cahoots. Or at the very least, Marie knows more than she told us during our little chat."

She explains how Marie very heavy-handedly pointed a finger at Cynthia, who is supposed to be a dear friend.

Courtney scribbles in her notebook.

Horrendous friend ✓ *Murderer?*

I chuckle, then stand, needing to move, to think. Our escapade has gotten us nowhere. I reach for my club, a practice swing a tried-and-true method for easing tension for me.

Then I realize something.

Then I say, "Oh no."

Chapter Seventeen

GINEVRA

Edith's "oh no" nearly has me choking on my gin. I cough, slapping my chest.

"What is it?" Courtney asks.

Outside, the wind howls, angry and desperate sounding.

I regain composure. "Yes, what Court said. What's wrong?"

Edith is on her feet. Her lips are twisted. "It appears," she begins, "I left my golf club upstairs with Murderess Marie."

I frown and use the voice I reserve for my children. "Edith."

She furrows her brow at me.

I go on. "How could you be so careless? First, Conrad saw you with the club outside the parlor, which puts you inside the room with Sarah after her death. Now it's upstairs. He'll know for certain we're up to something."

She rolls her eyes. "He'll know *I'm* up to something. You, dear Gin, are inculpable."

Courtney taps her book. "Minus your necklace on a dead body. And us covering for you *both*."

I sigh. "Yes, there is that."

Now Courtney's eyes widen. "What if E's golf club is involved in the next murder?"

"Stop that," I say, glancing at Edith, who appears utterly distracted, her mind elsewhere. "Let's not put that out into the universe. It's not as if there's to be a death every—"

The foyer's grandfather clock begins chiming the first of ten gongs.

Truly, the timing is fantastic, in the true meaning of the word. Enough to send Peg over the edge. "Are you okay?" I ask her.

She's crocheting at such a quick pace, the ball of yarn spinning. "Eddie, he'll be beside himself soon if I don't check in."

I lick my lips, looking in the direction of the foyer, where Conrad so bullishly yanked the telephone from the wall. While I understand his need to assert control in these challenging circumstances, I, too, have had to commandeer a room of twenty lively women. He used brute force. I used the teachings of Mrs. Burton Kingsland.

A woman need only to engage politely and exude an aura of composure and charm.

Composure is exactly what Peg needs from me now. I stand from my chair, cross to her, and gently take the hand she's now using to fan herself. "I'm going to have a quick peek at the telephone and see if I can't get it working again. In the meantime, why don't we shift you farther from the fire." I gesture to the chair I vacated.

She's agreeable.

I take a step to leave, then pause, eye catching on the fireplace poker. It's better to be safe than sorry. "While we're gone," I say, leaning the tool against Peg's chair, "it wouldn't be a horrible idea to have this close at hand."

With that, I must make good on what I've offered to do. If Lady Luck is on my side, Conrad will be behind closed doors again, and I'll be free to fix the telephone. I venture to the door, slowly turn the knob, and feel a breath tousling my hair.

Edith.

She says quietly, "Thought you'd like some company."

Very well. It's not as if any clues await us in the foyer.

To my dismay, the gold interrogation room doors are wide open when I crack open our door.

"He's still out there," Edith whispers, stating the obvious.

I puff out my cheeks, deciding whether we should turn back or at the very least wait until we're sure of Conrad's current location. But considering Edith is attached to my back, much like a baby squirrel monkey, I've no choice but to quietly step into the foyer.

I keep going, one delicate footstep after another, eyes peeled for any movement from the stairs, the coat closet hallway, the ballroom. The telephone is on the floor, the electrical cord and the cable both detached from the wall. The first should be easy enough to fix.

Before I kneel, I listen for sounds of Conrad. The storm continues on, determined and gusting. But the pings, groans, and roars are all I hear. I point Edith toward the electrical outlet. Task managed, I set my sights on the phone jack. If Lady Luck is still with me, it'll be as simple as reconnecting the cable.

I begin to reach for the cord.

The floorboards above us creak.

Edith's hand goes still, the plug half in the socket.

Then, footsteps align with the groaning wood.

E and I lock eyes.

It must be Conrad. The footsteps continue; then they quicken.

I gasp. I know the noise, the hasty footfalls of someone picking up speed as they go downstairs in a determined way. Usually it's my boys on Christmas morning.

Any moment, Conrad will reach the stairs' landing. He'll turn. He'll see us on our knees, trying to reconnect with the outside world.

Edith has my arm. I'm on my feet. There's no time to retreat to the library. Like the athlete she is, Edith hurdles the table blocking the entrance to the parlor. I've no choice but to scramble beneath.

There's only one spot in the room where we can't be seen.

Beside Sarah.

Edith is on one side of her.

I'm on the other.

Both our backs are against the wall.

I press a hand over my racing heart, trying to control my rapid breaths.

Over the top of Sarah's napkined head, Edith and I once again lock eyes.

Mine say: *That was close.*

Edith's say: *Shh.*

I scrunch my brows only to realize Conrad's footsteps are not going away from us—to the interrogation room—but toward us.

Holding my breath, I suck in my belly and pray the darkened room will conceal us. I'll forever regret wearing bejeweled scarlet this evening. Josephine, with her black attire, was much more prepared for an evening of murder and mayhem.

Ever so slowly, I twist my head to the left in an attempt to see out of the room and into the foyer. From my angle, there's only a sliver to be seen. But in that small space, I watch as Conrad presses his hands against the receiving table's top, only his fingertips in my line of vision. He drums his fingers. He lets out a long breath.

I question what he's doing.

I pray he won't decide to come any farther.

He taps.

He breathes.

He taps some more.

His fingers go still.

His fingertips whiten.

The side of his face appears, leaning forward, farther into the parlor's cased entryway.

Conrad's gaze is focused straight ahead, his eyebrows narrowed, his expression confounded looking.

I don't dare breathe.

But I do risk turning my head to assess what's captured his attention. It's the small tea table in the room's center.

At one time, Marie's brooch was there, along with my necklace, Edith's golf club, and, last, Josephine's framed pressed flower.

Now, the table is bare.

Chapter Eighteen

Edith

Six months ago
Onwentsia Club

"There you are," I hear.

I cringe, recognizing the honeyed voice.

Any one of my Big Four ladies would throw a faux grin and congenial greeting at Sarah Cudahy, but I'm not anyone.

"What do you want, Sarah?"

She scoffs. "Can't I say a simple hello to a friend?"

We're in the ladies' dressing room. I've one foot up on a bench, switching into my walking boots. I stand to my full height, towering over Sarah. "Forgive me, but I can't recall a time you said hello without an ulterior motive."

She taps her satin pump impatiently against the wood floor. "Fine. I do need a favor."

I roll my eyes and lift my other foot to the bench. "No."

Sarah repositions herself, inserting herself into my bubble. "Oh, come on. It's a tiny favor. You're teeing off soon."

I sigh. "Yes. I'm set to play with—"

"Not anymore. She's sick."

"And how would you know that?"

"I was with the receptionist when the call came in." Sarah shrugs. "I offered to tell you, and, fortunate for you, I'm available to play."

"You want to play?"

"I do. And I'd like to suggest a third."

Sarah's wrapped in satin from bow to heel, dressed for a scandal, not a sand trap.

"I'd change, of course."

I tie my laces. "So my favor is you playing a round with me? I may be the best, but I fail to see how this actually benefits you."

Sarah raises her chin farther. "I'd like you to ask Thomas Winchester to be our third."

I scrunch my brows. "Tommy's father? Why would I do that?"

"You've played with him before."

I give her an expression that's borderline petulant and broadcasts a single word: *So?*

"Listen, Edith. Deals are made on the golf course, right?"

"I'm here only to pla—"

Sarah raises her chin. "I'm not. I'm here to find a husband."

I snort. "Sorry, but Thomas is spoken for. Marie got to him first."

Poor man probably signed his marriage certificate and death certificate the same day.

Sarah edges closer. "It's not Thomas Sr. I'm after."

"Ah," I say, it making more sense. "Tommy is a dish. I should know."

That narrows Sarah's eyes, and I can tell two things. The first is that Sarah wants to insult me in this very moment, something along the lines of how I was only a blip in Tommy's dating history. But the second is that she needs me. Thus, her face softens as she says, "You'd also know why I've an interest in him, then."

I clear my throat. I'm dressed. It's a beautiful day. Why waste it? I can suffer through eighteen holes with Sarah. If nothing else, watching her curry favor with Mr. Winchester will be amusing.

"Fine," I say.

"Really?" Sarah questions.

"Don't make me change my mind."

Sarah quickly backpedals. "I'll change. Mr. Winchester is in the barroom. I'll meet you there lickety-split."

Ginevra is going to have a field day when I call her later.

I find Thomas Winchester right where Sarah said, a martini in front of him despite the early hour, and I pull out the chair beside him.

He notices, smiles. "Well, if it isn't the Fairway Flapper."

He forgot the *unflappable* portion of my nickname: Unflappable Fairway Flapper. But that's okay. As the name denotes, I'm unruffled.

"Hello, Mr. Winchester."

"Thomas. I've told you many times to call me Thomas."

"If you insist."

He sips his drink and smiles, ever the charmer.

"Say," I begin, "I was set to tee off in a few moments, but my second is sick. Would you have any interest in joining me?"

He whistles, again with the charm. "With the national women's golf champion herself? I'd be honored. Do we need a third? I can always ask Miller to play."

Miller? "Has he been a member long?"

"He's my caddy, the best there is."

I pat his arm. "As it is, I was just approached by someone eager to play in with us."

There's a question in his bright blue eyes.

"Miss Cudahy," I answer.

The question morphs into a lack of enthusiasm. "That socialite who my Marie runs around town with? A voice only a dog can hear? The temperament of a chihuahua?"

I press my lips together to hold in my laugh. "Now, Thomas, don't be cruel. We both know Sarah is more a Doberman."

He bellows, then throws back the remainder of his drink. "Only for you, Miss Cummings."

I raise a brow at him, correcting, "Edith."

He leans closer. "You know, Edith, if I didn't already have someone in mind for my Tommy, you'd be first on my list." At that, he winks.

Also at that, Sarah walks into the room, no longer in head-to-toe silk but in a matching plum-colored two-piece set with a pleated skirt. Atop her short brunette hair, she even wears a purple flat cap. If Sarah were indeed a Doberman, she'd easily take first prize at the Westminster show.

"Ah," I say, "our third has arrived. Shall we?"

"First," Sarah says, joining us, "a round on me. Well, on my daddy." She smiles winningly. "Wasn't it F. Scott Fitzgerald who said, 'Too much of anything is bad, but too much champagne is just right'?"

Sarah's attention is on Thomas, yet I get an odd sensation that her words are meant for me. Or rather, for Ginevra, with me as the proxy. It was only the other day that Gin called me in a panic about Scott's newest novel and how she and I are believed to be his muses.

"Now, Sarah," I say, sweet as an arsenic bonbon, "you're giving Scott too much credit. Twain said that line long before Fitzgerald was scribbling drunken love letters."

I'll have to remember to thank Courtney for that tidbit of knowledge.

"Doesn't matter to me who said it," Thomas says congenially, "as long as there's champagne. The man, whoever he may be, is not wrong."

I laugh.

Sarah laughs.

We all laugh.

Sarah sees to procuring our fluted drinks.

Which we clink. We drink. Soon, we're on the links.

The weather is perfect, even if the company is less than. Sarah talks off Thomas's ear. Does he know that her father is known as the beef baron? Or that they own 150 acres on Mackinac Island? She goes on. I tune her out, letting my head fall back to capture the sun. I'll have freckles. But I'm not currently after a man in the same way Sarah is. Society pooh-poohs the idea of me being a career woman and a wife, so why bother?

By the time Thomas's caddy announces the sixth hole, a German lilt to his voice, it's grown warm. All the dew has left the grass. Perspiration has gathered on my forehead, even more so on poor Thomas's. He tugs at his collared shirt. Sarah suggests he remove his argyle vest—Miller can hold it along with our clubs—but the recommendation seems to ruffle Thomas's feathers.

"Your shot," I say, sensing his annoyance. I hope returning our focus to the game will help.

But no. He shoots a glare at me, eyes wild. "I very well know it's my turn. I've been second in order to tee off all morning, have I not?"

For a moment, I think I've misheard him. Or at the very least, I'm confused by his irritation toward me. Toward Sarah, yes, I could believe that. But Thomas has been nothing but complimentary of me since I've said hello.

"Of course," I say. "I didn't mean anything—"

Thomas snorts and yanks a driver from the bag Miller holds, his face turning a shade of red that worries me.

"I apologize," Sarah says, stepping in. "Edith can be pushy and overbearing."

"Excuse me?" I say, but my rebuke is cut short. Thomas wobbles. He staggers. He drops to a knee. Then he keels over.

Sarah screams, rushing to his side, propping his head in her lap. She leans over him, talking softly. Sarah's head jerks up, and she snaps at the caddy to bring them water immediately. Then, Hyde gives way to Jekyll, and she's nurturing again, telling Thomas that he's going to be okay.

He stares up at Sarah's face, his eyes round, his face even redder than before. Sarah rips the water from Miller's hand and raises it to Thomas's lips. He takes a small sip, coughs. Sarah coos at him, promising him it'll pass, he'll be fine. Then he wrenches a hand over his heart, his fingertips digging into his chest.

What happens next happens so fast: his hand going limp, his head lolling to the side. Sarah jerking her head up again, this time setting her sights on me. "What have you done?" she screams at me.

What have *I* done?

I'm at a loss for words.

I've done nothing.

Sarah releases an animallike noise before unleashing on the caddy, first telling him to stop standing there brain dead and hurry for a doctor. Then, changing her mind, telling Miller there's no use. It's too late.

I backpedal a handful of steps, distancing myself, shaking out my arms, much like I do before I tee off to loosen up and relax. I tell myself not to look at Thomas—that'll only make my brain seize even further with confusion. Thomas was fine at the club. He was in good spirits, despite Sarah's overassertiveness, the first five holes. Then, as if a switch was flipped, he became aggressive. At me. And now, did his heart give out?

I can't help myself. I look at Thomas. Unmoving. Red faced. Appearing very much unalive. Yet I can't help but ask, "Is he dead?"

Sarah is on her knees beside him. She glares at me as if I'm also brain dead. "He's certainly not sleeping, Edith."

I step closer, my club outstretched. Perhaps if we shake him or prod him, he'll come to.

Sarah knocks away my club. "Stop that. Can't you see? He's gone." Standing, Sarah brushes the dirt from her pleated skirt. "We all saw what happened here. It's a warm day. Mr. Winchester became overheated. The poor man's heart gave out." She looks pointedly at me before addressing the caddy. "Bring him back to the club. I'll join you, explain what happened."

The caddy steps forward, bearlike in his demeanor, but makes no move toward Thomas. "Forgive me if I don't trust you to tell the truth, ma'am."

A gasp slips from Sarah. "Whatever do you mean? We all saw what happened here. He became—"

"I have ears. I heard you the first time," Miller says, the German in his voice becoming more abrupt, clipped. "I also have eyes. And what I witnessed is an innocent man who was healthy as a horse becoming increasingly agitated because of the two of you."

My hand flies to my chest. "No," I breathe, at which Sarah says more confidently, "Do not be ridiculous. I was *helping* him. Besides, it'll be your word versus mine."

She looks him up and down.

To which he puffs his chest. "That's right, a man's word versus a hysterical woman's."

I don't like this man. I don't like him one bit.

Sarah's eyes narrow. "Well, if anyone provoked him, it was Edith." She looks snidely at me. "You're the one who got his wind up. Like the caddy said, he was fine until he teed off with you. It was you he snapped at. You he was arguing with when he grabbed his heart. You've ruined everything."

"Sarah," I try, stepping closer, speaking more softly, making this conversation more intimate between the two of us, "we know that isn't what happened—"

"I'll have you know," Sarah cuts in, actually raising her voice instead of lowering it like I've done, as if she wants an audience, "it's punishable by law to cause a cardiac arrest in another person, Edith. What you've done is considered homicide."

Homicide?

I'm at a loss for words once more. But I'm horrified.

Sarah is now calling this a homicide and is blaming it on me?

I glance at the caddy, then behind him, thankful no other golfers are waiting on us or trying to play through. "Let's keep our voices down."

"Whatever for?" She gestures lazily at Miller. "He's just a caddy. He may be a man, but he's a penniless one at that."

My head's spinning. This man will tell his version of the story. Sarah will tell hers. In either case, by the afternoon, I'll no longer be the Unflappable Fairway Flapper but the Sly Fairway Slayer. "Please," I say to both Sarah and Miller, "I didn't mean for him to get upset. I only told him it was his turn. You have to see I'm innocent. It's unfortunate what happened here, but it's not anyone's fault. We can fix this."

I'm not even sure what I mean by that. I can't make someone undead. But I'll do and say whatever is needed to save my ass. "Sarah, please. The narrative won't only be about me. You'll be the one who could have saved him but didn't. Couldn't. How will that look to Tommy or Marie?"

Murderess Marie, who now has to bury husband number three, a husband she seemed to genuinely take to.

Sarah licks her lips. "Perhaps you're right, Edith. It's no one's fault. It was simply Mr. Winchester's time. Perhaps he wasn't even with us at all. Any of us." Sarah sets her eyes on the caddy. "How much will it take to adequately bury this situation, Mr. Miller?"

The caddy's slow grin is wolfish. "A lot."

"It just so happens I have a lot. So I take it we're all on the same page now?"

Her attention shifts from the caddy to me and back to the caddy. I give a weak nod.

"Fine," he says gruffly.

"Perfect," Sarah chimes.

The question is, can the caddy be trusted? Can Sarah? She was entirely too quick to throw me under the bus only moments ago. The colossal problem is, my hands feel tied. Unless I find a way to take matters into my own hands to ensure I'm not implicated in Thomas's untimely end.

Chapter Nineteen

GINEVRA

I pray Conrad isn't one of those detectives with a sixth sense. He continues to stare at the table that is now void of any donations. But if he does have the intuition to look around the corner, he'll find Edith and me, a very dead Sarah between us.

Guilty, party of two.

I don't allow for even an iota of breath to leave my lips.

After some time, I begin to grow dizzy from lack of oxygen. Finally, Conrad retreats a step before stalking off.

I immediately fill my lungs with air.

Me: *That was close.*

Edith:

She's staring blankly, her expression aghast, as if she's seen a ghost. I do hope it's not Sarah. I shiver, imagining her haunting the Bellevue forever more, and reach across Sarah's body to snap in front of E's face.

She blinks and startles. My friend has mentally gone adrift a few times tonight, once upstairs while talking to Marie, again in the library, and just now. What is she not telling me? Is it related to whatever Josephine overheard in this very room? Or maybe some startling clue she's working out in her head, angling to unearth our killer before I do?

In either case, I'm not going to press her. I, too, have decided to keep my lips sealed, and I won't be telling her about the missing flower if she hasn't spotted it for herself. It means someone has been in this room. Someone other than Conrad. And that someone took the flower. The question is, why?

To murder again?

To hide their culpability?

To dispose of the murder weapon?

The possibilities.

I shudder.

Edith has returned to the here and now. I say to her, "Let's reconvene with Court and Peg."

My friend spares Sarah's draped head another glance, then scurries away. I've taken only a single step when paper crinkles beneath my foot. It's a newspaper.

I rack my memory, but I don't recall seeing it in here earlier. Unless it was beneath the objects on the table. And perhaps was swept aside when the framed flower was retrieved. As Edith continues toward the door connecting this room to the library, I swoop to pick it up.

The folio lists it as today's paper.

That itself isn't peculiar.

But the newspaper has been folded to a specific page. On it, wedding announcements are featured. My heartbeat quickens when I notice that a crude square has been torn from the paper.

I open my mouth to tell Edith, excitement getting the better of me. Then I snap it closed. She disappears into the library. It'll only be moments before E realizes I'm not behind her.

I look back at Sarah, at the diamond on her finger, recalling how she boasted only hours ago about her engagement being listed this morning. Sarah herself could have torn out this portion. But if it were her, she'd have done so neatly and precisely. I run my finger down the rough edge of the paper. So who actually did the deed? And what was the meaning behind such an action?

I tuck the newspaper out of sight beneath Sarah's chair.

As some man from ages ago once said, "The plot thickens."

Earlier, I felt a thrill about having a mystery on my hands and being the first to solve it. But now, after two bodies and the threat of more, unease courses through me.

So does alarm when I once again hear footsteps. I recognize them as Conrad's; he's the only one here not in stocking feet or heels. However, someone with heels does follow him. And the twosome continues on until a door closes. Most likely the interrogation room's. It's entirely too enticing not to discover who is in the room with him. I crawl beneath the receiving table. But it's too risky to put an ear to this door of the interrogation room, which could open again at any moment. Fortunately, there's a second, the one the servants use from the kitchen.

My bottom lip between my teeth, I set off. I'm about to push through the doors to the kitchen when I say, "E, I know you're behind me. No need to breathe down my neck this time."

She laughs, sounding more like herself. Of that I'm glad. She asks, "Going to eavesdrop on the detective?"

"You know me well."

Together, we creep through the kitchen, down the servants' hallway, and to the back entrance of the interrogation room.

On the other side of the door, Conrad is indeed speaking with a woman.

"Cynthia," Edith mouths.

I rub my hands together. We know little of Cynthia thus far, beyond the fact she's not a fan of me. Or Sarah. But does she dislike us enough to murder Sarah and the attendant and to try to pin the deaths on me?

I press my ear against the door, a particularly loud howl of the wind making it hard to hear. Then comes Conrad's voice. "Okay, then—tell me about Ms. King Mitchell. What, in your mind, makes her complicit?"

"Beyond the fact her necklace was found around the victim's neck?"

"Yes."

"Okay, well how about the fact Sarah was telling everyone that she was Daisy—"

"I already know that."

"But do you know that her husband was having an—"

"Yes. Do you have anything else to add?"

"I saw him."

Who? I think to myself, just as Conrad also says, "Who?"

"Bill, Ginevra's husband. I live nearby, off Walton, and was taking a walk earlier. I saw Bill coming out of the Bellevue."

"Wasn't it quite cold for a walk?"

"Yes, but fresh air serves me well."

"What time was this?"

A very good question, I think, clenching my teeth together. I thought Bill was home all day.

Cynthia answers, "Not long before the drive was set to begin. I can't think of a reason for him to be here except for purposes of seeing Sarah."

My cheeks heat from anger but also from humiliation. Yes, I tell Edith everything. But I do so on my own terms, when I'm ready, and in my own words. Not like this, where Edith hears everything raw at the same time I do.

My stomach turns. My mind whirls. I picture Bill and Sarah upstairs in the four-poster bed. The sheets tangling. But wait, didn't Bill claim he'd taken care of the situation with Sarah?

Unless, of course, he was lying. It wouldn't be the first time. It makes me wonder how he looked as he was leaving.

Conrad's voice comes next. "How did Mr. King appear to you?"

Bless him for asking.

"As he was leaving?" Cynthia clarifies. "He couldn't get away fast enough."

There's a pause.

I press harder against the door.

Finally, Conrad says, "Is there anyone else who could have known about what was going on between Mr. King and Miss Cudahy?"

"Edith, of course. Ginevra and Edith are thick as thieves."

"Of course," Conrad parrots. "As someone who is close with Mrs. Morgan, I wanted to see if you could shed some light on her husbands."

Beside me, Edith stiffens, whereas I jerk my head at the sudden topic change. How did we go from my cheating scoundrel of a husband, to Edith, to Marie's deceased husband in a matter of seconds?

Cynthia asks, "Shed some light?"

"It's peculiar, no, that she's had so many of them die?"

A choking sound follows, which I can only attribute to Cynthia feeling scandalized by his implication. "I'll have you know," Cynthia says, with more gall than I've ever given her credit for, "that Marie was devoted to each and every one of her husbands. She was distraught after each of their passings, especially Thomas's."

"Ah, yes," Conrad says, "Thomas Winchester the first. If I have my information correct, his son's engagement was announced only this morning to Miss Cudahy. Mrs. Morgan did not like Sarah much, from what I've been able to gather."

"No one cared for Sarah overly much," Cynthia says in a flat tone. "Marie is no exception."

"So I'm piecing together. Yet, I wonder how Mrs. Morgan reacted to the news of Miss Cudahy marrying her former stepson. Were Mrs. Morgan and Thomas Winchester Jr. close? Could Mrs. Morgan view this marriage as a mistake? Would she be willing to do anything to stop it from happening? Even murder?"

Cynthia sputters incoherently.

I close my eyes, wishing poor Cynthia had more composure. Though the woman seemed well enough while talking about the indiscretions of my husband.

"Miss McCormick?" Conrad says.

The name dangles in the air until Cynthia replies, "Yes?"

"Give me a reason why Mrs. Morgan shouldn't be my prime suspect."

"I don't wish to say anymore."

"Come now, Miss McCormick. Cynthia. Two people have died this evening. I'm only trying to figure out who is behind it. If you protect that somebody, it'll spell a lot of trouble for you too."

"I don't want to say," she mutters, emotion thick in her voice.

Silence follows.

Conrad is waiting her out. No doubt he's staring bullets into her. Sweat will be forming on her brow. It'd be no use if she averted her eyes; they'd only fall on the elk's.

Oddly enough, Edith also seems unsettled, breathing only through her nose, her fingertips white where they press against the door.

"Fine," Conrad finally says. "If you've nothing else—"

She groans, a noise I interpret as acquiescence. "What I'm about to say could very well make it seem like Marie has an even greater motive to dispose of Sarah. But Marie's not the murderer."

"And you know this how?"

"I have a condition that makes my mind work in a certain way. It makes me horrible at playing cards and evenings like this one especially dreadful. But I'm very observant. My brain catalogs details more efficiently than most. I was at the country club the day Thomas died. So was Sarah. So was Edith."

I glance at Edith. She's shifting her weight uncomfortably.

Cynthia goes on. "I saw things. Things that make me believe that Thomas didn't die of natural causes. Marie and I both believe that Sarah had a hand in his death."

A chair scrapes against the flooring, and I picture Conrad sitting up straighter, his chair shifting closer to the mahogany dining room table. "Mrs. Morgan believes that Miss Cudahy killed her husband? Yet you want me to believe that doesn't establish motive?"

"Yes. Because it isn't only Sarah we suspect. Edith too."

My jaw drops open.

Cynthia continues, more conviction in her voice than before. "The two of them conspired about the whole thing. And I think Edith wanted to keep Sarah quiet afterward."

"Miss Cummings, eh?" Conrad says. His chair scrapes again, causing Edith to startle. It sounds as if he has moved to stand. "How interesting."

Edith staggers backward.

I watch her take another step, her expression laced with fear. Then she turns on her heel and runs.

Chapter Twenty

I have to get out of here. Not only is Ginevra gawking at me as if she doesn't recognize me, but Cynthia has all but put a flashing billboard above my head. And the scraping of the detective's chair can only mean one thing: he's coming for me.

But I know a way out.

As I run, my earlier conversation with Detective Davis races through my head.

He said there's something called homicide by heart attack.

He said a medical examiner could deem Sarah's death the result of cardiac arrest upon agitation—as a result of me.

Cynthia told him Thomas Winchester's death involved me . . .

"Edith," Ginevra whisper-shouts at me, giving chase.

I don't stop, rushing toward the exit off the dressing room, my stocking feet making my gait awkward as I slip and slide. I feel as if I'm in a dream, trying to run for my life yet unable to gain any traction, no matter how hard I pump my arms.

My brain rockets back to Thomas's death, another moment where I felt like I was barely moving, yet Sarah had her hands all over me, pushing me at a frenzied pace away from the body, pushing me toward the clubhouse, pushing me to my car, telling me not to utter a single word. All would be taken care of.

I didn't breathe a word. In fact, I felt as if I barely breathed over the next few days and weeks. Golf lost its luster. I could barely look Marie in the eye. I couldn't tell Ginevra. I couldn't tell anyone. I've been living like a paper doll version of myself—flat, fragile, and one gust away from collapse. And now the wind's howling.

Gin continues to softly call my name from between her teeth.

In the ballroom, I leap up the stairs, circumventing the three steps to the performance stage.

"Oh, come on," Ginevra mutters, breathing heavy.

But in the time it takes me to undo the lock, she's upon me.

Ginevra seethes, "You are entirely too fast. And stupid. What on earth do you think you're doing?"

"Leaving."

She grips my hand and yanks it free from the lock.

"Get a hold of yourself, E. You aren't even wearing shoes. You'll lose a toe to frostbite. And you'll make yourself look ridiculously guilty. Which cannot be the case. Whatever Cynthia said, I will not accept it as truth. Which is saying something, because I am livid with you for not telling me about that day, whatever happened." She's talking a mile a minute. "But I do care. And when Conrad gets to the library, your backside needs to be seated in one of those chairs."

She pushes me. For a shorter, more slender woman, Ginevra puts some real oomph behind it. I stumble backward. She pushes again. She pins me with a look that almost has me cowering.

"Fine," I grumble.

She shoves me a final time for good measure, and once more I feel as if I'm running for my life. I beeline for one of the doors that connects this room to the library. Across the foyer, I have a straight line of sight to the interrogation room, where the doors slide open, Cynthia exiting first, still in conversation with the detective. Buying me precious seconds. I'll forever be grateful she's a tall and hearty woman, blocking his view of me.

I throw open the door to our Big Four room.

Peg screeches and bunches her crochet in her lap.

Courtney fumbles and drops her notebook to the ground.

I race to sit down and heave in air.

The other door flies open, not so much as a knock first, and I hold my breath, the best way I can think of to negate the rapid rise and fall of my chest, my heart pounding from both exertion and fear.

The detective's gaze jumps from Peg to Courtney to me, our armchairs in a semicircle around the fireplace. He eyes the empty fourth chair, his jaw tightening. But all he says is "Miss Cummings."

I discreetly take a shallow breath, willing myself to look as cool as a cucumber. "Yes?"

Beside me, Courtney is also being discreet, using her foot to slide her notebook beneath the skirt of her chair. Smart. Very smart.

I add, "How can I help you?"

"I'd like you to come with me."

I smile politely. "May I ask where?"

"I have a few more questions to ask you in the dining room."

"You are welcome to ask me here. I have no secrets from my friends."

Though that's a lie that leaves my stomach feeling slimy. Ginevra's hurt face springs to mind.

He shakes his head.

"Of course," I amend, standing and taking a moment to smooth out my dress. I make a show of putting on my shoes. "I wouldn't want to traipse around in my stocking feet."

I see him growing impatient. I realize I may've misplayed this moment. I wanted to broadcast composure and calm. What I've done is make him grow more agitated with me.

Wouldn't it be something if he keeled over too? The irony alone would deserve its own headline.

But his mustache and beard don't so much as twitch as he stares me down.

Slowly, I follow him from the room, my mind once again racing with the question of how I'm going to get myself out of this one. I've done it before on the course, a bogey followed by two well-played birdies. But how to play myself out of not one but two murders is novel ground for me.

Chapter Twenty-One

GINEVRA

I slink into the library, quiet as a mouse, as soon as I hear Edith leave the room with Conrad.

"I cannot believe her," I say to the backs of Peg and Courtney, at which Peg nearly jumps out of her skin.

"Will you two *stop* that?" she admonishes.

"Huh?"

"You and Edith," she hisses. "This is the fourth time the two of you have barged into the room and scared us."

"Oh, *her*."

Courtney quirks a brow. "Where have you been? The detective just pulled Edith again."

I sigh. "I'm aware."

"And?" Courtney presses.

And . . . "I'm not pleased."

"That he wants to talk to her again?"

"About *why* he does."

I'm still processing everything I overheard Cynthia say. It's clear my friends know nothing. Not as if Edith had time to tell them what Cynthia is accusing her of.

"Why *does* he want to talk to her again?" Courtney asks, impatience in her voice.

I choose one of the empty chairs. As I sit, I pat Peg's knee. Her project is growing by the minute. "How are you faring?"

She frowns, her crochet hook pausing only long enough for her to say, "Are you not going to answer Courtney?"

"Sorry," I say, rubbing my temples. I'm both overwhelmed and annoyed. I can't fathom that Edith was actually involved in Thomas's death. What did Cynthia say?

I saw things. Things that make me believe that Thomas didn't die of natural causes. Marie and I both believe that Sarah had a hand in his death . . . Edith too.

But that can't be true. It's merely the rambling and active imagination of a woman who likes to poke her nose where it doesn't belong.

Still, I'm upset. While I don't think my best friend killed Thomas Winchester, something happened that day that she's chosen not to tell me. Something that's made Edith behave in a way I've never seen her act before. Completely panicked. Something between her and Sarah. Maybe the same something that Josephine overheard them talking about before Sarah's death?

I continue to rub on either side of my temples before looking Courtney and then Peg in the eyes. "Edith has been accused of murder." Even saying it out loud feels wrong. "Courtney, could you please pass my flask?"

She doesn't move an inch. "This doesn't seem like the time for drinking."

"I'm not sure there's ever been a better time."

Peg is shaking her head. "Explain. This is all sounding ridiculous. Edith killed Sarah? I won't believe it."

"Yes, well, it's not Sarah that Conrad is speaking to Edith about this very minute."

Courtney scratches along her brow with the back of her pen. "The attendant?"

"No, not him. Do you recall Marie's third husband?"

"Thomas Winchester, yes," Peg says. "My father played golf with him."

"Apparently," I say, again, still processing, still feeling ruffled at my best friend keeping this from me, whatever *this* is, "Edith did as well. She was playing golf with him the very day he died. We overheard Cynthia talking with Conrad. She's convinced him that Thomas Sr.'s death was Edith's doing."

Courtney says, "I'm confused."

I lean toward her, hoping yet failing to spot my flask beside her on her chair. "Get in line."

"But she couldn't have," Peg says. "Mr. Winchester suffered a heart attack."

"It appears there's more to the story."

I don't mean for my voice to sound flippant. It's just that I'm having a hard time reconciling Cynthia's accusation with what Edith has purposely kept from me. I sigh, feeling the drain of the night on me. A night that was supposed to be fun and games. That began with Edith and me at the top. But now, two people have died, more of us may be at risk, and Edith is the main suspect. I'm likely the next in line.

Oh, how far we've fallen.

But I am not someone who folds. I'm beginning to recognize that within myself.

Neither are my friends.

I clasp either side of my chair. "We must press on with our investigation. For our own safety. And for Edith. While I do not think she's guilty of killing Thomas, we'd be naive to call her an innocent bystander. In fact, we must consider how Thomas's death could have had a hand in everything that's happening this evening. We must think of all avenues. As it is, I have new clues for our Keeper of Clues to record."

Courtney bends forward and pats the ground beneath her chair, coming up with her notebook.

I don't bother to ask why it was tucked away. After hearing about E being accused of a death that occurred six months ago, I don't think anything else could cause me surprise this evening.

Courtney flips open the book, and it falls to the suspect page. She meets my gaze. She officially writes Edith's name. She writes mine.

"Excuse me," I say.

Peg looks up from her stitching.

I point her attention toward the book.

Courtney shrugs. "I'm putting myself in the shoes of the detective. I've been thinking about it, and I think I'd pen the novel from his perspective. As far as our detective, he must have noticed you missing when he came for Edith."

I realize that.

She adds, "That'd be suspicious and something worthy of writing down."

I sigh, waving her off. Peg returns to her stitching, but at an even more feverish pace. I say, "It's an unfortunate turn of events. But it's Edith who's currently the bigger fish."

Speaking of which, I'm twitching to eavesdrop on her conversation with Conrad. But if he finishes with her and finds me once again missing from this room, it could cast greater suspicion on me. My time is best spent talking through what I've learned with Peg and Court.

"Okay," I say, trying to blot out the storm's gusts and roars, which seem to die down only to begin again with a vengeance when the time has come for me to think. "I first want to address something—or rather someone—who is quite irksome to me."

"Who?" the girls ask in unison.

"Bill. Apparently, he was here. At the Bellevue."

"When?" Courtney asks, pen hovering above the page and a quizzical expression on her face.

"Prior to tonight's activities, while Sarah was here getting everything ready. Or at least that's my assumption. I hadn't realized he left the house.

He was late to dinner, though that's not uncommon. Then we quarreled before I left. Sarah put that nonsense about Daisy in his ear."

"He came to see her?" Peg asks timidly.

I frown. "Appears so. Cannot say if I believe him or not, but Bill insisted he put an end to their affair."

Or at least that's how I interpreted him saying *the situation is handled.*

But what if *handled* means something entirely different from what I've imagined?

I furrow my brow, and a pain builds between my eyes. I press on the spot. "Enough about my future ex-husband."

Peg's mouth falls open. "You'd actually leave him?"

I don't even know. My head fully throbs even considering it. Who am I besides Bill's wife and the mother of his children?

I blow out a breath. "Let's focus on our current predicament. In fact, let's back up prior to eavesdropping on Cynthia. Oh, Peg, we had no luck with the phone." I've completely forgotten that's why we left the library to begin with. "We'd only begun to try to fix it when Conrad came down the stairs and we hid in the parlor."

Peg shivers, no doubt picturing Sarah in the corner.

"Anyhoo," I say, my word choice meant to lighten the mood, but even I hear how strange it sounds coming out of my mouth. I shake my head and go on, saying, "While in the room, I discovered that two things have gone missing. The first is the pressed flower that was used to poison Sarah. The second is Sarah's engagement announcement. Someone hastily tore it from a newspaper."

I watch, satisfied, as Courtney adds both my new clues.

"Initials, please," I say, pointing to the page.

"You're still playing?" Courtney questions.

She leaves off "Even after a second murder? Even with Edith in hot water?"

"Edith hasn't said otherwise, so I see no reason to take my foot off the gas. Besides, don't pretend you haven't already penned the first chapter or two of your novel, Court." I look pointedly at her, and she presses a hand atop her notebook. "And you, Peg, you've been stitching up your own storm. But I know while you do, your mind is whirling faster than the wind outside in an attempt to unearth our perpetrator. So you may as well share what it is you're thinking."

I lift an eyebrow at her.

Peg momentarily puts down her crochet, as if she's about to protest. But she's as hardheaded as I am. Peg picks up her hook again, hands unsteady, and raises her voice over the howling wind to say, "You're right, I can't resist. But I've figured out nothing. What do these new clues even mean? Do we think someone will use the flower a second time to poison someone else?"

Beyond the quick movements of her hands, Peg is as stiff as a board and in desperate need of comfort. "Stay exactly where you are, don't eat anything or drink anything, and you'll be fine," I assure her. "It's the women who are wandering about who—"

The storm's gusto gives way to the sound of someone . . . wandering about, directly on the other side of our door. If not Edith and me, who could it be?

Chapter Twenty-Two

The Ginevra from hours ago would not be jumping to the edge of her seat, seconds away from throwing open the door and confronting whoever is on the other side. Yes, I've taken charge this evening. I often do. But up until this evening, I've done so in a calculated manner. I've been content to antagonize in a socially acceptable manner. I've done Mrs. Burton Kingsland proud.

Alas, tonight, I've begun to throw caution to the wind. Besides, it'd be horrid to wear the same tired clothes for an entire year.

Any one of the women could be on the other side of the door.

Any number of them could wish me harm.

I find it comical that I want it to be Josephine, the most logical person to have swiped the toxic flower. Or the tactful, multilayered Marie, who I'd wager knows a whole lot more than she's let on and who may be using this evening to avenge her husband's death.

I'd like to question them both further.

I don't waste a second longer. I throw open the door, once again brandishing one of my heels.

The person standing in front of me is the complete opposite of those femme fatales. It's the simpering, blubbering, two-faced Cynthia.

"Shh," I immediately say, tossing my gaze toward the interrogation room doors. "Conrad will hear you."

"Who?" she mutters taking two steps one direction before going three steps in another.

I wave her off. "What has gotten into you? Never mind," I say, considering all that's transpired this evening. "Get in here." I drag her into the library and close the door. Peg looks none too pleased that I've done so.

"Now, tell me," I say to Cynthia. "What has gotten you so visibly worked up?"

Cynthia says something incoherent.

I push down my irritation and use the voice I don when my husband is sick and unbearable. "You're okay. Why don't you take a deep breath and tell us what's happened?"

I can't reveal that when I heard her only minutes ago, she was stable. I'd even go so far as to say she was confident and self-assured while she was diming out my best friend.

What on earth could have transpired between then and now?

"The new girl," Cynthia manages.

I look to Courtney and Peg for help deciphering who she's referring to, but they don't seem to know either.

"What new girl?"

"In . . . in the white dress."

"Marie? I'm not following, Cynthia."

She shakes her head. "No, not Marie. The other woman tonight, who was at your table for the first round."

Ah. "Do you mean Greta?"

Cynthia's head bobs, her bottom lip trembling.

"Okay, then—what about Greta?"

Cynthia takes a shaky breath, and I'm glad to see it fortifies her enough to say, "After I spoke with the detective, I used the lavatory before going back to my room. But before . . . before I could get there, I found her."

"You found Greta?"

"Yes. It looks like she's been struck in the head."

"She's been what? Where is she now?"

Cynthia points up, her finger trembling. "In the hallway on the second floor."

I hate to ask it, but I must, avoiding eye contact with both Cynthia and Peg as I do. "Is she dead?"

With some stuttering, Cynthia says she doesn't know.

"Wait here," I say.

Cynthia is little more than a marionette doll, her body moving where I take her, settling her into a chair. But when I reach the door, she says a single word: "Edith."

"Excuse me?"

"Her golf club. It's lying next to Greta."

I curse internally. Of course it'd be Edith's golf club that thunked Greta upside the head.

"I'll be back," I tell the room. To Courtney: "Stay here."

I hope she knows the direction isn't for her but to ensure that Cynthia doesn't leave the room. The last thing we need is Cynthia running amok and inciting all the other women.

I creep into the foyer. The gold doors to the interrogation room are closed. That would mean that Edith is still inside with him, yes? I can only imagine the questions he's throwing at her and the dodging Edith is doing in return. I can't imagine him pinning anything on her. She's too good. She's savvy.

I'm careful on the stairs not to make a peep. As silently as possible, I push open the door at the top of the stairs, and it thunks into something solid. I edge my way through the small opening and see that the something solid is Greta.

She's face down, head turned away from me. If Cynthia hadn't forewarned me, I would scream, the entire house alerted to another gruesome scene.

On the floor runner beside Greta is her discarded headpiece. But also, Edith's club, speckled with blood. It's something else I'm prepared to find, yet a development I find interesting, considering I know that Edith forgot her driver in Marie's room.

I narrow my eyes in that direction. In fact, I'm tempted to do my special knock on Marie's door and ask her how the club got from there to here.

But my conscience stops me. It'd be in poor taste to step over Greta's lifeless body without checking on her first. My husband has accused me many times of wearing blinders when focused on a task. And I've chastised him in turn for comparing me to a horse.

I do the compassionate thing and wipe the hair from Greta's face. I touch my fingertips to her neck, relieved to find a pulse. Then, not sure what else to do, I give her a gentle shake, all the while whispering her name.

She stirs.

I'm further relieved.

Greta blinks and lets out a soft moan.

"It's me. Ginevra. You've been struck in the head. Can you sit up?"

She swallows roughly. "I think so."

I help her, rearranging her white dress to keep her decent, forcing myself to count to ten before I ask, "Do you remember what happened?"

Greta touches the back of her head, cringing as she makes contact. When she lowers her hand, blood stains her white gloves. "No. I don't know. I heard someone behind me, but that's the last I remember."

"Do you know who attacked you?"

She begins sobbing, too distraught to answer.

"It's okay. You're okay," I say. "You wait here. I'll fetch the detective."

She grips my hand. "No, don't leave me alone."

"Very well. I could help you downstairs—"

"No." Greta's eyes are fearful as she looks up and down the hallway, eyes landing on the discarded club. "Edith is out there."

A third alternative, then? "Would you like me to help you to your room? You can barricade the door, and you'll be safe in there until the detective joins you. Is anyone sharing it with you?"

"I don't know anyone else here tonight. I've been by myself."

"In that room there?" I ask, nodding to the closest one, even though I know the answer. It's the only room on this floor that was empty when Edith and I explored each one while looking for Josephine. The green room, I think now. With all the furniture covered, only the green wallpaper and green lamp are visible.

Before I move her, I study her eyes. They are brimming with tears but otherwise lucid, a good sign. Greta answering some simple questions to prove her brain is functioning properly will be another one. "Are you new to Chicago?"

She nods, grimacing at the movement. "I lived overseas until recently."

"Ah, so you likely know Miss Marian Ellison?"

"I, uh, do not think I've met her yet tonight."

I chuckle softly, unsurprised she hasn't seen Miss Ellison this evening, considering the woman lives in the United Kingdom, where she runs a prominent etiquette school. "I daresay you've taken quite the blow. What were you doing out of your room?"

"It'll sound foolish."

"Try me," I say with an encouraging smile.

"Sarah's been kind to me. After she died, I convinced myself I could help."

"You wanted to find her killer?"

Greta nods, much like my William and Charles do after I ask them if they'd like a cookie, after catching them with their hands in the cookie jar.

"That's very noble of you. Now"—I help Greta to her feet—"let's get you back to your room."

I remove a sheet from a chair-shaped object and settle her in, and then I'm on my way back downstairs.

The interrogation room doors are still closed. I'm sure Edith will appreciate the interruption. I knock sharply, then enter, without waiting for a response.

Conrad is seated at the table, his elbows bent against it, cradling his head in his hands.

He jerks to attention.

My brow furrows.

"Where's Edith?" I ask him.

Chapter Twenty-Three

The interrogation room is empty, save for Conrad. He stares at me, nothing behind his eyes. Though I sense I've caught him deep in thought. His body language doesn't evoke confidence in his ability to solve the case. Or maybe his conversation with Edith has shaken him? Left him befuddled? Didn't go as expected?

It could be any number of outcomes. I'm surprised, considering it was Edith in the hot seat. Yet I also am unsurprised. Some believe one of E's greatest assets is her physical strength, second only to her wealth. But those closest to her know it's her mind. Honestly, it's an unfair advantage of bank, beauty, brawn, and brains. I've said it before—Edith's savvy.

Which, again, brings me back to my question: Where is my brilliant—and also deceitfully tight-lipped—best friend?

Conrad hasn't answered me.

I mentally pivot, focusing on the reason why I barged into the room in the first place. It certainly wasn't to see the elk, which follows me with its eyes as I approach the table. "I have unfortunate news."

Conrad rubs along his brow. "What now?"

"There's been another incident with one of the women. Rest assured this one is still with us, but Miss—" I cock my head. "Well,

I only know her as Greta. It appears Greta's been struck. I've come to fetch you so you can hear firsthand what's happened."

This breathes life back into the man. He launches to his feet and brushes past me.

"She's in the room at the top of the stairs," I inform his back, then say under my breath, "You're welcome."

But I'm pleased he rushes off. I, myself, need to find Edith so I can lay into her, first about why she didn't tell me about the day Thomas died and second about what exchange happened with Conrad to leave him so catatonic. The library is the logical place to start, where we've reconvened all evening. But as I enter—more gingerly this time so as not to cause Peg more unrest—I'm immediately chilled that E is nowhere to be seen. It's only Peg, Courtney, and Cynthia, the last woman still simpering.

So again, for the second time this night, I ask, "Where is Edith?"

My question is met with confusion, and before they can suggest she's with Conrad, I add, "She *was* with Conrad. Whatever transpired between them left him quite rattled. But she's no longer in the interrogation room with him."

Which means not only is Josephine missing but Edith is too. Instinctively, I rub my bare arms. Could Edith have tried to flee again? Or could she be following a lead, something she's gleaned while talking with Conrad? Of course, there's another possibility I don't wish to vocalize.

I'm not obtuse to the fact I can be hardheaded, that I often make a game of things, or that I've been known to hide behind my glib nature to shelter myself from internalizing certain situations. Hasn't Peg made such comments all night?

But the current reality is that Edith could have been bested and now be lying somewhere unconscious, another victim of her own club or some yet-to-be-discovered murder weapon.

I shake my head; it's not something I'm willing to entertain any further. I'd prefer to bull on, to unearth the killer—or killers—and, hell, why not win my son some golf lessons along the way.

Cynthia's whimpers increase in volume. It's hard to think over the noise. "Cynthia, dear, why don't we get you some tea? I drank some earlier, and I'm still alive and well."

I extend an arm toward the door connecting us to the ballroom. She proceeds in that direction, and I promptly prepare her a cup of tea, glad to see the kettle is still piping hot. I make note of the brand for future events.

"There," I say, once she has a cup between her two hands. "Now, have a seat here and I'll be back in a jiffy. I need to use the little girls' room."

Except that's not where I go. Heart beating out of my chest, I try the external door off the dressing room, relieved to find no footprints. E hasn't left. I let loose a breath. Surely she would have fled if she believed herself to be in danger.

I rub my lips together, dismissing the idea of E being in trouble and replacing it with the fact she's following a lead. This very second she could be a step closer than me to figuring out who killed Sarah and the attendant, along with who whopped Greta upside the head. And that won't do.

I return to the ballroom. Cynthia hasn't moved, beyond slowly raising her teacup to her mouth. "Thattagirl," I say in a soft voice. "I'm going to have a quick chat in the library. I think it's best if you stay here, as what we discuss may not be of the delicate sort."

Her hands tighten around the china.

I leave her to her tea and slip back in with my friends. I choose to pace rather than sit. "So," I say to the girls, "to appropriately summarize the last few minutes. Greta is not dead. And Edith is somewhere in the house, likely following leads without informing the rest of us."

Peg's crochet fully covers her lap now. I notice she's begun to stitch what appear to be a few letters. An *H*, perhaps. The garment is folding in such a way it's hard to tell. At the pace she's working, it won't be long until she's done. I fear she'll get a cramp. She says pointedly, not bringing up Edith at all, "What a relief no one else has died. But what happened to Greta?"

"I don't know much," I say. "She claims someone came up behind her and hit her."

"She didn't see who?" Courtney asks, pen posed.

"She claims Edith. But Edith was in with Conrad. Any guesses?"

Peg says, "I couldn't tell you the first thing about the girl, so it's hard to say who'd want her dead."

"I'm not sure any of us know a lick about her," I say, "except for the deceased. I remember Sarah saying she'd taken Greta under her wing."

"Poor girl," Peg says under her breath.

Courtney taps her pen against the paper. "We know nothing else?"

"We know whoever hit her took the club from Marie's room and left it at the scene of the crime. When I found Greta, Edith's club was beside her, covered in blood. We may need you to stitch her up, Peg."

But even as I say it, I realize I didn't actually see a significant amount of blood on Greta. I lick my lips, still pacing, then add, "Greta's dress is white. Yet there wasn't so much as a speck of red on it. Only on her glove, after she touched her head."

"Peculiar," Peg says, stitching away.

"Very," I say.

I slump into a chair and move to clutch my pearls but then remember once again that they're around someone else's neck.

"What?" Courtney asks, no doubt reading my perplexed expression.

"Well, it's two things." I tap my neckline. "My pearls were used, not to murder, but to point a finger at me."

Court suggests, "Which is interesting. Most everyone likes you."

"Most?" I counter.

Peg smirks, and Court answers coyly, "There *must* be someone who finds you tiresome if they're willing to frame you."

"I don't love your choice of words. But you're not wrong. Cynthia, for one, dislikes me."

"The question is," Courtney goes on, "what have you done to make someone wish to pin the murder on you? That's a little more serious than Sarah taking this whist drive from you."

I throw up a hand. "Sarah hasn't taken a thing from me. I chose not to run this one. But that's not the point. What matters to this conversation is no one is ever rude to my face. The Breuers I don't know well. Greta I don't know at all. If anything, Elizabeth Field and the Swifts pity me." I frown, but only momentarily, because a thought comes to me. "Though Henrietta Swift is clearly not a fan of Edith's."

Courtney says, "I'd surmise because of Jacob."

"Edith wouldn't give up golf for him," Peg says matter-of-factly.

It's a shame too. She never lets herself get close to men.

Courtney scribbles in her notebook. "If we can ever make heads or tails of what's going on, this story truly will be phenomenal." She looks up. "Oh, you said there were two things, Gin. What's the other?"

"Edith's club," I say, circling back to it. "I've gotten hit in the shins by a wayward club when William was swinging. He truly is horrific. And that was the force of a tiny human. Imagine a grown woman striking hard enough to draw blood. You know, if there was blood."

Courtney nods. "She'd likely be dead."

"Exactly. And yet Greta is upstairs as we speak, telling her tale to Conrad. Which leads me to believe that someone hit her, but not hard enough to kill her."

"No blood on her dress, you said."

"That's right." I cluck, thinking, and tilt my head back, looking toward the second level. "Maybe I missed something. I could go upstairs—" I trail off, a new train of thought coming to me.

"What is it?" Courtney asks.

Peg's head perks up too.

I lower my voice to say, "Cynthia told me that Greta was on the second floor. Which *is* where I found her, just beyond the stairwell door. However, Edith and I searched all the rooms when we were looking for

Josephine. Here, write down what room each woman is in, Court." I wait for her to flip to a new page, to label it. Then I dive in: "Marie is in the farthest room on the second floor, a dressing room. Elizabeth Field used to be with Marie. I'll come back to Elizabeth. Josephine was in the middle room, the bedroom, before she disappeared. God knows where she is now. That leaves Rose and Daisy Pullman in the bedroom by themselves. When we were searching, there was an empty room—I've been calling it the green room in my head—that I now know belongs to Greta. Then we have the third floor." I pause, licking my lips. "We really should have written this down earlier. Let's see . . . Henrietta, Rebecca, and Marjorie are in the smoking room. There are two empty rooms. Ruth Armour and her twins are in the game room. Elizabeth is with them, too, after the switcheroo. Then the last room is the Breuers and Cynthia, in the screening room."

"Got it," Courtney says.

"Do you?" I ask.

"I thought so," Court says, turning her book to show me.

"No, it's not that. I'm sure you scribed superbly. It's Cynthia." I lower my voice again. "Her room is on the third floor. There's a door at the top of each stairwell before you enter the hallway. Greta was on the *other* side of that door, yet Cynthia found Greta on her way to the third floor. Unless she can see through doors, how did she find her?"

Court's eyes go wide.

Peg brings a new color of yarn from her bag, this one a pale green. She's intent on whatever she's stitching, but still asks, "And then Cynthia runs down to tell us, instead of telling the detective? This is making very little sense to me."

Unfortunately, to me too. "Something isn't adding up. Either Cynthia is lying and deliberately made a show of Greta getting whopped upside the head. Or she was on the second floor for a reason unbeknownst to us. Anyone care to take a gander?"

Courtney scratches along her hairline with her hand. "Maybe it'd help if we nailed down motives? Formulated a theory or two?"

I say, "An excellent idea."

Courtney flips to that page of her notebook, pen at the ready, her eyes on me.

Peg cuts in. "I don't know. Is this actually getting us anywhere? What about Edith? Shouldn't we be looking for her? I worry that she's missing."

"Peg," I say, "you're not leaving this room. Not in your condition. And I'd rather you have someone with you." The fireplace poker still leans against a chair, at the ready. "I'll go after Edith. But first I think it'd behoove us to list what we've unearthed and what we know. Right now, that's the only real weapon we have."

Peg sighs before I'm met with agreeable expressions. I rack my brain, beginning as early in the evening as I can remember. "Josephine was not only one of the first to arrive, but she also tried to leave first. Marie took back her brooch. Someone purposely switched off our electricity." I twist my lips. I hate to say it, but it's true, so I do. "Then Edith's hat was found near the power box. Daisy Pullman is covered in scratches along her neck that could very well be defensive. She and Sarah have a history, mainly Sarah trying to ruin Daisy's debut and blackmailing the Pullmans into an open invitation to any event they throw for the rest of time." I pause, glancing at Courtney, who is flipping through her notebook, checking off facts, making notes, and nodding along. I continue. "I found one of Ruth Armour's daughters dangling from a window. The poisonous flower goes missing. Cynthia accuses Sarah and Edith of killing Thomas Winchester. Greta is attacked. Cynthia was on the second floor for some odd reason. Hmm. I'm not certain I've gotten all that in the correct order. But that's what I can think of for now. Maybe it'd also help if we discuss a specific person of interest."

As I've just mentioned Cynthia, she comes to mind first. So, "Cynthia," I say, "who we know didn't want to be here this evening. Marie asked her to come."

I reposition, crossing my left ankle over my right. It feels awkward. I go back to my original position. "I don't recall seeing Cynthia in the ballroom while Sarah was taking her final breaths in the parlor. Let's say Sarah blackmailed her into coming . . ." I search my brain for a reason why. "Oh! Cynthia's father was doing nefarious business in a corner with Sarah's father and Josephine's father. They could've been doing it on behalf of their daughters."

Court asks, "Are you speculating, or—"

"No," I say, "this rendezvous truly happened. Henrietta Swift told me that her husband saw Edward Cudahy, Thomas Winchester, Jagger McCormick, and Marcus Bamford together. Then, Edward gave Marcus money. Or it could've been the other way around, Josephine's daddy slipping Sarah's daddy money. Though Henrietta did question if Josephine killed Sarah because of this meeting. It'd make more sense for Josephine to pay off Sarah in this scenario. Which leaves the question of why a Winchester or a McCormick was even at the table. Cynthia told Conrad she's observant. She proclaimed how she witnessed *things*"—I put air quotes around the word—"the morning Thomas Winchester died. What if Sarah found out? What if Sarah threatened Cynthia?"

"But," Courtney says, "your original suggestion was that Sarah blackmailed Cynthia. In your scenario, it'd be more likely that Cynthia would blackmail Sarah."

"Tomayto, tomahto," I say.

Peg cocks her head. "Ginevra, dear, I don't think you used that correctly."

I wave her off. "Fine. New scenario: What if Cynthia is the mastermind behind everything this evening? She killed Sarah with Josephine's flower. She strangled the attendant, then added my necklace to the scene. She hit Greta using Edith's golf club. She went into a state of theatrics to divert suspicion from herself. Now she's quietly sipping tea in the next room, planning her next move. She could be trying to set up everybody else for tonight's misadventures."

Courtney glances in Cynthia's direction, no doubt pleased there's a wall separating us. "But why?"

I groan. "I don't know. Being a detective is actually a very difficult profession. Remind me to increase my contribution to the Chicago Police Department this December." I take a deep breath. "Let's put Cynthia aside for the moment before my brain implodes. Marie is the most obvious, after all."

"Which is very Agatha Christie," Courtney points out. "She's known to hide her murderer in plain sight. Though she tends to make her murderer unassuming."

I twirl a strand around my finger, my hair growing more limp as the evening progresses. "Marie is anything but meek. But as I said, the most apparent. She took back the brooch she donated, which belonged to Thomas, who *Cynthia* claims was killed by Sarah"—I sigh—"and Edith. Then there's the fact Sarah was set to marry Marie's former stepson, something Marie may have wanted to stop at all costs. But it feels like there's another layer we're missing, unless it's as simple as Marie wanting revenge against Sarah."

Courtney points out, "It doesn't account for the attendant and Greta."

"No," I say, gripping the arms of the chair. "It does not. Love, money, revenge. What other reasons are there to murder?"

"You've already mentioned it, but blackmail?" Courtney suggests. "It's not a favorite of Agatha Christie, but she does use it as a plot element from time to time."

"Blackmail," I parrot, my mind spinning on how I can relate it to someone else with the clues we have. I wiggle my fingers for Courtney's notebook. She hands it over. *That* she gives me, but not my flask? But it's fine; better to be clearheaded.

I flip through the pages, and my eye catches on my initials, next to a clue I'd forgotten about entirely: the newspaper clipping.

"Sarah's engagement announcement was ripped out of the paper. This could be about Sarah's entanglements." I roll my eyes. "Beyond Bill."

Courtney takes back her notebook. "She *was* dating Henrietta Swift's son, Jacob."

Peg asks, "Was that before or after Edith?"

"I can't recall," I say. "But things progressed with Tommy rather quickly. They were seated next to each other at that dinner at . . . at . . ."

"The Pullmans'," Peg offers.

"Yes, that's it." The night I asked Rose Pullman to switch my husband's seat with Tommy's. Would you look at that? I'm a matchmaker. Sarah should have been thanking me, not antagonizing me.

"Still—" Courtney begins.

"I know; Sarah potentially dropping Jacob for Tommy doesn't give Henrietta Swift a motive for killing Sarah, especially as Marjorie stepped in to marry him. Besides, the attendant and Greta add a wrinkle that's making my head pound again. We'd likely come to the same obstacle if we were to think through Josephine's motive."

Though all night my gut has been telling me Josephine is involved in some way.

Still stitching, without averting her gaze, Peg says, "As you said, Gin, Josephine was the first who tried to leave after Sarah's body was discovered. She also was one of the first to arrive this evening, which gave her an opportunity to poison Sarah without watchful eyes. Considering Josephine has gone into hiding and the poisoning flower is missing, we can assume the two are together. I'd also assume blackmail of some sort, considering her father was part of that clandestine meeting. We all know Sarah thrives on collecting secrets, either of her own making or ones she unearths. Why would Josephine bring a poisonous flower, if not to use it? Let us not forget that Josephine has been suspected of poisoning to solve a prior problem."

She finishes, continues to crochet.

"Peg," I begin, "how very astute—"

"As far as the attendant," she goes on. "Scott's book has two murders, but not by the same person. If memory serves, the person who helped to cover up the first murder later becomes the victim of the second murder. What if the attendant stumbled upon the first murder and needed to be removed? Or what if he was involved in the first to begin with, and then someone killed him to silence him?"

I'm utterly amused with Peg at the current moment. What she's saying is ghastly, of course. But what tickles me is how she so plainly laid out a plausible means for murder, piecing this all together, while being seemingly distracted and shaken to the core.

"Though," Peg muses, and I cannot wait to hear what comes out of her mouth next, "there is something that's been causing me particular distress all evening. The detective. It's never been answered how he knew to come this evening. And now you're telling us that Edith has said something to him that left him rattled. Something isn't adding up. We need to find Edith."

She's right. Edith may have the answers. But could there also be a chance that Edith is in danger?

Chapter Twenty-Four

EDITH

Hands firm on the sink's edge, I stare into the lavatory mirror. And at who I've become.

A murderer. A liar. A cheat.

I'll stop there. No need to continue listing my less-than-favorable attributes.

After the detective dismissed me, I escaped to the restroom off the stage's dressing room. His words were delivered in an authoritative way. "You can go now," he said.

But I think his posture—gaze steady, chest puffed—was a facade. A debutante knows a thing or two about pretense. For years, I've seen my friends put up their own fronts. Ginevra, for one, is the queen of compartmentalization. She does it with her husband, her children, and she's been doing it this very night—turning an evening of murder into a frivolous competition.

Though maybe I was the one to initiate our game? I can't recall. Which is part of my own facade. I'm calm, cool, unbothered. The Unflappable Fairway Flapper who always walks away unscathed. Truth is—I'm flapped and scathed.

After demanding I join him again in the interrogation room, the detective took an aggressive approach off the tee. I waltzed into the room. He commanded me to sit. He stroked his beard in what I believe he thought was an intimidating manner. He ordered me to tell him every detail about my involvement with Thomas's death. All things I was expecting, even the intimidation.

Then the unexpected happened. It was like the sun emerged from behind a cloud on an overcast day, allowing me to see minuscule peaks and valleys on the green that I might have otherwise missed. I turned the tables on him. I ruffled his feathers. He choked up on his metaphorical club, even if he didn't outwardly show it.

And now I'm hidden away in the restroom, having a good, hard look at myself in the mirror about how I got here. And what's next for me.

All I know is that it wouldn't be prudent for me to leave this room when I don't know how this night will end. It's gone off the rails.

And I don't think I can win.

I drop my chin toward my chest, only for my head to pop up again at a crashing sound. Seconds later, a muted screech follows. I know instantly it's come from Ginevra.

I shouldn't, but I burst from the lavatory and stop on the stage, appraising the scene.

A light-haired woman in a blue dress is lying crumpled on the ground, a teacup beside her, dark tea splashed onto the floor, a half-eaten smoked-salmon-with-cream-cheese sandwich (most likely mushy and stale) still clutched in her hand.

Cynthia.

As she fell, she pulled down the serving table's cloth, breaking more china, piling tiny sandwiches all around herself.

Ginevra is the palest I've ever seen her. She's kneeling over Cynthia, her rounded eyes jumping from the unbroken teacup beside Cynthia and back to Cynthia's unmoving body.

"It was an accident." Ginevra palms her mouth. "I wasn't thinking."

I'm not sure what she means. Peg and Courtney join her from the Big Four room. "What's happened?" Peg questions, arms hugging her stomach. "Is she breathing?"

Courtney, hand trembling, checks and then nods.

"Water," Peg suggests. As she does, she lifts her head, meeting my gaze from where I've been standing unnoticed across the room. She palms her chest, a relieved expression washing over her face. I smile—a lie—letting her know I'm okay. Then I motion toward the kitchen, letting her know I'll get the water.

My mind whirls through possibilities, the most obvious being that Cynthia has also been poisoned. In the kitchen, I snatch a crystal glass and begin to fill it from the sink.

Water gushes noisily into the cup. Enough to muffle the sounds of footfalls closing in behind me, until my stomach sparks with heat. And a hand covers my mouth.

Chapter Twenty-Five

GINEVRA

I'm kneeling over Cynthia, willing her to open her eyes, when I catch a dash of mustard yellow from my peripheral vision. It's Edith. She disappears into the kitchen.

On my knees, I gasp and shuffle, trying to get my feet under me, but Peg stills me, saying, "I saw her too. She looks unharmed. She's getting water for Cynthia."

Water.

Unharmed.

Both very good.

Water is one of those things that people always call upon. An elixir to help all ailments. In this case, hopefully a small dose of poison, for which I'm unfortunately responsible.

Earlier, I left behind the poisoned teacup in the ballroom when Marie's screams interrupted my investigating. And only minutes ago, in my haste to get Cynthia out of my hair so I could focus on the case and theorize with my girls, I must have made her tea with that very cup.

Conrad bursts into the room. "What is all this commotion—"

Both his body and his words stop short.

"She's not dead," I say, standing and wiping the floor's invisible grime from my hands. "But I'm fairly positive that she's ingested a very tiny amount—a dusting at most—of poison." I pinch my fingers together. "Diluted and very marginal."

Conrad shakes his head, his gaze jumping from me to Peg to Courtney, then around the room, as if he's looking for additional people. "She's been poisoned? What on earth is wrong with you women? There's something new every—"

You cannot make this up: The grandfather clock once again begins to strike a new hour.

Conrad says something, but the gonging is quite loud in the otherwise quiet house. I'm just now realizing the storm has called a ceasefire. He tries to repeat himself, only for a gong to interrupt him again. And again. Conrad presses his mouth closed, frustration etched across his forehead. The clock chimes the number eight, nine, ten.

We all wait.

Finally, the eleventh.

Right now, we should all be pushing back our chairs and saying our goodbyes. E and I would have been tonight's whist champions. Instead, I'm standing over the fourth body of the night.

It's guilt that prompts me to add honey to my voice and address Conrad. "What is it you were saying, Detective?"

He points demonstratively to Cynthia. "I'm asking how it is even possible that someone else has been targeted. How do you know she's been poisoned?"

I point to the teacup.

"And how do you know she's not dead?"

I glance at Cynthia, still sprawled on the ground. Body slack. Eyes closed. But breathing. "Don't you see the rise and fall of her chest?"

Conrad palms his face, running a hand over his short beard. His mannerism is not that of an abashed man but that of an exasperated one.

"I must ask," I say. "Do you have any suspects?"

"I'm not at liberty to answer that."

"So you have no leads? Have you questioned everyone? You must have speculations. Perhaps if you shared your intel, we could—"

"There is no 'we,' Mrs. King Mitchell."

Such a stubborn human being, who has quickly lost control of the evening, if he's ever had control from the moment he conveniently arrived—as Peg has only just reminded us.

I could press him on that. Or I could show more consideration to the woman I've accidentally poisoned. "Someone should check to make sure there isn't any sandwich in Cynthia's mouth. She could choke."

By someone, I mean Conrad. He's the trained professional. I widen my eyes at him. At which he appears vexed, his jaw tight.

Peg offers, "I'll do it."

"No," Conrad says in a stern voice. "Everyone out. Back to your rooms. There is a killer on the loose, and you're gallivanting around the house like it's nothing."

I do not like his tone. I am not some child. I cross my arms. Peg does too. "There has been no gallivanting," I insist. "But I am confused. You won't let us help Cynthia?"

And where is Edith with the water? Does she not want to show her face with Conrad in the room? If only I'd been a fly on the wall during their conversation.

Peg exhales very loudly. "I'm going to help her."

Conrad responds—again in that same tone—but I stop listening. Instead, with Conrad's attention on Peg and Peg safe with Conrad, I backpedal, slipping away toward the kitchen.

I've never before realized how large the ballroom is. One tiny step after another. Plenty of time for Conrad to catch me very suspiciously and slowly fleeing the room.

But Peg is doing a fabulous job of holding his attention, even if it's not for my benefit but for Cynthia's, and Courtney repositions where she stands to block his view of me—for my benefit.

A girl could not ask for better friends.

As soon as I enter the kitchen, I hear it: water. The faucet is running. But the room is empty. I palm my chest, my heart racing as I cross to the sink and whisper, "Edith?"

I was completely wrong when I said this evening couldn't surprise me any further. First Greta. Then Cynthia. Now Edith, missing again, but in a more dramatic fashion. One that legitimately gives me pause this time. What would cause her to flee, but leave the faucet running? Not only that, but a glass is in shatters within the metal sink, a splash of blood on the basin's side. At my feet, there are larger drops of red, one smeared as if someone walked through it.

The little voice inside my head is growing louder, cracking my carefully constructed resolve. Telling me that tonight is more than a mystery Edith and I have been racing to solve before each other. Demanding that I take this seriously. Shouting at me that Edith could truly be in danger.

Chapter Twenty-Six

GINEVRA

I told Peg I would go after Edith. And now, more than ever, I need to. But first, my friends need to know what I've found. If I don't return from my search for E . . .

That's not a line of thought I care to follow.

Upon my reentry into the ballroom, Conrad reacts to my sudden appearance in a few ways. First, he growls, unaware that I wandered off. Second, he commandeers the glass I've filled with water for Cynthia, as if he's the only one capable of properly handing it to her. Third, he demands I remove myself to the library. Fourth, he also demands I take my friends with me.

Peg is reluctant to leave but acquiesces once Cynthia shows signs of life, at first a moaning sound, and then pushing onto her elbow to sit up.

Courtney raises her chin, not keen on being told what to do. Her first husband tried that. But she gives in when Peg finally does.

I lead the way.

As soon as all three of us are in the room and the door is closed, Peg whirls on me.

"That was incredibly irresponsible, Ginevra."

I make no attempt to hide what happened with Cynthia.

"I know."

She's not done. "You carelessly left the poisoned teacup alongside the clean ones, and then you used it to make her tea."

"I know," I repeat. "I'm sorry."

"It's not us you should apologize to."

"I'll apologize to Cynthia when she's more lucid. I'll also say—you've already mastered the tone of a disappointed mother, Peg."

That gets a crack of a smile from her as she crosses toward her chair.

"It's the least you can . . ."

When she doesn't finish, I ask her, "What's wrong? You aren't one to leave a good dressing down unsaid."

Peg doesn't answer. Her back is to me as she stands just beyond the four chairs.

"Peg?" I ask. "Is it the baby? Are you all right?"

She faces Courtney and me, her pale complexion even more washed out. "Someone's been in here."

Courtney storms forward. "Tell me my notebook hasn't been taken." She stops in her tracks.

I'm almost afraid to look. Edith is the bravest of our Big Four, but Courtney is fearless in her own ways, always willing to tackle whatever task or foe awaits.

She tells me, "It's your necklace, Gin."

Oh.

That is strange.

Did someone remove it from the attendant's neck and return it to me? It's a necklace I'm quite fond of, but . . . I begin to cross the library to my friends. "I don't think I want it back."

I also stop in my tracks.

It is indeed my necklace, lying innocently on the seat of the chair I was in earlier. Stained with and dripping with blood.

My own blood runs cold. I cross my arms, rubbing my hands up and down my goosefleshed skin. So many questions swirl in my head. Who and why and how and what on earth this means.

I blink a few times, urging my senses to return to me instead of feeling scattered. "Girls, it's not often I'm speechless, but I'm at a loss for what to make of this. But coupled with what I just found in the kitchen, it's making me feel a bit woozy."

"What do you mean?" Court asks, worry dripping from her voice. "What did you find?"

"The water still running. Blood in the sink and on the floor. But no Edith. I've grown legitimately worried she's in danger." I risk another look at my pearls. "Maybe all of us are."

Where Peg was pale moments ago, her skin has now taken on a green hue closely resembling that of her emerald dress. She crosses to the window, unlocks it, shoves it open, and sticks her head out into the night air.

Frigid air floods the room.

I survey Courtney, who is faring better than my other friend. Still, she's clearly rattled, wringing one hand into the other. She points at my crimson-stained pearls. "It feels like a message."

Peg returns, skin now rosy from the cold air. "This changes everything, you realize that, yes?"

"It certainly feels more personal," I say. "Why cover or dip or splatter or whatever they did to my pearls with blood? How grotesque. Could Courtney be right? What type of message is this meant to send?"

Peg sidesteps the now-tainted chair to get to her own. She sits, positioning her crochet in her lap. It's taking on a rectangular shape. Definitely an *H* and three other letters, but the way the fabric is bunched makes it impossible to tell. She kneads into the fabric, much like a cat. Clench. Unclench. Clench. Unclench.

She lifts her head. "Ginevra."

"Yes?"

"I think we should tell the detective."

I bite my lip. "I don't know. I'm still ruminating on your question, Peg, about his apparition here this evening. Then how he treated us only moments ago. How he seemed less than concerned about Cynthia. He'd only bark at us to stay in this room." And I must leave it again.

Peg knows this. Courtney too. I see it in how they both take a long inhale. Then Peg's shaky voice says, "What if the pearls mean that the blood is on your hands?"

I ask, "Whatever do you mean?"

"What if someone believes you're responsible for everything happening this evening?"

I palm my chest. Peg is quite intelligent. Her baby will likely be a genius, taking into account Eddie's intellect as well. But I'm failing to see how my pearls doused in blood means anything more than the fact someone here tonight is greatly disturbed. I rub my arms again.

Peg explains, "Your necklace is one of the murder weapons."

I shake my head. "We already established it's not strong enough to kill—"

"True," Peg says, clasping her hook, "but the necklace is depicted as the murder weapon. And now that murder weapon is covered in blood. There's a passage in the Bible that speaks of a watchman's responsibility to warn people of impending danger, and if he fails to do so and they die, their blood is on his hands."

"I can't fathom how I'm responsible for everything."

Nor can I stomach how this person must view me. As a monster? As a callous human being? I can't help it—Daisy Buchanan edges into my brain. Did Scott not depict her as callous? As someone who lacked empathy, particularly when it came to the consequences of her actions? Was she charming? Yes. But did her choices prioritize her own comforts and desires? Also yes.

Is this how I'm seen? Is it being insinuated that my missteps and attempts to protect my image have propelled tonight's events into motion?

I still can't make heads or tails of the accusation and how this is all my doing. Even in Scott's novel, Daisy doesn't bear the full brunt; Tom and Gatsby are also responsible for the tragedies that take place.

I spot my flask, tucked into the side of Courtney's chair. I snatch it, uncap it, and begin to take a long draw, finishing its contents.

Nothing like some liquid courage; I may need it. If someone out there has sent me a message, then I'll answer it. "I'm going to get to the bottom of this. Both my necklace and Edith."

"How?" Courtney asks.

"Simple. I'll talk to the women again. Determine who is behind this"—I point to my pearls—"spectacle. The same person must be behind whatever has happened with Edith. I won't allow myself to believe anything other than her being okay."

Neither of my friends says anything at first. I'll lose my nerve if I hesitate. "Peg, I'll need you to ensure Conrad stays in the ballroom with Cynthia. And Courtney, review our notes. There must be something we're overlooking. Or rather, someone. Oh, and keep the poker within arm's length at all times."

I take one last pull from my flask, then turn to leave.

"Wait!" Courtney says.

I whip toward her, part of me relieved she's delayed my exit.

"What if whoever left your pearls here knows that you'll immediately investigate? They could be lying in wait. You could be tonight's grand finale. Sarah, the attendant, Greta, and lastly you."

She leaves Edith out of the list. I'm glad for it.

"We could also add Josephine," Peg says. "No one has seen her in hours. There could be a perilous reason for that. Unless, of course, she's the one behind all this."

Peg's hypothesis almost has me changing my plans. I could hide out in this room until Conrad apprehends the perpetrator. But what if that's exactly what the culprit wants? What if I'm getting close and my bloodied pearls are meant to be a warning, to scare me into paralysis?

I lift my chin. "This all shall be over soon. Either I'm going to find the murderer, or I'm going to die trying."

Chapter Twenty-Seven

I'm a liar. The sentiment that I'd die trying felt brave as I made the proclamation, but reality quickly sets in. And I do not want to be another victim sitting properly in a chair with a napkin draped over my head or with my legs and feet sticking out from beneath a row of coats.

I once uttered the phrase *beautiful little fool* to Scott. In his novel, he uses it in a different context. His meaning is more applicable to Edith's experience, how societal expectations limit her. I suppose I fall into that boat too. But then and now, I meant it as a woman who follows her heart instead of her head.

Currently, it doesn't very much feel like I'm using my head.

I may be bold when it comes to bossing around others or inciting games with my friends, but the atmosphere in the house suddenly feels ominous. The lights flicker. The wind howls once more. There's a peculiar dripping sound, though I can't determine where it's coming from.

"Sarah," I whisper. "If that's you, cut it out."

I cannot take any additional emotional distress after Edith not trusting me with whatever happened with Thomas Winchester—and now her possibly being in mortal danger. Then there's the threat against me, along with my accidental poisoning of Cynthia.

It's a lot.

But I'm convinced if I can find whoever has threatened me, it'll lead to Edith and also to whoever murdered Sarah and the attendant. Three birds with one stone, as they say.

Unless I'm found first. I truly am a fool, standing outside the library like a sitting duck. I shouldn't dawdle for that reason alone, but also because of Conrad. Peg's high-pitched voice is currently arguing with his deeper tone. But he could march out of the ballroom at any moment.

I beeline it toward the stairs, once again only in my stockings to move as noiselessly as possible. I pause at the top of the first flight, listening intently for any movement. I'd also be a fool to think I'm the only woman creeping around. Edith could be. Josephine. A possible third, who may be responsible for Greta's attack.

Whoever that person is, they retrieved the golf club from Marie's room. I take a step in that direction, stopping as floorboards creak above me. It sounds like multiple people are moving about.

I've never been a fan of the idiom that curiosity killed the cat.

Curiosity can lead to answers.

What if that movement is my murderer? I could uncover a crucial piece of evidence, ending this once and for all. We'll be safe. Sarah's murderer will be brought to justice. Then I'll promptly schedule William's golf lessons with E. My shins will be the true winner.

I proceed up the stairs to the third level. I once saw in a film a woman use a compact to peek around the corner. I have such a thing—in my clutch downstairs. I'm left to do it the old-fashioned way, poking my head into the hallway. It's empty, and it appears the game room with Elizabeth Field, Ruth Armour, and her twins is the offender of all the noise.

I press my ear to their door, hearing voices, mostly at a whispered level. I'm unable to make out what they're saying. The brass doorknob is cold to the touch. Frigid air seeps beneath the door, chilling my toes through my sheer stockings.

As quietly as possible, I turn the knob.

I promptly stifle my response, putting a hand over my mouth, taken aback by what I've walked in on. Once I understand what is going on here, I surprise them, saying, "I see you've taken matters into your own hands."

I'm met with heads swinging in my direction and gasps. I quickly count heads. All four women are accounted for, not like on my last visit to this room, when one of the twins was dangling out the window.

Now linens have been knotted together to create a rope of sorts. And said sheets are hanging out the open window, tied around the leg of the billiard table.

"Let me guess," I say barely above a whisper. "None of you have been brave enough to descend?"

"We're on the third level," one of the twins says matter-of-factly.

"And we'd still have to fall quite a ways," the other says. "We were testing the length."

"It appears I need to make another trip to the linen closet," Elizabeth says as she shivers.

Icy snow drifts in from the window, which Ruth shoves closed as she says, "We've used all the sheets on this floor we can find."

"The second story, then," Elizabeth suggests.

I raise my brows, nodding my head, unable to help myself from being utterly amused by their antics. "Before you do that, I must ask—why do you believe that the 'blood is on my hands,' as the saying goes?"

Elizabeth's gaze drops to my palms, and her forehead wrinkles.

Ruth also appears confused. "I believe what, now?"

"It's a theory," I say simply, their responses indicating they likely aren't the ones who threatened me with my pearls. "Apparently somebody believes tonight is my doing."

Elizabeth steps closer to me and clasps my hands. Hers are ice cold. "May I speak plainly?"

"Please," I say.

"Ginevra, you are many things. Charismatic, sophisticated, and endlessly hospitable. Superficial, self-serving, and, at times, unmindful. But do I think you killed anyone this evening?" She shakes her head. "Do I think your previous actions may've influenced Sarah's death? I won't count it out. You and your Big Four have your fingerprints on most everything. Sarah has long wanted to be one of you. If not a friend, perhaps that's why she fell into the role of foe. Though honestly, I don't blame you for your distaste for her. If she was carrying on with my husband and tarnishing my reputation, I'd give a thought to what I could set into motion to cut her off at the knees."

She smiles sweetly.

I insist, "But I did no such thing."

There's that sugared smile again. "That you know of."

I blow out a breath. This conversation has been heavier than expected. It's also illuminated nothing new.

I turn on my heels. "There's a linen closet on the second floor, should you want to continue with your escape. But I'll warn you that the detective is not currently in the dining room."

Elizabeth cocks her head. "Where is he, then?"

I swallow roughly, debating how much of the truth to reveal. Hell, the jig is up with these particular women. "The detective is seeing to Cynthia in the ballroom. She's a bit under the weather. I may have mistakenly fixed her a cup of tea with the same china Sarah drank from, and that, well, left her unwell."

I wrinkle my nose—I've had to admit this twice now—and then clear my throat. "So as I've said, be careful wandering about. If the detective knows what you're up to, he'll certainly thwart your escape efforts."

And he'd certainly thwart my detective efforts, something I'm adamant about continuing via a second conversation with Marie.

I need to move about without being seen. Which makes me remember the back staircase that Edith and I discovered in the kitchen—before I learned about her keeping things from me. Even today, she kept putting me off, hiding whatever happened that day with Thomas. I growl internally, doing my best to put my so-called best friend out of my mind, as I quickly locate the stairwell and begin to descend. I'm about to slip through a door onto the second floor when there's a gruff cough. A low voice. The knob begins to turn. Eyes wide, I panic, looking for a place to hide. I could run up or down the stairs, but it'd cause a great deal of noise. Or I'd slip in my stockings and break a leg. Neither is ideal. My gaze locks on the dumbwaiter.

I've long envied Edith for her height. In this moment, I'm grateful for my small frame. My *grand-mère* would roll over in her grave if she saw me now, hiking up my beaded red dress to crawl inside. I close the door the best I can, a small crack letting in a sliver of light.

The hallway door creaks open.

I hold my breath, a challenge with my knees pushing into my rib cage. William once hid in our dumbwaiter during hide-and-seek. It was the fact he couldn't fully close it that gave him away, though Ingrid and I pretended we couldn't see the laces of his shoes.

I curl my toes, pleading not to be seen, wishing my vantage point gave me an idea of who was on the other side of the thin dumbwaiter door.

Then, just as the mystery person came, they go.

I release my held breath and wipe away the perspiration that's gathered on my brow. What a ridiculous predicament I've put myself in. It'd do me good to get out of here immediately before I give myself a cramp. I shift, freeing a leg. I put my hand down for support. My fingers touch something hard and smooth. I hold it before my eyes.

It's a black feather.

Chapter Twenty-Eight

Edith

Half an hour ago, give or take

A hand covers my mouth. An arm snakes around my waist, pulling me tight against a lithe body.

The crystal glass slips through my fingertips and clashes against the bottom of the sink. As I thrash about to free myself, my hand catches on a shard of glass.

I grasp onto the side of the sink, fighting for purchase as I continue to struggle, but my assailant is stronger than I anticipated.

"Shh, Edith."

It's said at a whisper directly into my ear.

It's a woman's voice, but that's not a shock in a house of women. Her perfume is earthy. She's shorter than me. My first instinct was to knock my head back, but I'd only strike air. I've tried to kick her shins. She has sidestepped every attempt. I've caught a glimpse of a black dress and black gloves, and she truly may be a ninja dressed in all black with how she's restraining me.

"I'm going to release you," she says. "Please don't scream. I just want to talk."

I nod.

Her fingertips loosen across my mouth, as does her grip around my waist. I whirl to face her, at the ready to strike.

"Josephine," I breathe.

She holds up her palms but doesn't say anything more.

I've been assessing women for years. On the course, Glenna Collett-Vare blinks rapidly when she's unsure of her putt. Joyce Wethered goes stiff as a board if she fears she won't make par.

The woman standing in front of me, her hands now clenched together across her stomach, appears fearful as opposed to violent.

Of course, it could all be an act.

"You said you wanted to talk?" Blood drips from my hand onto the floor.

She nods. "But not here." She crosses the room quickly and opens the door to a dumbwaiter. From it, she pulls the framed flower. Josephine faces me, eyes as large as those of a doe caught in the crosshairs.

"Is that where you've been hiding?"

Josephine is small boned, but the square space is barely large enough to fit a child.

Her words come out rushed and whispered. "Follow me. Please."

Doing as Josephine says may be the daffiest decision I've ever flirted with. All I know about her is that we overlapped at the Westover School for a year. That she was expelled from her previous boarding school because she was accused of poisoning another student. That her family may be even wealthier than my own. That she generally doesn't come to social events, but when she does, I've found her intelligent and sarcastic, with a dry sense of humor. That she's the leading botanist in the country. That she stealthily took the toxic flower. That she overheard me with Sarah earlier.

That last one changes things. I need to know what she knows. And what she plans to do with the information. I told myself earlier I'd resolve things here, tonight.

Josephine's head jerks, as if she heard a noise. With the water running behind me, I heard nothing.

"Hurry, Edith. Please trust me."

I make the decision—and hastily follow her straight down into the cellar that gave Ginevra and me the heebie-jeebies earlier this evening.

It's dark. It's dank. It's a regular death trap. The kind of place a gumshoe finds the victim.

In the pitch black, Josephine's voice sounds detached from her body. "I can't turn on the light. Someone may find us, and I really need to tell you what happened."

Tell *me* what happened?

"I'm listening," I say, then suck on my fingertip to stop the bleeding from where the glass cut me.

Josephine exhales.

"Thank you. That's very kind of you."

She may be giving me too much credit. It's her I need information from. But perhaps she also knows something that can help me get out of this pickle. "Go on."

"It started six months ago, at the Onwentsia Club."

The darkness cloaks my reaction; otherwise, she would've seen the split second my nostrils flared in alarm. "What do you mean?"

"The day Thomas Winchester died."

My heart's pounding. "Sarah told you about that day?"

Or is she pulling from what she overheard? I rack my brain, trying to remember what words were spoken moments before Sarah's death. The club. That's all we called it. Never the Onwentsia Club. After Sarah berated me about Tommy, she mentioned Thomas. Sarah was panicked about our secret being revealed.

By Josephine?

She shakes her head. "No, Sarah didn't tell me directly. She approached me a week or so before Mr. Winchester's death. She wanted to know about toxins. Specifically, a flower that could create a certain effect if consumed."

"What type of effect?"

"Momentary paralysis. I said I knew of such a flower, but I wouldn't tell her the species without knowing why she wanted to know. Of course, she refused to tell me. So I also didn't share more. But I should have. If a nominal amount is ingested, paralysis can be preceded by aggression or agitation. But if too large a quantity is consumed, the effects could be—"

"Deadly," I answer.

"Yes, the plant is highly toxic and contains atropine and other tropane alkaloids that can disrupt the nervous system and affect heart rate and rhythm. The disruption of vital functions can lead to a cascade of effects, including increased heart rate and sweating, and potentially fatal respiratory failure, which causes a lack of oxygen in the blood, strains the heart, and damages its tissues. A heart attack is possible."

"A heart attack . . ."

Josephine pauses before she says, "That is my professional conclusion, yes."

My mind is whirling. It's transporting me back to that morning, back to the clubhouse, when Sarah approached me. She told me that my golf partner called the club to say she was sick and unable to play. I never asked Ginevra afterward about being under the weather. The next day, I left for a tournament, and was adamant about not uttering a word about that day. But now I see that moment for what it was: a lie. Sarah simply wanted Ginevra's place. Then she wanted Mr. Winchester to join us. What did she say . . .

"'Deals are made on the golf course,'" I recite to Josephine. "That's why Sarah wanted to play with me. And with Thomas. She wanted to get close to him to ultimately get close to his son." I rub my lips together. "Sarah suggested we have a round of champagne before we teed off."

Josephine asks, "Was she ever alone with the drinks?"

Was she?

I suck in a breath. "She fetched them and passed them out."

Josephine curses under her breath. "So she easily could have doctored Mr. Winchester's drink."

I tell her more about what happened. "On the sixth hole, Thomas suddenly became angry with me. Sarah immediately stepped in to help him. But then he clutched his heart. Sarah screamed at me that I had provoked his heart attack. But—"

You've ruined everything, Sarah screamed at me.

What you've done is considered homicide.

"Sarah poisoned him." Josephine's voice is thick with emotion. My eyes have adjusted enough to see the tremble of her bottom lip.

I reach out to touch her arm. "It's not your fault."

"Nor is it yours."

My breath hiccups. I didn't know how badly I needed to hear that.

Josephine exhales, then says, "It's Sarah's fault, I know that. But if I'd told her the species and stressed how deadly it was, perhaps she wouldn't have sought out the plant on her own. She would have understood the severity of using the flower, in any amount."

"She was trying to cause paralysis, wasn't she? Her plan was to incapacitate Thomas, then swoop in as the hero. She wanted to gain his favor, which in turn would go a long way with winning Tommy." I knead my neck. "She killed him, yet she still got Tommy in the end."

"I cannot handle when women like that come out on top."

"Josephine, I have to ask—did you poison Sarah?"

Her head shakes aggressively. "No. I'd never do that."

I don't understand. "Then why did you bring the flower tonight?"

"I didn't. Sarah did."

I really don't understand.

Josephine goes on, "Sarah brought the flower. I was one of the first to arrive tonight. Sarah immediately asked me to join her in the parlor. There was the flower—the very one I alluded to months earlier—on the table. I asked her why she had it, and she told me it was an insurance policy. Of course, I had no idea what she meant. Then Sarah became hysterical, first blaming me for her giving Thomas Winchester too great a dose. If I would have just told her the proper amount . . ."

I touch her arm.

"Sarah's hysterics turned to anger then, and she demanded to know why I'd threatened her."

"Why did you—"

"I didn't. But she insisted that I sent her a note that said something along the lines of *I know what you did.* But I never sent it. She must have believed me, because she began muttering about who else could know. Then, she threatened me, saying how if a finger was pointed at her for Thomas's death, she'd take me down with her."

"But how?"

Josephine swallows roughly. "The incident I was involved with back home. Apparently, Sarah dug up information that could end my career."

"So she brought the flower tonight to scare you and to keep you quiet?"

"Yes. But then, I don't know when, or by who, the flower was ground up and added to the tea."

"Who had already arrived by the time Sarah was done blackmailing you?"

"A lot of women. The Breuers, Marie Morgan, Cynthia McCormick, Peg Carry Cudahy, Greta Fischer. After we walked out together, Sarah launched into perfect hostess mode."

Perfect, my foot. "I'm sorry you got caught up in all this, Josephine. This is all Sarah's doing."

Even though she tried to pin the whole rotten mess on me. For months, I've agonized over having a hand in Thomas's death. It's sullied being on a golf course for me. It's made me question if I should stop playing golf altogether. When, all along, it had nothing to do with me. I didn't stop Thomas's heart. Sarah did. Josephine would have had more reason than most to kill Sarah. But if she didn't do it, will the real killer be unearthed?

"I'll get to the bottom of this," I tell Josephine. "Keep hiding until I do."

She nods, her bottom lip trembling once again.

But before I go, a thought pops into my head. "What if," I begin, "one of the women was eavesdropping on the two of you?"

So much of that has been happening, Josephine even doing it herself to me and Sarah.

Josephine puffs out a breath. "Then Sarah basically told whoever that could be how to murder her. And how to make the whole thing look like natural causes."

Bingo.

If ever there was a time for Sarah to cry for a mulligan.

"Though," Josephine adds, clutching the framed flower to her chest, "I don't believe the nominal amount administered to Sarah would have killed her outright."

Chapter Twenty-Nine

Ginevra

Josephine.

I twirl the black feather from her hairpiece between two fingers. I was eyeing it earlier, impressed with her fashionable yet macabre ensemble.

So the dumbwaiter is where she's been hiding. But if she's not here, where is she now? And why is she mobile? Could she have Edith?

I'm biting my bottom lip, worried, thinking, when I hear yet another noise. It's getting increasingly harder to move about. Women are growing impatient and anxious, taking matters into their own hands, such as by preparing to rappel down the side of a three-story building. Society will be talking about this night for years to come. That is, if we make it out to tell the tale. This time, the creeping sound has come from beneath me, from the servant stairs. Which means whoever it is ventured from the kitchen. Or the cellar.

I need to see who it is. I don't bother to be quiet. I dash down the dimly lit stairs, catching a glimpse of orange.

"Edith," I whisper-shout, relieved, but now that I know she's safe, there's a little venom in my voice.

She stops in her tracks. "Ginevra, what are you doing?"

What an asinine question, considering we've been slinking around the house together most of the night, until, of course, she went AWOL.

Not in danger. Not taken by the murderer. But still on the case. So naturally, I respond, "What are *you* doing?"

"I'm returning to our Big Four room to tell you what I've learned."

"And where have you been? I saw blood in the kitchen. I was worried."

"I'll explain when—"

I snort. "Typical. You'll explain when it's convenient for you. I'm only surprised to hear that you're sharing now instead of six months from now."

We're standing on the landing that leads to the kitchen. Not the best location to hash this out, especially when I know I sound like a petulant child who believes they've been wronged. It's all too similar to a petty, emotional conversation my two boys would have after one irks the other. But I do not care. My emotions are frayed, and the one person I trusted most in the world has deceived me. So it must be done, and I go on, "What happened that day? I still don't even know what actually happened, only that Cynthia saw *something* that made her think you killed Thomas Winchester."

"I didn't."

"Of course I know that, you dumb Dora."

"Dumb Dora?" As soon as the question leaves Edith's lips, she bursts into quiet laughter. "Is that what I am?"

Her laughter is contagious. It's thawing. I join in too; I really am acting juvenile.

"Gin, look," E says, regaining composure. "I'm sorry I haven't told you. I was afraid."

"Of me?" I ask incredulously.

"Not of you, but of what happened and my role in it. I thought I killed a man, Ginevra." She goes on, telling me about being out on the course with Sarah and Thomas Winchester. Him growing agitated. Him dying. Sarah insisting Edith could be charged with murder. Sarah, the caddy, and Edith coming to a truce. She rubs her forehead. "So you see, I don't think it's unreasonable for me to sit with that for a while."

"For six months," I say, palming my chest, feeling for my friend.

"Just be glad you weren't actually there that day."

"What do you mean?"

"Remember, you called the club to say you couldn't make it because you were sick."

I shake my head; that's untrue. I think back. It's not difficult to pinpoint the day. It was a few weeks prior to the Summer Soiree. Edith was in Chicago before and after, traveling in between. I don't play with her often, but when she's home, I make an effort to go to her. And I know one thing for certain: "I never called the club that day. Someone called *me*."

I see my friend is clearly befuddled.

I go on, "They told me you had to cancel to rest for your tournament. I'll admit I was miffed because you had to leave the next day, and I wouldn't have an opportunity to see you. But being the good friend I am, I understood."

Edith shakes her head. "That wasn't me. It was Sarah. Or at least Sarah telling the receptionist what to say." She pauses, then resumes shaking her head. "And I bet you anything Cynthia witnessed it all. That must be how she knew something underhanded was going on that day."

"Unbelievable. Perhaps we should call her Sensational Cynthia from now on. Sarah 'the Snake' Cudahy still rings true."

Edith chuckles. "Listen, Gin, I really am sorry I didn't tell you about that day. It's been haunting me ever since. I should have gone to you with it."

"You should have. I tell you everything. And let me emphasize the 'you.' I went to you first about Bill's infidelity, about Scott's novel, about that odd rash I had." I scrunch my nose. "I love our Big Four, but it's you I want skulking beside me as we track down a murderer. I don't even care anymore if I win."

"Liar."

I smile. "Okay, maybe I do care. William is simply horrid at golf." I take her hands. "But I am concerned about your safety. All of our safety, especially baby Carry Cudahy. Now let's go before I'm startled by yet another noise." I bop her with the feather. "Josephine is out there somewhere."

"Oh," Edith says, a sly smile on her face, "you'll be all ears when I share what I've learned from her."

I cock my head. "You spoke with her?"

She waggles her brows in an "I sure did" manner. "Is the detective still in the ballroom?"

"Last I checked, he was in there with Cynthia."

"You accidentally poisoned her, didn't you?"

I scrunch my nose. "She's fine. It was a trace amount. She was already sitting up when I left. Stop shaking your head at me."

"I make no promises. Now come on."

We're able to quickly and successfully navigate to our Big Four room without any sightings of Conrad or Cynthia.

So as not to repeat prior offenses and scare the living bejesus out of Peg, I softly knock on the door before opening. It was unnecessary. My heart rate quickens. "Where's Peg?" I ask Courtney.

"The interrogation room." She looks from me to E. "Edith, there you are. We've been worried."

I smile. "She's just fine. Edith is unshakable."

"Actually," Court says, "I've been trying my hand at a scene, and that's how I've been portraying you, Edith."

I question, "You've written another scene?"

She cringes. "Is it callous of me?"

"Am I in it?" I ask.

Courtney nods.

"Then," I say, "not callous at all."

Of course, I'm trying to lighten the mood, but Courtney still twists her lips. "Sarah's body isn't even cold."

Edith makes her own lighthearted attempt, saying, "She's probably moderately cool by now."

We really are two peas in a pod. And it does the trick, Courtney shifts into author mode, saying, "I recently read in *The Murder of Roger Ackroyd* a line where Agatha Christie said how the body was quite cold after two hours. She worked as a dispenser during the war and has a decent understanding of pharmacology and basic forensic concepts,"

I say, "Well, there you have it. Sarah is likely cold. Speaking of cool, either we see to our fire or we'll all be freezing soon." The building doesn't yet have the modern convenience of heat. "Does either of you know how to do that?"

I spot the fire poker leaned against the chair and approach it slowly. The chair. Not the poker. "Oh, wonderful," I say, "the blood is gone. Did Peg see to that?"

Courtney nods. "A quick flip of the cushion."

Edith kneels in front of the fireplace, saying over her shoulder, "The blood?"

I say, "There's much to catch you up on, E. But we should wait for Peg—otherwise, we'll repeat ourselves." And because I want Perceptive Peggie's take on things. But to help pass the time, I say, "Courtney, why don't you read us a sample? I must say I'm curious."

"I haven't been writing in chronological order, just whatever speaks to me. And this isn't from the perspective of the detective, as it predates his entrance into my novel." She clears her throat and flips back a page. "I'm going to start mid-scene. *The women, hands to throats and mouths agape, stood around the body, utterly dumbfounded as to what lay before them. The lady in red stepped forward, the obvious choice, as Giselle often dictated their movements in society—*"

"Oh!" I proclaim. "Is that me?"

She shushes me as Edith begins stabbing the fire with the poker.

"*The obvious choice*, yada yada yada," she says skipping what she's already read, "*and she took stock of the darkened room. The fireplace was roaring, casting light onto the victim. There was no obvious murder weapon.*

No blood. No signs of a struggle. Serena had been young, healthy, and with the constitution of a viper. Natural causes could and would easily be ruled out. The body itself was perfectly posed, feet crossed at the ankles. One could and would also assume care had been taken in staging Serena after death came for her. Suddenly, there was a gasp, a thud, an eruption of startled women as one of the ladies fainted. The horrific turn of events was penetrating their meticulously crafted facades. A woman was dead. And one of them was the likely culprit. Chaos would ensue unless Giselle took charge of the women and the room. First things first, Serena's staring eyes were too much. A napkin was procured to cover her face, keeping the dwindling composure of the women intact. Second, Giselle said, 'You there,' to a young woman, Gertrude, who was closest to the parlor's entry. 'Call the police.' Gertrude left with no hesitation. It was when she returned that the equilibrium of the room truly shifted. 'The phone lines are dead,' Gertrude illuminated them. 'I'm unable to call for help—"

My eyes narrow. I tap my finger to my lip. I say, "Wait a minute."

Chapter Thirty

My mind has whirled numerous times this evening, the most I've used my brain in quite a while. It's been fun to flex muscles that lie largely dormant in my day-to-day. For my boys, we've adopted the theory that engaging in intellectual activities, such as chess and memorization games, will strengthen their mental acuity. Very similar to how physical exercise builds physical muscles. So why is it that, for myself, the most exertion my mind gets is crafting shopping lists, redesigning rooms, and keeping up with societal gossip?

After tonight, this must change.

Edith stands from the fireplace, having reignited the embers. She turns to face us again. What's interesting, I realize as I study Edith's keen gray eyes and her pressed lips, is that she's courting a similar reaction, as if something Courtney has written has sparked her own revelation.

"What is it?" I ask E.

"Something Courtney has said."

I feel energized. "Same. You first."

"No, you," Edith says, peering toward the parlor. "I need to investigate my line of thinking more."

"By going in there again?" I shiver. "Fine, I'll share first. But I wish Peg were here. It's about something she said earlier."

Perhaps the night's fortune is shifting in our favor; at that very moment, Peg enters, swift enough for the three of us to jump from our skin. The payback feels fair.

"Are you all right?" I ask her as she hurries to the chair she's occupied much of the evening. Her crochet is lying in a heap. Without a word, she pulls one long loop through and ties a great big knot in it, not even bothering to bind it off properly, let alone weave in the ends or cut off the last remaining spool. She takes the whole kit and caboodle and crosses toward the window.

Edith, Courtney, and I watch with bated breath, unsure how her movements will end.

Peg unlocks and then heaves open the white-dusted window, snow tumbling into the room and light shining in from the portico sconces. She shakes out her crochet, and it falls to its full size—the making of a baby blanket in yellows, blues, and greens. It's unfinished, only half the final row completed, but my eye catches on the *H* from earlier. And now also an *E*, *L*, and *P*.

She positions the blanket outside so it's hanging from our first-floor window, then calls for us to close the frame as she holds the afghan in place.

We do.

I'm astonished.

"This is what you've been doing all evening, Peg? Crafting an SOS message?"

She nods, out of breath.

"But why the sudden urgency to put it out now? What's happened?"

She palms her forehead, and I lead her to a chair. "There's something about him," she says.

"Who? Conrad?"

"Yes. I have a feeling I was his final interview and now that he's done, he's about to take action in some way. An accusation, perhaps? But I don't trust him—"

Edith cuts in. "It's because he's not who he says he is."

"Explain," I say. "What have you found out?"

Edith flexes and unflexes her hands, like she wishes she were gripping her club, and stares at the door to the foyer as if Conrad is going to barge in any moment. "It all started back at the club."

She shares with Peg and Courtney about that fateful morning. About Sarah's deadly ploy. This I know. Then she mentions Josephine. The toxic flower. Josephine's involvement leading up to that day. How Sarah received a threatening note, the sender unknown. I'm rapt. "All I know for sure," Edith concludes, "is that Josephine is no more guilty than any of us in this room."

I question, "How can you be so certain she's not involved? And what on earth does this have to do with Conrad?"

"That day on the course," Edith continues, "Thomas Winchester's caddy was forgettable. He looked like any other handsome fella. Tall, clean shaven. Didn't speak much, at first. But I remember him announcing the sixth hole. The combination of the s, i, and x tripped him up, although I couldn't detect an accent until he got worked up and angry. Then tonight, when the detective pulled me again, he made mention of how I was the sixth woman he'd spoken to tonight, but the only one he needed to have a second conversation with. The way he said 'sixth' sent off alarm bells in my head. I'd heard it before. Remove the beard, put him in golf attire, and—"

"He's the caddy," Courtney says, astonished.

"He's Miller," I confirm. "Only tonight he introduced himself as Detective Davis. I had no reason to put two and two together."

I'm aghast. "How did you not lead with this revelation?"

"Context is important," Court answers for her.

"I should've kept my mouth shut about knowing who he really is," Edith says. "But I challenged him."

Peg glances at her crochet hanging from the window, a hopeful yet fearful expression across her face. "You told him you knew who he was?"

E nods.

I'm further aghast. "When you were alone with him?"

"Adrenaline," she says with a shrug. "I asked him if he was a caddy, a detective, or both. He took so long to respond I questioned if he even heard me. But then his face rearranged into something I couldn't quite place, and he told me I was mistaken. He excused me after that, and I wasn't about to try to stick around."

"So what does this mean?" Peg asks. "That he knew or surmised what actually happened with Thomas Winchester on the sixth hole and is here this evening for retribution? Were they close?"

"I'm not sure," Edith says. "I usually go with whatever caddy is available. They all know the course equally well. Though Thomas did offer for Miller to play as our third. That speaks to a level of intimateness."

"Certainly. But then he doesn't show his face here until after Sarah died," I add. "Although"—the pieces begin to form in my head, including the point I wanted to bring up after Peg returned—"Peg, you were able to call Eddie earlier, correct?"

"Yes."

"The lights went out, but your phone call wasn't disconnected," I clarify, the pieces falling even more snugly into place.

"That's right."

"Then," I say, my voice an octave higher than usual, "why did Greta say the telephone was down? Which leads to the question we've circled all evening: How did Conrad the Caddy know to come when he did?"

Unless he was in on it from the get-go.

The last portion goes unsaid, but there's no doubt we're all thinking it. For the first time tonight, I feel as if we're making progress and getting close to figuring out who is behind this god-forsaken evening.

"What have we learned?" I ask. "Let's summarize."

We talk over each other as Courtney scribbles, the gist being that . . .

Josephine is innocent.

Greta lied about the telephone lines being down.

Miller, who had a first-row seat to the killing of Thomas Winchester, is here this evening, passing himself off as a Detective Davis, and arrived only moments after Sarah's death.

Very suspicious.

Also: "Very good. Now what's left for us to solve?"

"Well," Courtney says, "why Miller would pose as Davis. He's going through the motions of conducting interviews. But why?"

"To find the best person to pin the murders on, perhaps," Peg suggests.

I raise my brows. "Such as planting Edith's hat next to the electrical box."

We all exchange looks. Again, no need for words to know we're all thinking the same thing: *How curious.*

"Okay," I say. "What else is left to solve?"

Edith's laugh is dry. "Only who is killing everyone."

"Yes, that," I say. "I must get back upstairs."

Peg is incredulous. "To do what?"

"Well, first," I say, "I want to talk to Marie. I never closed the loop on Edith's golf club, which feels like an integral part of the equation. If you remember, Conrad was interrogating Edith at the time Greta was struck. So unless Conrad and Edith are working together . . ." I give E a cheeky smile. "That means Conrad didn't have a direct hand in Greta's attack. I'd also like to speak with her again—with Greta." I make eye contact with Edith. "I can go alone. You shouldn't wander about with Conrad knowing you've placed him."

"And this has nothing to do with you wanting to go alone so you can win?" But she says it in her own cheeky voice. "Go. I've a hunch to see to in the parlor."

"Reconvene after?"

It almost feels as if we should do a huddle and a cheer before Edith and I are sent off. I only hope we're both able to make it back unscathed now that Edith has shown her cards.

Chapter Thirty-One

EDITH

I don't envy Ginevra—tiptoeing over creaky floorboards and through shadowy halls like she's in a haunted picture show, half expecting a wallop to the head. I only have to venture to the adjacent room. And for once, I'm eager to see Sarah.

I enter the parlor. The fireplace is little more than embers, darkening the room to my advantage.

When Courtney was regaling us with her first draft, she mentioned how the body was perfectly posed, feet crossed at the ankles. And how obvious care was taken in staging Serena.

I'm the one who told the girls about this detail. I'm also the one who saw Thomas Winchester as he succumbed to the very same poison. He writhed. He clutched his heart. His face grew red. He'd been given a proper dose.

But Josephine said the missing petals wouldn't have been enough to kill Sarah outright, not unless other factors were involved.

Which is exactly why I'm currently creeping closer to Sarah. If poison didn't kill her, what has?

Before, I planned to use my club to remove the silk linen that Marie draped over Sarah's face, curiosity about what the effects of poison looked like on a person getting the better of me. What can I say? I'm only human.

But more time has passed. She's gone cold, confirmed by Agatha Christie herself. Small mercies—there isn't yet a smell.

I reach out a hand, willing away any tremble. I've seen too much and come too far to let the sight of Sarah stop me.

I pinch the bottom of the napkin, right where it falls against the embroidered collar of her dress.

And I yank.

Sarah is revealed.

To my astonishment, her face isn't colored with heat like Thomas's was. Hers has a bluish-purple hue.

Horribly, I've seen this shade before. Twice. Only hours ago beneath Ginevra's pearls. And months earlier at the Christmas Gala, where Ruth Armour nearly choked on her shrimp cocktail. Moments passed, hysteria growing in the room, before Ruth's husband whacked her on the back and the chunk of crustacean shot across the room.

A very close call, which turned her lips and fingertips a periwinkle color. Just like Sarah's.

Her mouth is parted ever so slightly. And she's staring straight at me.

I chastise myself for so hastily removing the linen. I decide there's no need for me to see the upper half of her face, only the lower portion that could be involved in asphyxiation: her mouth.

I cover her back up, the napkin falling just short of her plum-colored lips. What caused Sarah to suffocate? There are no marks on her throat, like there were on the attendant's. A quick survey of the room doesn't reveal any pillows. She clearly didn't drown. That leaves choking.

I hesitate, but steel myself to bend at the waist and peer into the small opening of Sarah's mouth. Sarah would just about drop dead—again—if she knew I was eyeballing all this silver in her mouth. But then I gasp, seeing something else of grave importance.

Chapter Thirty-Two

Ginevra

I do the prearranged knock, then promptly swallow my fear.

Tapping the opening to "Sweet Georgia Brown," a favorite of mine, actually helps a smidge to sooth my unease.

Marie opens immediately and ushers me inside. "I expected you sooner." She lodges a chair beneath the doorknob again, then swipes a stray strand of hair from her face. Her eyes, once perfectly smoky, have raccooned ever so slightly, and her blue eye shadow is smeared beneath one of them. "Have you figured out who has ruined a perfectly good evening?"

She is certainly cutting right to the chase. Before, I felt as if Marie was playing games with me. This late in the evening, my tolerance for any funny business is waning.

I sit.

Marie sits.

This time she chooses the spot beside me on the bench.

She's kept her fire going with impressive know-how. The room is smaller and a much more pleasant temperature than the library.

I answer, "I'm afraid the woman who I thought to be behind everything is indeed innocent. I may even call her a victim."

"Oh?"

I pivot, needing to address something off the bat. "I know you believe Edith had a hand in your late husband's death."

Her eyebrow quirks.

"Cynthia said as much," I say plainly. "But we've gotten to the bottom of it. Sarah's wholly responsible."

Marie huffs. "I actually feel relieved the secret is out. Of course, the detective and I spoke about it as well, considering the connection to Sarah. Though I wonder if you know the full story. Yes, Sarah wanted to get her claws into Tommy. But do you know why she had to go to such extreme measures to try to impress my Thomas?"

I do not.

"It may come as a surprise, but we all don't come from the same background. My Thomas had a ward, a young woman who was the daughter of a man he met during the war. Henrich and his daughter were German. As such, this wasn't a relationship Thomas broadcast after the war. But I assure you, the Fischers were not sympathetic to their fatherland. Unfortunately, Henrich did not survive the war, but his dying wish was for his daughter to be cared for, and Thomas was resolute to uphold this final request. The daughter was to marry Tommy, a way to ensure she'd always be cared for."

"And Tommy was in favor of the plan? If I'm not mistaken, he has an extensive dating history. He could have married any one of them. How he landed on Sarah is still a mystery to me."

"Is it?" Marie says. "Do you not recall the dinner Rose Pullman put on?"

Vaguely.

"For whatever reason," Marie continues, "though I'm almost certain it was your doing, she switched your husband and Tommy. It put Tommy directly beside Sarah. And the rest, as they say, is history. A confusing and frustrating history, but history nevertheless."

"Confusing in what manner?"

"Tommy had been more than agreeable to marrying his father's ward. She didn't come from money. Nor did she have the proper schooling. Marrying her would've been quite beneath him, actually. But for Thomas's ward, it would have been life changing. She'd never want for anything ever again. And you see"—Marie twists her lips, as if debating how much to reveal—"by marrying him, she offered Tommy the thing he wanted most."

"Which was?"

"Freedom. Tommy may have had a long list of suitors, but it was all for appearances. He only wished to marry so he could carry on in secret with who his heart truly desired. Thomas's ward was receptive to this. When she came to the States, a beau followed her and became quite close with our family. An agreement was struck. They could all be with who they wanted, under the guise of holy matrimony."

"And Thomas was keen on this as well?"

Marie barks out a laugh. "Oh, my sweet Thomas didn't have the foggiest clue. I was the captain of that ship. If he could hear me now, he'd be rolling over in his grave. Alas, Sarah swooped in and ruined everything."

"But how did Sarah convince Tommy to marry her instead?"

"Isn't it obvious? Sarah unearthed his secret. She knew *all* our secrets, and it was only a matter of time until she divulged them for her own benefit. Each time she did, she left a devastating wake. Think of all the women here this evening. Did you not talk to Daisy Pullman, for example? Sarah somehow put her on a blacklist unless—"

"Yes," I say. "Say no more. Sarah had learned Daisy's secret and used it against her."

"And yours. And mine. And Josephine's. And Edith's. And Greta's. And I could go on."

I press my lips together. I have to know. Asking the question outright may be extremely daft of me. But I say, "Marie, did you kill Sarah?"

Marie titters a laugh, a hand palming her chest. Finally, she says, "No. I did not kill her."

She said the same thing regarding the attendant earlier . . .

Marie adds, "Someone saved me from having to do it, though."

The smile she gives me is unnerving, and I do not think she's being facetious.

"However," she says, wrapping one of her curls around her finger, trying to breathe life back into her hair, "I did threaten her. It's important to me that my husband's cause is not abandoned. Sarah must be held accountable."

She rises then and crosses to the vanity. A bag sits on top, from which she retrieves a small box of Kleenex and begins dabbing at her smeared eye shadow.

I fight to hide my reaction. "You told her that you knew she was responsible for Thomas's death?"

"I believe the words I used were *I know what you did*. Just a simple note on ordinary paper. I paid an errand boy to bring it by her home." Marie shrugs, casting a quick glance at me in the mirror, so quick her expression is unreadable. "Someone had to finally put her in her place. I must say, it was fun watching her squirm. You could have done the same. There," she says, done with the tissue, her makeup all cleaned up. Gone is the frazzled girl. She meets my eyes again. "Why you let Sarah carry on with your husband is a mystery to me."

It's becoming more and more unclear to me as well.

Marie twists on the stool to face me. "I'll have you know, you're the catalyst for this entire mess we're in. The reason I had to write the note to begin with. Had you gone to the country club that day—"

"My housekeeper received a call saying Edith canceled—"

"And then, had you not played puppeteer and sat Sarah next to Tommy . . ."

"Oh, surely she would have cornered him at the next event or the one after that. You can't pin this all on me. Even earlier, you claimed Cynthia would have liked to frame me."

Another shrug. "Merely making suggestions, albeit far-fetched. Cynthia is too mousy to implicate a person."

"She implicated Edith."

"Touché. As far as all the happenings tonight, though, all I'm saying is you've put everything in motion."

I frown. "And you're certain you didn't put an end to it all?"

Marie looks me dead in the eye. "Sarah is responsible for her own death. She killed herself."

Hiding my reactions is something I can no longer do. My jaw nearly drops to the floor. Out of all the things that have made no sense this evening, this takes the cake, along with making me shiver at Marie's deadpan delivery. A moment later, the room feels too warm. Sweltering even. I swallow. "You're saying Sarah poisoned herself?"

"It would be poetic, wouldn't it?"

I have to avert my eyes from Marie's steady gaze, my attention straying to where Edith left her golf club earlier. "How did Edith's driver become a possible murder weapon?"

"I gave it to Detective Miller. Who had it after that, I can't say."

Interesting; her pupils don't expand, and she's not fidgeting; thus I don't believe she's lying. But the Big Four and I only just deduced that it couldn't have been Conrad who struck Greta. The timing is off. So whose hands did the golf club end up in? Furthermore, who was bold enough to unravel my pearls from the attendant's neck to ruffle my feathers?

"I assume you also don't know who got their hands on my pearls?"

"To kill the attendant?"

The fact she even asks the question is curious. Only the perpetrator and my girls know about the sullied pearls left in the library for me to find. Wouldn't that mean there'd be no reason for Marie to ask an elucidative question? For Marie, the pearls would only be connected to the attendant. She would know nothing of the threat against me. Or does she? Or am I overthinking? By this point in the night, I'd hope for more clarity and far less questioning. But I still get the sense that Marie is playing her cards close to her vest. She knows more than she's letting on. She has all night. She has for the past six months, and likely well before then. Sarah may have used people's secrets against them, but Marie was a collector of them.

Now she sighs. "You really don't know who killed Sarah, do you?"

"We have theories," I say. "In fact, I should reconvene with the others." I stand to leave, then decide to divulge, "The detective has completed all his interrogations. Let's hope a close to this horrid night is imminent."

"Yes, let's hope."

I'm eager to return to my friends, though I'm unsure what of importance I've gleaned, if anything. It's frustrating. I'm unaccustomed to feeling a lack of control. Even in veiling my husband's infidelity, I've convinced myself that it allows me jurisdiction over my own life. Though now I'm beginning to realize I've gone about it in all the wrong ways.

I sigh as I close the door behind me.

A hand snakes out and grabs me. Then a face appears. I barely hold in a scream. "Edith," I whisper. "I thought someone was about to kill me. What are you doing?"

"I was listening."

"And?" I ask as we begin to silently make our way toward the stairs.

"And we have much to talk about."

"Do we?" I say. Then I admit, "I can't quite put my finger on her. But—"

Hushed voices drift from the room across from the stairs. It's the green room.

Apparently, the word of the night is *eavesdropping*. So why should we cease doing it now? Remembering the door off the butler's pantry, I lead Edith and myself in that direction.

God bless keyholes.

E looks first, then all but shoves my face toward the opening.

And for the seemingly millionth time this evening, I gasp, taken aback by what I'm witnessing.

Chapter Thirty-Three

Well, that's a doozy of a twist. But it's all making sense now. I nudge Ginevra ahead of me on the stairs to go more quickly. Peg's and Courtney's heads are going to explode when we tell them what we just saw, coupled with what Marie revealed.

Ginevra shoots a warning look over her shoulder. "Stop pushing. You'll trip me."

She's fine, always so dramatic.

We round the landing of the stairwell, the first floor coming into view.

Suddenly, there's a massive bang, and the front door of the house flies open. Snow and wind pour in, a miniature blizzard momentarily obstructing the foyer.

Ginevra and I stop dead in our tracks, our holds on the handrail keeping us from tumbling forward.

A police officer appears, barreling into the foyer. Then another uniform, along with a man—Eddie?—and also a woman.

"Oh my goodness," Ginevra says. "Is that an Armour twin? I cannot believe she actually went out the window."

And was plucked from the side of the building as she tried to escape.

"What rotten luck," I say.

Ginevra blindly reaches back to take my hand. "Come on."

I begin to step but then grind in my heel. The officers have brought the Armour twin back. They'll do their own line of questioning. It's my cloche hat that was found next to the electrical box. My golf club that was used to crack Greta upside the head. It was me who was seen with Sarah the day she killed Thomas Winchester. I was alone with Sarah in the parlor moments before she died.

This has frame-up written all over it.

In fact, it's exactly how Miller slash Davis hoped it'd look.

I withdraw a step.

Then another.

Ginevra looks over her shoulder again, her forehead wrinkling at my obvious retreat.

"I'll be blamed," I whisper, pulling free my hand. Isn't it what Miller wanted all along?

Ginevra's green eyes bore into my gray ones.

In unison, we nod.

Above us, floorboards creak. There's an uptick of voices. My window to escape is rapidly closing. I take the stairs two at a time, going up, going away from the officers, until I slam into a body.

Greta.

Her mouth opens. I barrel past her before a scream can form. But then there's Marie. There are Daisy and Rose Pullman.

"I—" I begin to say to them. But I don't know how to finish it, nor is there time for pleasantries. I hightail it toward the servants' staircase, needing to get away.

Chapter Thirty-Four

Oh, Edith, I think.

I question going after her, but it won't do either of us any good if we both appear guilty.

So instead, I flurry into the foyer and grip the officer's arm. "Thank goodness you've come."

"Ginevra," I hear, Peg's husband stepping out from behind one of the officers.

"Eddie! Thank goodness. Aren't you a sight for sore eyes."

Even if his suit is rumpled, his hair is askew, and his expression is crazed. "Where's Peg?"

I take his arm. "Just this way." I stop, realizing the officer may not agree. "If that's all right with you."

He has kind eyes. Young too. Even younger than Conrad. Though I can see he's about to deny me exit. Turns out, he doesn't have to. The library door is thrown open, and Peg emerges.

Husband and wife rush to each other.

Eddie palms her face.

Peg gives him a peck on the lips.

I smile. Good for them, throwing modesty and restraint out the window. Especially for all to see. By now, Courtney has joined us, along with Greta, Marie, Elizabeth, Rose, Daisy, Henrietta, Rebecca, Marjorie, Ruth, both twins, Jasmine, Cordelia, and even Cynthia, looking sturdier on her feet, a balm for my conscience.

It's quite the gathering. If not for unforeseen circumstances, tonight's event would have surely been a success. If only death had not also been on the guest list.

I note the missing. Edith, of course. But also Josephine and Conrad—who suddenly appears from his makeshift interrogation room, slightly out of breath. He tugs on his suit jacket, straightening it. I see him scouring the room, likely for Edith. Without her here, Conrad can continue his ruse. "Officers, I'm Detective Davis," he says in an authoritative tone. "I take it the storm has calmed enough for you to move about the city again. If you'll join me, I'll fill you in on this evening's happenings."

In Eddie's arms, Peg stiffens.

We're all standing just beyond the parlor, and it's as if all heads turn in that direction at once.

"What *has* happened?" Eddie asks his wife. "You're all right, aren't you? We saw the blanket hanging from the window. Then we found Miss Armour dangling from another window . . ."

Peg bites her bottom lip to keep it steady as she nods, eyes swimming with tears.

In the past, I'd be brash, drawing the attention to me, proclaiming that Conrad is a fraud and announcing that Sarah is dead. The latter is what I did earlier, come to think of it. Now I stand aside, not yet wanting to reveal Conrad's true identity, but more importantly letting Peg artfully tell her husband that his sister is no longer with us.

He's confused, rightfully so, sputtering for words about what happened, along with how it happened.

Peg is discreet, but I hear a single word.

"Murdered?" he responds stoically from the center of the room. Surrounding him are all the women who could have potentially done it. He turns to address Conrad, his gaze twitching over the possible perpetrators. Eddie's stoicism turns to anger. "I need answers. Now."

"Of course." Conrad gestures to the interrogation room. "Gentlemen," he says to the young officers, also inviting them inside—where Conrad slash Miller slash Davis will do nothing but spew lies and false accusations.

While I bit my tongue moments ago, minding my place, that time is now over. I step forward. "No."

"No?" one of the officers says.

"That's right. No. The men will not go off and sequester themselves to talk about what this man"—I point at Conrad—"claims happened here this evening. *Everyone*, please join me in the ballroom. As it is, *I* would like to make an accusation."

"You'd like to make an accusation?" Conrad says, incredulously.

"It appears you understood me perfectly. Shall we?"

Eddie has known me since childhood. On many occasions and in various scenarios, he's witnessed me take control, maintain order, and perfectly execute a plan. So it gives me great pride when he leads Peg by the arm toward the ballroom. One by one, the others follow.

I take my spot at the front of the room, ascending the steps to the stage, like Sarah did to begin this evening, telling everyone to "please, take a seat." But I don't take the stage for the obvious purpose of wanting to commandeer the room. I want a better vantage point. I want to see everyone's faces, their reactions, how they shift in their seats. I want to see if anyone acts accusable, after which I will effectively accuse them.

Until then, I need to draw out the murderer.

And I think I know how to do it.

"For our newcomers in navy blue and for dear Eddie, allow me to provide a digest on tonight's unusual and regrettable events." I pause, assessing the room. Cynthia is doe-like, but behind her wide eyes is a watchful mind I know is spinning on all cylinders. Marie is as angelic looking as ever. Elizabeth Field and Ruth Armour both have their heads tilted, hanging on my every word. The Armour twins wear sour expressions, no doubt because one of them was feet away from freedom. The Breuers have expressions that are hard to decipher. Unlike Greta, who is beyond frightened, hands clasped tightly in her lap and a bandage wrapped snugly around her head. That leaves the Swifts, the three of them on the edge of their seats, and the Pullmans, who still appear like they'd rather be anywhere else in the world than in this very room, in this very house, about to learn who killed Sarah. Though the only person giving off a similar yet stronger sensation is Conrad. Hands shoved in his pockets, he stands on the opposite side of the room from me, closest to the doors to the foyer. Flanking him are the two officers.

I meet Conrad's gaze before I continue with a summary of events. He's calm, save for the discreet tapping of his fingertips within his right pocket. I say, "Shortly after our games commenced this evening, Sarah and Edith went to the parlor together. Soon after, the electricity went out, mayhem ensued, and Sarah was found dead. To our great relief, Detective Davis came to our rescue and began his investigation."

All heads turn toward him. Some of the women appear grateful for his diligence. Others narrow their eyes on account of his brute treatment of us throughout the night.

I continue, "A few details quickly revealed themselves. Sarah had been poisoned. Edith was the last to see her alive. Edith's hat was found beside the electrical box." I pause, gauging the reaction from the policemen. I see them scouring the women, wondering who this Edith is. From the corner of my eye, I watch as the kitchen door is cracked open and a strand of strawberry blond hair appears. She's listening. I swallow roughly, as much for my own composure as for optics. It'll bring me no joy to divulge this information about my best friend . . .

"Then there was the second death. Our attendant this evening."

The policemen's eyebrows shoot up. Eddie grips more tightly to Peg.

I share, "My pearls were used. Pearls that Edith had access to in the parlor. Then, of course, we all saw Edith bring her golf club this evening. A golf club that was used in an attack against Greta. How are you faring, sweet Greta?"

Suddenly, there is a flash of light, stealing Greta's response from me. The room's occupants exclaim, heads whipping toward the glass doors. Seconds later, a crack of thunder seemingly shakes the frame of the house.

Of course tonight's blizzard would be followed by something so uncharacteristic as a thunderstorm.

I palm my chest. "This is incredibly difficult for me, in particular, but the evidence is clear. The identity of our murderer is likewise clear." I meet Conrad's gaze again. His expression has shifted from uncertainty to confidence. Hasn't he been hoping to frame Edith? And here I am wrapping up the accusations for him with a bow. He nods at me, a show of solidarity. All that's left to do is to say it.

To say, "Edith is our killer."

Chapter Thirty-Five

EDITH

She did it. Ginevra pinned the murder on me. It's very apt for the woman being compared to Daisy Buchanan. She sacrifices Jay Gatsby, after all.

And now she's sacrificed me.

It's all unfolding as I hoped it would.

It's why I said *I'll be blamed* before I retreated up the stairs, prompting one of our unspoken conversations.

Ginevra: *Without a doubt.*

Me: *So sell it. It's the only way.*

Peering out from the kitchen, I instinctively narrow the gap between the door and its frame. The response in the room is as expected. Gasps. So many gasps. Heads on swivels. Hands over hearts. Expressions of bewilderment. Peg and Courtney feign surprise, though they must know Ginevra is up to something. Then, of course, Miller's look of utter satisfaction.

Ginevra goes on, "I can see how my revealing this information comes as a surprise to many of you, especially with Edith being one of my dearest friends. But unfortunately the evidence doesn't lie. Nor does the fact that Edith was involved in a scandal with Sarah six months ago."

Ginevra dips her head toward Marie, as if saying, "Let me help you reveal the truth." Marie presses her palms together, a show of gratitude.

Gin continues, "It was during this unfortunate scandal that Thomas Winchester lost his life to a poison administered by Sarah and communicated to society as an untimely heart attack. Afterward, Sarah and Edith covered up their transgressions. Though Edith has never trusted Sarah not to incriminate her. Threats were made against Sarah. Tonight, Edith took action."

Shock waves are felt across the room in response to Ginevra's carefully worded accusation. The officers reposition on their feet, eager to now take their own action. I've surmised that the fact they're greenhorns has made them amenable to listening. A more seasoned officer would never have let Ginevra take the stage. But also, the old-timers are home in their slippers, leaving the night watch to these babes in blue. They're the ones who've answered Eddie's call in the middle of the night during an unheard-of autumn snowstorm.

One of the officers—Baby Face, I'll call him—steps forward. "Where is this Edith?"

Ginevra frowns dramatically. "She's missing, holed up somewhere in the house."

"I saw her," Greta says, face stricken. "Edith barreled straight into me, then ran off again."

This sends the women into a frenzy of overlapping dialogue, Daisy and her mother proclaiming how they saw me too. Baby Face and his partner, Tall, Dark, and Handsome, try to quiet the room. But leave it to Ginevra. "Now, now!" she yells. "We are all safe if we stay together under the protection of these fine officers. It's only when we wander about on our own that we are in danger. Greta can speak to that firsthand."

All heads turn in Greta's direction.

She raises a hand to the back of her head and cringes. Her voice trembles as she says, "Edith hit me. She must be held accountable for this and all the other deaths she's been involved in, may God rest their souls."

Greta and Miller lock eyes—and hold their gaze long enough to raise a few pencil-thin brows. His faintly veiled grin speaks to what he's been jonesing for all night: to pin the murder on me to draw attention away from his own involvement.

But what is his role in this tangled web?

Here's what I've come to know. His materialization this evening, sporting a badge, was no mistake. He came here tonight to finish what began at the Onwentsia Club six months ago. But not only did Miller have an intimateness with Thomas Winchester, he also shared one with Thomas's ward. Miller followed her across the Atlantic, with a deep desire to remain together.

That was proven only moments ago, when Ginevra and I looked through the keyhole and saw him embracing this very same ward.

Greta.

Chapter Thirty-Six

GINEVRA

Greta, Greta, Greta.

I've long suspected her. The outsider. Seemingly meek yet brave, voicing to me earlier how she sought to find Sarah's murderer. She wouldn't have to look far.

Certainly, the girl doth protest too much with that longing look at Conrad. Along with her declarations only moments ago.

Edith hit me.

Edith barreled straight into me, then ran off again.

Except earlier, Greta never identified Edith as her assailant. Sure, she implied as much. Naturally, she acted terrified of her too. What did she say?

Edith is out there.

But would it not be incredibly obtuse of Edith to use her own golf club to attack Greta? It's too neat. Too convenient. And I'm not ready to abandon that particular line of questioning.

"Officers," I call, loudening my voice. They stand farthest from me, the gaggle of women in between. "As you can see, Greta is on her feet, but perhaps she's in need of medical attention. A golf club to the head is no small thing."

I let that statement hang in the air.

I watch as Elizabeth Field narrows an eye. Is she of like mind, that such a blow could be fatal? And that it's peculiar that Greta's clothing, save for the fingertips of her glove, are free of any bloodstains? And that, ultimately, Greta staged the whole thing?

"No," Greta says hastily, lowering her hand from the back of her bandaged head. "I assure you I am fine. Only a bump that'll go away with time. I'm more concerned with the location of Edith."

And I'm more concerned with how I can prove Greta is not as innocent as she appears. It's she who likely called Conrad this evening. When she returned to the parlor after claiming the telephone line was down, her cheeks were rosy. I assumed the rise in her color was due to exertion. Now I believe it to be from excitement. And the lingering adrenaline that accompanied poisoning another human being.

What I do not yet know are the particulars of her pulling off this feat. But shall I up the ante? Perhaps try to ferret out an answer? I believe it's due time everyone knows of her relationship with Conrad.

I soften my voice and say, "I understand your urgency to find our culprit." I palm my chest. "I share in that conviction. I only want to assure your well-being. Is there anyone who can call on you after you go home? You said earlier you are relatively new to the country. Do you have a sponsor or companion? Oh, your suitor. You mentioned earlier a Mr. Donahue?"

Conrad stiffens at the mention of another man's name. He followed her from another country, after all.

"You're mistaken," Greta says. "I didn't mention a Mr. Donahue."

"Oh." I laugh lightly. "It's been a night. Who was it, then? A Mr. Simpson? No, that's not right either." I smile and raise my pointer finger. "I've remembered. I very clearly recall a Mr. Miller."

Greta is too surprised to react, a deer caught in headlights. But Conrad projects a different story—that of a man who once believed himself to be untouchable. Yet I witness the stiffening of his shoulders at the mention of his God-given surname. His mouth parts. He reflexively pulls his hands from his pockets.

The man looks guilty as sin.

"Yes," I say, staring into him. "It was a Mr. Miller. I saw the two of you together with my very own eyes." I also let this linger, before I add, "Only mere moments ago. Upstairs in the first room. Isn't that right, Mr. Miller?"

I raise my chin to peer over the women between us. At my side, I subtly use my thumb to crack my knuckles one by one, feeling quite satisfied with myself. Conrad knew I was sneaking around, yet he never considered that I might unearth the truth about his involvement.

"Ginevra?" Elizabeth Field questions. "Why have you called Detective Davis by another name?"

"I have done no such thing. You see, Mr. Miller is only *posing* as a detective. Isn't that right?"

I glance at Edith in the kitchen's doorway. "Well done," she mouths to me. Anyone looking could see her lurking. But the air of confusion in the room is keeping everyone's attention on me.

And on Miller.

Who takes a small step backward. Then a larger one. I see the moment he means to run. Only, the officers recognize it as well. "Hold up," the younger-looking officer says.

But Miller does the opposite, trying to flee.

The taller officer seizes him.

"What is the meaning of this?" Miller growls. In his anger, his German accent is revealed, seeping into his voice. "I've done nothing wrong."

The taller officer says, "Then why the sudden urge to leave?"

"Exactly," I say.

If looks could kill . . .

I press, "Greta called you this evening, and you arrived, posing as a detective."

"But I didn't," Greta breathes.

"That's not true," Miller seethes. "You are going to believe this woman over me? I have a badge, if you'll only unhand me."

I shake my head. "Don't you mean a *hysterical* woman?" I ask, a smile playing on my lips.

It takes a moment—his mind has to travel back six months, after all—but I see when he registers my words and how they have mimicked his own. *Yes,* I say with my eyes, *Edith told me everything.*

"As to the badge," I go on, shifting my attention back to the rapt room, "my children have similar ones from Halloween. Shall I call for them to help investigate this evening as well?"

"Show us," the younger officer demands. But with the taller officer holding Miller's arms behind his back, he chooses to fish the badge out of Miller's breast pocket himself. "It says Jefferson Davis."

The younger officer scoffs. "Ain't that something—Jefferson Davis retired months ago."

Eddie chimes in, "Yes, a celebration was held in his honor. I attended."

I bet he wasn't the only one. I also bet poor Jefferson Davis has been looking for his badge ever since.

It's in this moment that two things happen. First, the tenor of the room changes. Whereas before, the women may've thought I was up to my normal theatrics—and I'd wager a number of them, especially Peg and Courtney, saw straight through my incrimination of Edith—they now know my accusation was not only strategic but also multilayered. Second, Miller slings a derogatory name at me. Why do men resort to this type of behavior when cornered? At least dignified women only think it in their heads.

He wrestles against the taller officer.

"Mr. Miller," I say, capturing his attention again. He stills. "Why don't you explain to everyone your involvement in this evening?"

The noise he makes is animallike, and his struggle continues.

"Very well, I'll try on your behalf. After Greta poisoned Sarah—"

"No," Greta interrupts.

I focus on Miller. "Greta called you to carry out your shared plan."

Greta interrupts again, denying my claim, desperation filling her pitched voice.

The Pullmans noisily move their chairs away from her.

I say, "Sarah's betrothal turned everything on its head. Greta was meant to marry Tommy Winchester. Greta would be taken care of. It was a promise Thomas Winchester made to her father on his deathbed. Here's where things get particularly interesting." I once again speak to the room of women. "Tommy and Greta had a unique arrangement. Their matrimony was to be fictitious. It would allow Greta and Mr. Miller to discreetly carry on, while Tommy was free to pursue his own affair." I stop there, Tommy's secret not mine to tell. I also take this moment to wave a hand toward Miller, the women following my gesture to find an extremely surly-looking young man. "See, there's no denial on his part. *But* it all went to hell in a handbasket when Sarah became involved. With her engagement to Tommy, not only would Greta lose her cushy life, but Mr. Miller would too. Now . . . after drinking a toxic cup of tea, Sarah's no longer an obstacle."

"No," Greta cries.

Adrenaline courses through me, words continuing to spill out of me. "With Sarah no longer a factor, Tommy is free to marry again. Greta can ride off into the sunset with Mr. Miller while pretending to be married to Tommy. They'll have that comfortable life. Honestly, people kill for much less."

"I didn't," Greta says, desperation in her voice. "I had to."

The room murmurs. I cock my head. "Which one is it, Greta?"

Her eyes are wild. "Sarah was going to poison *me*. I had no choice. I couldn't . . . I switched our cups."

I fight to keep my jaw from hitting the ground. "When?"

"During whist. While I shuffled, I purposely dropped the deck. Then, while the cards were being picked up, I changed Sarah's tea with mine."

And here I thought the reason for her fumbling the cards was her nervousness. But no, she was scheming to save her life.

"Clever," I say, because it's true. It also creates a gray area, in my opinion. The officers see it differently. Greta doesn't yet realize, but the baby-faced one is crossing the room toward her. I hold up my hand. "If you'll give me one more moment, gentlemen."

Greta turns, sucks in air at the sight of him. Her voice becomes shrill. "Sarah did this to herself. She prepared the poison. She brought me a cup. Ginevra, you were at the table when she did it. She meant to kill *me*. All I did was swap our tea and let Sarah get a taste of her own medicine."

Again, that gray area . . .

Greta frantically searches the room, pausing on each startled face. She speaks to the Pullmans, the Swifts, the Armours, the Breuers. To Elizabeth Field and to Cynthia. "Sarah did this. She's done horrible things to all of us. You heard her at our table, Ginevra . . . how I'd have a bright future ahead of me if only I'd been born the other Greta. That starlet Greta Garbo."

My heart goes out to her. Just like Jay Gatsby and Myrtle, Greta is an outsider and social climber, trying to reinvent herself. Only it's gone so very wrong.

Greta's voice hiccups. "Sarah was mocking me. She stole Tommy. She stole my future. Then, because I knew she killed Thomas, she tried to poison me."

I purposely shoot up an eyebrow, hoping Edith sees my reaction to that final bit. "I do wonder about that. How did you know to swap your teas?"

She hesitates. "I didn't trust Sarah. Would you?"

I smile in earnest. "Of course not. But if all you did was swap teas, why did you later fake your head injury?"

"I didn't. Edith—"

"Edith did not. Nor is there a wound on your head. We could unwind your bandages, but we both know there is no need to do such a thing. That means you lied, which is quite beneath you. You're protecting someone. Someone told you to pretend Edith hit you in the head. Who is that someone?"

Greta is as white as a ghost. She shoots to her feet, her head shaking wildly from side to side. The baby-faced officer quickly apprehends her. That does it; composure waning, her gaze flicks toward one of the women.

A very interesting flick.

A telling flick.

Mrs. Burton Kingsland wouldn't be pleased at this facial tic. But I'm thrilled by it—it confirms a suspicion I've held since my second exchange with Marie.

It's important to me that my husband's cause is not abandoned.

I scrutinize Greta further. Her clothing is not comme il faut for a young lady who is without proper financial support. In fact, her white frock is something I would have had made for my own wardrobe. Greta, who is unfortunately not a starlet on the rise, wouldn't be able to afford such a dress for herself.

But Marie would be able to purchase it for her.

I slowly turn my head toward Marie. "You told me you didn't kill Sarah."

The room choruses, "What?" while Marie does something I'm beginning to recognize as a veneer: She titters, as if the situation or the comment or the circumstance is utterly absurd and only worth half a laugh.

When, I believe, I've actually hit a nerve.

"Let's not be silly," Marie says lightly. "I've done no such thing."

There's another sharp cracking noise.

My first thought is that there's been another clap of thunder. My head whips toward the booming sound. But it's not the storm. It's

Edith. She's thrown open the kitchen door, and it's cracked against the wall, creating quite the memorable entrance. I both love her and hate her for it.

Women cower and mewl and make for the door. But Edith's commanding voice stops everyone in their tracks. "If you didn't kill Sarah, Marie, then why did I find this in her mouth?"

Chapter Thirty-Seven

EDITH

I hold up the wrinkled newspaper clipping.

Ginevra's nose wrinkles. "That's from inside Sarah's mouth?"

"Yes," I say, "and in the parlor, you'll find a very blue-faced—"

"Miss," Tall, Dark, and Handsome interrupts. "You've removed it from the victim? That's evidence."

Well, drat. "Sorry, I'm new to murder. Well, second time around, but it's the first I've played detective."

I walk toward Baby Face, who's still restraining Greta, the closer of the two officers, and sheepishly hand the clipping to him.

Mrs. Armour asks, "What is it?"

I stand beside Ginevra, who is making a shushing noise and motioning for everyone to take their seats again.

Ginevra and I have played team golf before, where I tee off, she takes the next shot, I take the third, and so on. There have been some holes where Ginevra has left me in less-than-favorable hazards—bunkers, the rough, behind trees or other obstructions, and even out of bounds. But this time, she's put me on the green, only a short putt away from the cup.

Gin takes a step back, giving me the floor, and I announce, "It's the *actual* murder weapon, the engagement announcement for Sarah and Tommy. Not neatly cut from the newspaper, but hastily torn before Marie shoved it into Sarah's mouth, ultimately killing her."

First, I watch as genuine surprise crosses Greta's face. Second, I notice how Murderess Marie presses her lips together. "Edith, sweetie," she says, "that's certainly a colorful story, but it's simply untrue. Greta just admitted to Sarah poisoning herself."

In my head, I do a practice swing. "Greta did say as much. But there's also the small detail that Sarah displays signs of asphyxiation. Only, we didn't see it because you promptly covered her head with the linen. I think many of us are curious how the clipping came to be in Sarah's mouth."

Heads nod. A very tired-looking Mrs. Armour cries out, "I know I am."

Marie shrugs a shoulder. "It wasn't by my hand."

I test her. "Greta, perhaps? The poison wouldn't have killed Sarah straightaway. Paralysis can occur first, like we saw with poor Cynthia."

A detail, I quickly realize from the rapid turns of heads in Cynthia's direction, that most women did not know about. My error. I clear my throat and continue. "Unless I'm mistaken, Greta was the only one who knew the tea had been poisoned."

Marie smiles sweetly. "Greta is only responsible for switching the teas."

"So you both say. It's admirable how protective you are of Greta. There must be a reason for that. Care to share it with the room?"

Marie sighs. "If you must know—"

"I must."

"I've been looking after Greta in Thomas's absence. I saw no reason for Greta to suffer on account of Sarah's actions."

"So you knew that Sarah killed Thomas?"

Marie doesn't respond straightaway, likely running scenarios through her pretty little head. Finally, she says, "You know that I know that, Edith." There's a testiness to her voice now. "Seeing to Greta's financial stability is not a crime, is it, officers?"

"No," I say answering for them. "But it would be neater if Tommy married Greta instead of Sarah."

Marie shrugs a delicate shoulder. "I won't deny that."

"And," I go on, "you must harbor resentment against Sarah for killing your husband and getting away with it."

"Anyone would," she says, encompassing all the guests in the sweep of her hand. "It took me two husbands before I found happiness with Thomas. I wanted to keep him. So yes, I do not think loathing her is an unreasonable response. But loathing her and killing her are two very different scenarios. And again, as established, Sarah was poisoned by her own doing."

"That is what Greta said. But Greta also said something else I found curious."

The room collectively holds its breath.

I look at Ginevra and raise a brow, just as she did to me. Of course, I knew what she was getting at with that reaction. "Greta said that Sarah tried to poison her because she knew about Sarah's involvement in Thomas's death."

"Yes?" Marie says. "Sarah wasn't as good of an actress as she took herself for."

I pause to address the others in the room. "Not as good as you."

"What's that rubbish supposed to mean?"

"I mean hiding your identity as the anonymous author of the threat you sent to Sarah, saying that you knew what she did."

I see again that Marie is choosing her words carefully. "Again, something that is not a crime."

"But why not tell the police that Sarah poisoned your Thomas?"

A few women murmur their agreement.

Marie changes the cross of her legs and fluffs her white dress. "I felt confident Sarah would be her own undoing. You've all borne witness to Sarah over the past few weeks. She's been more high strung than usual.

I've quite enjoyed seeing her squirm. Tonight, she accused Josephine of sending the threat."

"Why Josephine?" I ask, already knowing the answer.

"Isn't it obvious? We're talking about poison here. Sarah didn't poison my Thomas all on her own."

Baby Face asks, "Josephine?"

"Bamford," Marie provides.

Mrs. Pullman offers, "My daughter and I were sharing a room with her until she went missing."

"Missing?" Tall, Dark, and Handsome questions.

"Hiding," I correct. "It's a large house, and poor Josephine was worried she'd be blamed for tonight's deaths."

"Well, she did bring the toxic flower that ended up in Sarah's drink," Marie says.

I smirk. "One would think. But no. It was not Josephine. Sarah brought it as blackmail. And I think you know that, Marie."

"Excuse me?"

"You just said that Sarah accused Josephine. That happened in a private conversation. Which can only mean one thing: You were listening, an ear to the door." I raise my voice. "Isn't that right, Josephine?"

The Poisoning Posy enters the room. I glance at Courtney. She said earlier that Josephine would make the perfect subject in a mystery. And currently my friend is salivating at Josephine's sudden appearance after being missing most of the night. I give Court credit for not whipping out pen and paper.

I also give Josephine credit for squaring her shoulders—she prefers to be the woman behind the lens, not in the magnification of it—and addressing the room. "That is right. Earlier, Sarah threatened me. I suspect our conversation, one in which Sarah spoke plainly about the toxin she added to Thomas's drink, could have been easily overheard. Cynthia, Peg, Greta, Jasmine, Cordelia, Marie—they were all already in attendance when Sarah and I left the parlor."

Many feathers are ruffled with that final statement.

Cynthia fans herself.

Greta begins to sob.

The Breuers are mirrors of each other, hands over their mouths, words escaping about how they're innocent.

Peg leans into her husband and assures him, "I overheard nothing. I passed Josephine and Sarah when I went to telephone you that I'd arrived." She cocks her head, speaking more loudly. "Marie had been replacing the telephone in the cradle. I've thought nothing of it until now."

Could it be? The missing link? Not Greta, but Marie? "Is that when you called our friend here, Marie?" I ask, pointing toward a still very surly-looking Miller.

"Who I called is my own private business."

Baby Face begins, "Miss—"

But Marie interrupts him. "It's Mrs. Morgan."

Ginevra, who's been abnormally quiet, quips, "I give you immense credit for never having a slip of the tongue with your current surname."

"Williams," Josephine says under her breath.

"What's that?" I ask. "Who is Williams?"

Ginevra pipes up again. "There are entirely too many names to keep track of."

Josephine would camouflage into the dark draperies if she could.

"Josephine," I prod.

She blinks her eyes closed. "I'd rather not involve myself any more than I already have. But information that once seemed irrelevant may actually mean something. Years ago, I had an incident at university with another student. It was sincerely an accident, but she became gravely ill. My father saw to her medical expenses, along with any additional expenses. Her name was Marie Williams. Who shortly after her rise in station became Marie Alexander, then I presume Atkinson then Winchester.

And now Morgan. Though that girl and this woman barely resemble one another."

All eyes turn to Marie, and once more there is a universal gasp. It's quite the ladder our Marie has climbed, each surname adding additional zeros to her wealth.

Murderess Marie throws up her hands. "Honestly, I do not understand the hoopla. I saw an opportunity to make something better of myself. So I did and I have." Marie smooths her dress again.

Tall, Dark, and Handsome twists his lips. "Theodore Atkinson? Thomas Winchester?"

Marie rolls her eyes. "Familiar to you, I gather?"

"My old man spoke about those cases around the dinner table. Said how Atkinson died of mysterious causes. If I remember correctly, he grew ill after dinner."

"I assure you," Marie says, "that was a difficult night for everyone. It was horrendous to see Teddy suffer as he did. As I recall, it was the kitchen staff who mistook a daffodil bulb for an onion."

Josephine perks up at this, ever the scientist. "Yet you didn't also take ill? Abdominal pain, nausea, vomiting, loose bowels. I still feel horrible you experienced these very same symptoms on account of me all those years ago."

"Hmm," I say to myself. I've always believed that coincidences are not coincidental. Ginevra is thinking it, too, her head tilted subtly to the side. Yet . . . I'm going to pivot, following a hunch.

The grandfather clock causes us all to nearly jump from our skin. It's midnight, and I know we all want this ghastly night to be over. But we're on the back nine, victory in sight. "Officers, would it be okay if I laid forth a scenario?"

Baby Face, restraining Greta, and Tall, Dark, and Handsome, holding Miller, are the only other ones standing in the room. They must be growing tired of being on their feet. I know I am. I ignore Miller's glare and nod in turn to the officers. "I'll be quick, promise." I set my sights again on Marie. "Shall we recap? You heard Sarah accuse Josephine of threatening her with that letter. You knew Sarah would unravel further after Josephine denied it. You suspected Sarah would act and try to eliminate whoever threatened her. So you told Greta not to drink anything Sarah gave to her." I pause and look at Cynthia, who is making a meal of her nails. "And Cynthia too."

Marie swallows but says nothing.

I continue, "Imagine your delight when Greta switched the drinks. Sarah would consume the poison. She'd die in front of everyone, and everyone would assume it was a heart attack. It's what happened to Thomas. Poetic justice, no? But then Sarah and I went to the parlor. You followed, didn't you? You saw Josephine listening in. But after Josephine ran off and I left, you were in the clear. You slipped in and shoved the newspaper clipping in her mouth."

"We're back to that," Marie says in a deadpan voice. "Again, this is all a very colorful story. I do hope Courtney is taking sufficient notes."

I tap my temple. "I'm sure she is. Now, there is something I recall from earlier that shouldn't be overlooked. Upstairs, when you were talking about 'Detective Davis,' you actually misspoke his name."

Marie's gaze shoots to Ginevra, who she was having the conversation with at the time. "I did no such thing."

"But you did. You really never know who is listening at the door, do you? I heard you. Instead of 'Davis,' you said 'Miller.'"

No denial is forthcoming. She could try. It'd be her word against mine—and Ginevra's. But her teeth are clenched, and I think she's doing all she can to keep her mouth shut. So I go on. "This tells me you knew Miller prior to this evening. It wasn't Greta who called him, but you. You eavesdropped on Sarah and Josephine. You told Greta and Cynthia about the poison. You turned off the lights to create alarm. You shoved the clipping down Sarah's throat. It was you in the coatroom with the attendant. You struck Greta. All to avenge Thomas's death, the only husband you've ever cared for."

Marie laughs loudly. "I had no reason to strike Greta. And how do you suppose I did all those things myself? I'm only one person."

I smile. "Exactly. You had help. Where is he, Marie? I know he's not dead."

Chapter Thirty-Eight

GINEVRA

"Who?" I say—in unison with Marie. Though I wager she's not genuinely perplexed, unlike me.

Who is this *he*? Who is undead?

Edith crosses her arms. "You very well know who. Shall we go see if he's still lying there?"

Surely she can't be talking about the attendant. I saw him sprawled out on the coat closet floor, blue in the face, with my very own eyes.

Edith adds, "I bet my best custom-made driver that there will be no body."

"Mrs. Morgan?" the taller officer asks, adjusting his grip on Miller.

It appears the cat's got Mrs. Morgan's tongue.

I begin descending the stairs from the stage area. "Shall I lead the charge?"

Edith follows, and slowly, one by one, the other women stand from their seats. Marie is suddenly hesitant, meek. I notice Eddie hanging back to ensure she stays with the group.

I go straight to the coat closet, move aside the telephone table, and throw open the door.

I huff a perplexed laugh. "He's gone. The attendant is gone." I return to E in the foyer. "Last I checked, a dead man can't get up and walk away."

"Unless someone moved him," Elizabeth Field interjects.

I spread my arms wide. "Did anyone here move his body? Miller? Greta? Marie? I can keep naming names."

One person after another adamantly denies.

"What in tarnation is going on here?" the younger-looking officer demands. His eyes are simultaneously tired and charged as he holds Greta with her arms behind her back. I watch as she lifts her gaze to Marie's. As she pleads with Marie with that gaze. "Please," she says to her. "This has gotten out of hand. Let's just explain."

"Oh?" I say. How incriminating. "Eddie, it appears we have run out of officers. Would you be a dear and apprehend Marie? I get the sense she may be a—"

Flight risk.

Marie bolts toward the main entrance. She even manages to make it there, bowling past the Pullmans and Breuers, and yanks open the heavy door with impressive strength. To my utter surprise, the attendant stands on the threshold, very much alive.

"What are you doing?" Marie screeches at him.

"I couldn't let you take the fall," he says solemnly. "Stand aside, sweetheart."

Then the attendant stalks back into the foyer and closes the door behind him, once again entrapping us all inside, much to Marie's chagrin.

The attendant is unscathed, of course. The blue tint and markings on his skin and neck are gone, washed clean, with what I presume to be an eye shadow stain remaining on his collar. There's no sign that he's ever been strangled, certainly not with my necklace.

"So my pearls were never used. I was correct," I say, satisfied with my earlier conclusion.

Marie pins me with a glare, which she then transfers to Greta. "A simpleminded mistake. Anyone of means would assume pearls would snap."

"I didn't know," Greta says feebly.

Marie huffs. "Exactly."

"Leave her alone," Miller snaps. "You never should have asked her to fake his death. This is all your own doing."

"Which," I say, "I would absolutely love to hear about."

There's a chorus of agreement, after which the officers quiet down the women and gain a semblance of control.

Greta, Miller, Marie, and the attendant are each cuffed to a chair. The rest of us sit at our respective tables in the ballroom to listen.

Turns out, the attendant is none other than Marie's father, recently come from England. A working-class man, and also not a fan of Marie's fourth husband, he insisted on paying his own way. That's how he ended up working as an attendant at the Bellevue.

As luck has it, tonight's event was only his second gig. He wasn't expecting his daughter to overhear Sarah's conversations with Josephine. Nor did he expect his daughter to caution him not to eat or drink anything that evening. Not that he would.

Then we know what happened next. It's been well established. Greta switched her poisoned tea with Sarah's. Marie called Miller, recognizing an impromptu opportunity to exact justice. When Sarah keeled over in front of everyone, Miller would be the dutiful detective checking in on them on account of the storm. There'd be plenty of eyewitnesses to attest to Sarah's sudden collapse and demise.

But instead, Sarah left the room with Edith. When the coast was clear, the attendant slipped in and tore the announcement from the newspaper. Shoved it in Sarah's face as paralysis set in. Impulsively shoved it down her throat. Now, with no witnesses, someone would need to take the fall. Edith. She'd been with Sarah. And thus her hat was swiped from a ballroom table and left next to the electrical box. That was also the attendant's doing. The darkness would create alarm and disorientation upon the discovery of Sarah's body, and also allow him the discreetness to snatch Edith's hat from the ballroom table.

Throughout it all, Marie's hands were clean. All she's done, she insists, is seize an opportunity, as she's done throughout her entire life. In my opinion, a mastermind and also a puppeteer. Greta and Miller doing her bidding. Faking Greta's accident. Creating a case against Edith. Perhaps believing they owed Marie a debt for all she's done for them?

All this time, we thought the perpetrator was a woman. I once even questioned if it could have been Cynthia, silly me. And while the mastermind is indeed female, the true murderer is a man.

A father.

Sarah took a love from his daughter that she cherished. He is Scott's George Wilson, a man who acts with revenge, fueled by love and a warped sense of justice.

And if the attendant's to be believed, Marie knew nothing of his transgression. But it raises a curious question. If Marie was unaware, then why fake her father's death, ultimately diverting suspicion from him as the perpetrator? Oh, and another question: Would the attendant have thought to pose Sarah's body—all on his own—after suffocating her?

The devil is in the details.

Details that were meant to pin the deaths on Edith, but also on me.

"Why me?" I interrupt.

"Oh, Ginevra," Marie seethes. "You can't be that daft. I knew you'd put your nose in this. You always do. And when you did, you'd make a messy situation even messier. I mean, look at what you've done—inciting alarm, asking uncomfortable questions, poisoning innocent people. You selfishly put this night in motion months ago, and you kept it in motion tonight. It's why I gave you back your pearls. The blood is on your hands, Ginevra." She scoffs. "Sarah was right about one thing. You truly are Daisy Buchanan. Fickle and careless."

I snort a laugh. "If I'm Daisy, you're Jay Gatsby himself. You've fallen for cheap tricks, tried to pull one off yourself, and destroyed yourself along the way. You didn't think anyone would catch you, but we have."

"And you're smug as ever in doing so," Marie snarls.

I open my mouth to object. But I can feel the haughtiness of my features. My chin slightly lifted. My shoulders back. My lips in a tight smile. And I can see how the other women are looking at me. Not with gratitude for helping to unravel tonight's mystery, but with narrowed eyes (Cynthia), exasperation (Ruth Armour), and even disappointment (Henrietta Swift and Elizabeth Field).

Upstairs, Elizabeth called me self-serving and unmindful.

She may be right. Could I be one of the East Egg careless people of privilege, one who smashes up things, then returns to my world of the wealthy elite? I *have* been smashing up things all evening. Digging into other people's lives and secrets. Leaving damage in my wake. Not caring who I hurt—and even temporarily paralyze. I turned this night into a game. I perpetuated that game. I wanted to win. Needed to win. All because I want to be viewed a certain way, the perfect way, the way society expects me to be. I was acting great, but I wasn't being good.

I lower my chin and glance around the room—at Cynthia, Elizabeth, Ruth, Henrietta, even Marie. Women I've known for years. Women who've smiled, curtsied, hosted galas, and whispered behind one another's backs. Women who've kept secrets, borne slights, curated images. All of us were taught that survival—true social survival—depends on looking perfect, even if everything beneath the surface is unraveling. We've lied to protect reputations. Covered up betrayals. Turned a blind eye to cruelty. Hurt others because we were too afraid of being hurt ourselves. Because we were too afraid of being seen as less.

Earlier, I swore I had no hand in Sarah's death. But perhaps that's not the full truth. Like in *Gatsby*, it feels as if we've all played roles in tonight—through action or inaction, deceit or detachment. It was never just one person. It was all of us, bound by fear and vanity.

Now the night has come to a close. And while it's not only the four in handcuffs who've been unmasked, I do wonder: Will anything truly change?

I want to say yes.

I want to believe we can choose something better. That women like us—raised to smile, to nod, to accept, to scheme quietly in corners—can stop pretending. That we can rewrite the roles we've been given.

I'm meant to go home now. Back to a house built on pretense, a marriage exposed for what it is. But how can I return unchanged when everything tonight has cracked me open?

I think of Edith, told she can only be one thing. Of Peg, told if she's a wife, she should also be a mother. Of Courtney, taught that her beauty is her greatest achievement. Of Marie, who wielded the tools provided to her—manipulation and charm—until they cut her too.

I think of Scott and me, that sunlit morning, dreaming of a different future. Yet I made the same choice Daisy did, accepting the safe haven of money rather than waiting for a truer love. How did he ultimately end our story?

So we beat on, boats against the current, borne back ceaselessly into the past.

And maybe that's true. Maybe we are always pulled backward by who we once were, by what we were told to be.

But I say it can be different.

At the very least, it's worth trying.

Epilogue

GINEVRA

Sometime later

"I'm so very proud of you," I whisper to Courtney, coming up behind her, taking care not to tip my glass and give her a champagne bath. She's sitting at a table, personalizing a copy of her book to an M. Basil B. Zavoico.

The man is the last of quite the impressive signing line.

"I'm anxious to read it," this Basil says. "Alaska. And as a woman. That must have been harrowing."

She's polite, thanking him.

Truly, her work is groundbreaking. The first book in which a woman recorded her experiences in the Arctic. It was quite the departure from her original story idea. But as all the women left the Bellevue, we agreed not to speak of the night's happenings. Publicly, at least. There will never be a mention in the history of the Bellevue or the Civic Daughters. And while there are countless headlines about the kidnapping of Eddie Cudahy Jr. that can be dug up, there are none about his sister's murder. It's exactly as Peg wanted, reminding the women that the majority of us behaved in rare form that evening. We've all striven to do better.

As far as her book, Courtney quipped that Miller had accused us of acting like animals. So when her husband suggested a five-month voyage to Alaska to write about actual animals, the muse struck, and she swapped her lacy day wear for laced-up boots. Apparently killer bears and walruses are more civilized than the likes of us.

Speaking of which. "Where's that little hell-raiser of yours?" I ask Peg as she joins me sans child.

"Around here somewhere. Ideally not pilfering or breaking anything."

"They'll do that."

Motherhood suits her.

Peg sips her champagne. "Where's Edith?"

"Oh, around here somewhere," I parrot. In fact . . . "She appears to be up to no good."

E is hand in hand with her husband, walking our way between the bookshelves, a satisfied grin on her face.

"What have you done now?" I ask her.

She waggles her brows, pulling a deep laugh from Curtis. "Nothing scandalous. We've identified the recipient of next year's scholarship."

Ah, for the Curtis and Edith Munson Foundation. A worthy cause, and I was mistaken; she was up to loads of good. "Here, at Courtney's launch event?"

"No better time than the present," Curtis teases, the spitting image of Clark Gable.

"Especially," Edith says, "when you spot a bright-eyed young woman in the nonfiction section reaching for *Down the Fairway*. We got to talking, and she more than fits who we're looking for."

That is, a top female collegiate golfer who excels in academics.

I clink her glass. "This night has been a success for more than one of us, then."

Courtney finally pushes back from her chair, accepting the glass of champagne Curtis offers her. "Shall we toast to Courtney?" he suggests, ever the charmer.

I couldn't have picked a more suitable partner for Edith if I tried. A career in golf and marital bliss.

Peg's blur of a child runs past us, nearly toppling his mother, my children on his heels, and I smother a laugh at the sideways glance Edith gives her husband.

A career in golf, marital bliss, and *no* thoughts of children.

She has all she wants—and society has had absolutely no say in it.

I've taken a page from her book. I've dropped Mitchell from my name. Bill's free to canoodle with whoever he pleases. And so am I.

Damn him, but Scott springs to mind.

He has a habit of doing that—and has ever since we were kids and madly in love. Goodness, what a self-centered little ass I was back then. I cringe whenever I reread our old letters, which his daughter has sent me.

Yes, I'll come to Princeton, I said in one of them, Princeton where he attended school. *But only if you promise me something exciting will happen and that I'll be admired by all your friends.*

Oh, what a shallow motivation!

But there are worse lines.

Oh well, you'll win next time. I never expected you to be the editor, anyway.

Scott, you take things too seriously. You really must learn not to be so intense.

Could I not have simply supported the man?

Though this last one imprinted on my memory takes the cake.

I adore you. At least, I think I do. But don't expect me to act like it all the time.

It's no wonder he believes me to be fickle.

It's no wonder our last meeting didn't go well.

I went all the way to the Beverly Wilshire Hotel in Hollywood to meet him, but it was like he didn't want to see me at all. Later, his daughter told me how he'd faithfully avoided seeing me up to that moment to keep the illusion perfect of the first girl he had ever loved.

Scott had been on the wagon for some months. His hand twitched for a drink, I could tell. Then he gave in. Double shots of gin.

I worked up the nerve to ask him; I'd been wondering for years. "Scott," I said, "did I ever inspire a character in any of your novels?"

Along with Daisy Buchanan, Gloria Gilbert feels like another dead ringer. A wealthy, beautiful debutante from Chicago. Raised with privilege and high expectations. She's both admired and critiqued in his portrayal.

His blue eyes pierced into me after the question. I always adored his eyes. Cavern-like. Eyes I could get lost in, create dreams in. But that day, his gaze wasn't inspiring.

He spat a question at me, following it with a derisive laugh and another shot. "Which bitch do you think you are?"

I didn't answer him.

I left after that.

It'll be the last time I ever see him, I know it.

I went home to John.

"And where's your paramour this evening?" Courtney asks me, as if she can see the sparkle in my eye as I think about him.

"He sends his regards. He's on a hunting trip."

It's how we met, on a fox hunt. Courtney's excursion inspired me. I'd been on a horse, riding behind John, when his horse suddenly balked at a fence. He was unconscious as soon as he hit the ground. I leaped from my steed, ran to him, and stayed at his side until the ambulance came. When it did, I remained by his side, climbing right into the back with him. Then going into the hospital. Then, afterward, we continued to remain side by side, as if there was no other option for us.

Only the Big Four—and their husbands—know about my relationship with John. It's not that I'm hiding it from society. It's that this relationship is simply my own. Not for anyone else's consumption—or opinion.

Maybe I'll marry him one day. Maybe I won't. I could imagine a quiet ceremony. Nothing flashy. Though most certainly with champagne, I think, taking another sip. And my Big Four.

"I'm proud of you," I say to Court. "Of all of us."

I'm met with gleaming faces, women I've known since 1914, a year that is worlds away. Yet as I touch my pinkie ring, it feels like only yesterday.

"We must be off," Edith says, leaning in to kiss Courtney's cheek and speaking congratulations into her ear. "But I'll see you all tomorrow."

I joke, "And here I thought you were going to weasel out of it?"

"Out of a social event? Never," Edith says in a mocking tone.

I'm hosting a fundraiser for the Ladies' Guild of the American Cancer Society. It's something near and dear to me that I've founded, a way to leave the earth a better place than I found it.

I squeeze hands and kiss cheeks.

"Careful in the snow," Peg cautions.

"Could you imagine," Courtney begins, "if another storm trapped us all inside tomorrow night?"

"As long as no one dies," I say. "But don't worry; I've already checked. Death is *not* on the guest list."

A Note from the Author

Those who know me from my biographical fiction, I hope you've enjoyed my first foray into murder mysteries. What fun this was to write. In fact, a novel about the Big Four debutantes from Chicago is a story I've wanted to pen for years. I just didn't know the proper hook. From time to time, I'd reread the Wikipedia page devoted to the foursome to see if the muse would strike. One day, it did, my mind homing in on the fact that two of the women, Ginevra and Edith, inspired Daisy Buchanan and Jordan Baker. There was something there, but still, I wasn't sure what.

My inclination was to write biographical fiction or a fictional memoir. However, I struggled to find enough information to pen an authentic true-to-life storyline. Besides a nonfiction book that explores Ginevra's relationship with Fitzgerald and the few original sources Wikipedia pulls from, information on these dynamic ladies was limited.

I let my brain explore another option. Still historical. Still the Big Four. Still a focus on the two women who inspired characters from *The Great Gatsby*. But . . . what if I put Ginevra and Edith at the center of a murder mystery? There'd be *Clue* nods (Did you notice the colors of the dresses? Or how Ginevra and Miss Scarlett are both cunning and charming, using their allure to manipulate others and hide their secrets? Or how Edith and Colonel Mustard are both known to have past shady dealings?). I used the floor plan of the Bryan Lathrop House in Chicago to influence my fictional Bellevue House. I modeled the Civic Daughters after the Fortnightly women's group. The main characters would be inspired by their real-life counterparts (to the best of my ability). I placed Edith at a real golf club in Lake Forest, Illinois. Though, to my knowledge, a murder has never taken place at the Onwentsia Club.

In some instances, I may have done some of the historical figures dirty. Any ancestors, please forgive me! Bill Mitchell could very well have been a good man. For the purposes of my novel, however, he was the villain. I also reused the surnames of many influential families of the time (Morgan, Pullman, Swift, etc.), but their characters are all fictional. Sarah Cudahy is a complete figment of my imagination. However, Eddie Cudahy Jr. really was kidnapped as a child.

It's been great fun melding fact and fiction.

In the epilogue, I did some more melding. I wanted to end with a wrap-up of what came next for our Big Four. Only, Courtney's book was published by the Macmillan Company in 1928 (she really did write an inscription to M. Basil B. Zavoico, with Christmas greetings). Edith married in 1934. Ginevra met John T. Pirie in 1937. Ginevra saw F. Scott Fitzgerald for the last time in 1938 (he died two years later). None of these events aligned or coincided, and so for storytelling purposes, I mashed up all these varying years into a single scene.

An interesting tidbit I learned while researching this book involves the popularity of *The Great Gatsby*. Who knew that the novel was originally considered a commercial failure? In its initial print run, the novel sold fewer than twenty-five thousand copies, which was about half the sales of Fitzgerald's previous novels, *This Side of Paradise* and *The Beautiful and Damned*. Many critics failed to grasp the deeper themes and symbolism he intended. By the time Fitzgerald died in 1940, the book had fallen into obscurity. It wasn't until World War II that *The Great Gatsby* began to gain popularity and critical acclaim. In 1943, as part of the Armed Services Editions program, the novel was distributed to American soldiers serving overseas in an effort to boost morale and provide entertainment. It's said that the novel's themes of unrequited love and the elusive nature of the American dream resonated strongly with young soldiers. This led to substantial word of mouth (it's a powerful thing!) during and following the war. To date, more than thirty million copies of *The Great Gatsby* have been sold.

Part of me wonders what Ginevra would think of the book's eventual success. Or the fact Fitzgerald is said to have modeled a total of eight characters after her across his body of work. I daresay that'd be a great topic for a book club!

As always, I'd like to extend a big thank you to my agent, Shannon, my critique partner, Lindsay, and to the many people from Thomas & Mercer who made this novel possible: Jessica, Selina, Annie, Miranda, Katherine, Aimée, Ploy, Michael, Brittany, Allyson, and Nicole.

Pursuing my dreams as an author would be impossible without my husband and kids cheering me on, without my author village (you know who you are!), and without amazing support from so many bookstagrammers, book influencers, and online book groups (I'm looking at you Peloton Moms Book Club). I apologize for not listing individual names. I'm blessed to have so many of you in my life and I'll lose sleep if I left anyone out.

I'm so appreciative for the opportunity to do what I love. And thank you for going on this journey with me!

Book Club Questions

1. A locked-room murder mystery usually includes several core elements: the murder(s), an isolated location, a closed circle of suspects, a brilliant detective (or detectives), red herrings and misdirection, a "whodunit" reveal, and a strong atmosphere. Which aspect of this type of novel is your favorite?

2. How effective were the novel's clues and red herrings? Who did you suspect, and were you correct?

3. Did you enjoy seeing figures inspired by real-life women placed in a fully fictional setting and scenario?

4. How did the setting—1920s Chicago during a snowstorm—affect the characters, the plot, and the overall mood of the novel?

5. In what ways did the characters' attire and mannerisms influence your perceptions of who they were?

6. What similarities did you notice between Daisy Buchanan and Ginevra King Mitchell in this novel? What nods to Fitzgerald's work did you pick up on? (There are many!)

7. Discuss Ginevra's growth throughout the novel.

8. How do you think Ginevra would feel about the eventual popularity of *The Great Gatsby*? Knowing the novel's reputation today, were you surprised to learn it was initially released to near obscurity?

9. How did societal norms and expectations shape the characters' thoughts and actions in this novel?

10. Which of the Big Four—Ginevra, Edith, Courtney, or Peg—
    do you most identify with, and why?

11. When recommending this book to a friend (and please do!),
    which scene or character would you highlight as your favorite?

12. Who would you cast in a film or television adaptation? What
    songs would you include on the soundtrack?

Questions written by Marisa Gothie and Nicholle Thery-Williams of
the Bookend and Friends book club.

About the Author

Jenni L. Walsh is a *USA Today* bestselling author of over a dozen books. Her passion lies in transporting readers to another world, be it historical or contemporary. Jenni's historical novels for adults include *Sonora*; *Ace, Marvel, Spy*; *Unsinkable*; *The Call of the Wrens*; *A Betting Woman*; *Side by Side*; and *Becoming Bonnie*. She also writes books for children, like the nonfiction She Dared series and the novels *Outlook Unclear*, *The Bug Bandits*, *Operation: Happy*, *Over and Out*, *By the Light of Fireflies*, *I Am Defiance*, and *Hettie and the London Blitz*.

A proud member of Tall Poppy Writers, Jenni is a graduate of Villanova University and lives in the Philadelphia suburbs with her husband, daughter, son, and various pets. To learn more about Jenni and her books, please visit www.jennilwalsh.com or @jennilwalsh on social media.